Draw A Hard Line

An E.J. Kane Mystery

Micheal E. Jimerson

Elwood Jimerson Farms L.L.C.

Published by Elwood Jimerson Farms L.L.C.

Library of Congress Control Number: 2024904526

Ebook ISBN 979-8-218-37773-1 Print ISBN 979-8-218-37772-4

Cover design by Matthew Fielder

Proofreading Armadillo Editing Rachel Santino

Elwood Jimerson Farms L.L.C.

This novel is dedicated to all those engaged in the search for truth and justice.

The world loves to be amused by hollow professions, to be deceived by flattering appearances, to live in a state of hallucination; and can forgive anything except the plain, downright, simple, honest truth.

William Hazlitt

Chapter One

Bomb Disposal

"**A**re you bomb disposal?"

"No, ma'am, I'm the guy who drew the short straw. I enjoyed your talking fish movie." Oven-baked air stuffed E.J.'s throat with hot, fine dust rising from the combination of red clay and sugar sand. His head twisted, spitting out the thick grit.

Gazing beyond the movie star, he caught sight above the tracks through the thick glass windows and doors of the cab. E.J. had been around the oil field enough to learn operators called the rotating compartment above the tracks, the house. Like an object materialized from an alien world, a crude bomb stood out from behind the tall, transparent door. The device appeared primitive, like sticks of dynamite out of an old Western movie.

"Ma'am?" She shrieked like someone had stabbed her. Her athletic body pulled against the logging chains. The bonds fastened her through the massive track around an interior steel wheel. She slung her head back, ending the futile battle against the enormous dirt mover.

E.J. jumped across a deep vein the mechanical leviathan had cut into the earth. His arthritic knee buckled, causing him to regret the leap. Seventy feet of dried red dirt separated him from the green-needled pine trees standing arrow straight under a blazing sky.

Behind him lay the expanse of an unbroken pipeline easement parting a pine curtain. Raising his arms and lifting the leg eased his suffering.

"Hey, idiot," yelled the woman. "I call nine one one and they send me a geriatric cowboy with attention deficit disorder."

Pain permeated E.J.'s bones, stabbing into one another. Like brittle spindles threatening to snap the kneecap backward, his legs faltered.

E.J. gritted his teeth, self-conscious he must look like a modern Moses separating a vast sea of pine timber. Scent from an ocean of dry evergreens diffused throughout the scorched air, despite the lack of a breeze.

By placing his boots on the steps of the enormous industrial machine, he gained the ability to analyze the explosive device closely. The bomb looked old-school except for a plastic two-by-two-inch box and a modern blasting cap wrapped atop the red sticks with duct tape.

"Well?" she wailed.

"Can't rightly say," said E.J.

"What?"

"I don't know," said E.J.

"You don't know? You don't know? Why did they send you?" Her right hand struggled to lift a cell phone to her ear.

"No. We don't know what sets it off. Might be the radio waves. No way of knowing," said E.J.

"I'm going to die, and they send me the village idiot from inbred redneckland to diffuse a bomb who thinks mermaids are talking fish. Why didn't I ask Siri how to disarm the stupid thing?"

E.J. turned back to her. Googling the question didn't sound like a bad idea except for using a cell phone in proximity to the device. If he walked back some distance, he could ask a search engine. Surely there is some artificial intelligence floating in the ether of cyberspace that has the capability to formulate an answer.

Human intelligence had evidently concluded a person strapped to a colossal mechanical contraption topped by an incendiary device amounted to reason. One had the ability to only match the absurdity of the foolishness with the arrogance of giving credit to such boundless ignorance as scientific thought.

Reason dictated finding an alternative to such purported wisdom. Yet this woman acted as if he were the one acting stupid. She had put E.J. in a bad spot—worse, she put herself in extreme danger for nothing.

Still, her face drew his gaze back. He saw why she starred in movies. Even middle-aged, without makeup, and adorned in a white tee shirt with denim overalls, the woman exuded a brightness he could feel on his skin like the sunshine beating down.

Why couldn't he keep his mind on the task before him? Did death call a siren song audible only to him, or did others hear the tune?

Forcing himself back to the moment, he erupted. "Lady, I'm head of security for Devekon Energy, the company overseeing this pipeline project. I got sent to stop your little protest. Don't know anything about a nine-one-one call or a bomb." He drew a deep breath, then continued. "I'm all the cavalry you got."

She rolled her eyes, catching herself before speaking.

E.J. gritted his teeth. Who knew how you get rid of a bomb? Maybe he shouldn't have admitted the fact to a person already upset?

Sweat matted her blonde hair over her forehead. She looked down at her arms, then forced her chest against the chains, to no avail. "Cowboy, we need a plan."

E.J.'s head swung back from the force of her roar. "Got a plan. We get you out of here and let this behemoth blow up. What Devekon pays insurance for."

"I got no key." A shrill quality conveyed urgency.

"It's what you told the crew, but nobody locks themselves to a half-million-dollar piece of equipment without an exit strategy. Only a total idiot would do that."

"I'm the idiot? Chains symbolize our addiction to fossil fuels, so I don't have a key. Can't you see, humanity doesn't have a key? You idiot, humanity is throwing our key away literally every minute." She peered intently at him.

E.J. returned the puzzled stare. Was she so deep into this environmental cause, she couldn't see the glaring stupidity of this scheme?

"You don't see any of it, do you? Why I had to go to these lengths to get people like you to understand? The plan was the pipeline company would have to find some way to cut through the chains. It was meant to take time. News crews would come from everywhere, publicizing my plight as a concrete symbol for the murder of Mother Earth."

E.J. peered into her dark eyes. She was as mentally unsettled as the crowd of pipeline workers over a quarter mile distant had claimed. However, the oil field workers had proclaimed their psychological assessment in the more graphic and vulgar language of the oil field. Would explosives sheering her flesh into a million concrete symbols save the planet?

He needed to end the ignorance now before this true believer got herself killed over nothing. "There is a little plastic rectangle near the blasting cap. An electronic device, a counter, or a clock are all possibilities. Understand? Time might be ticking down to detonation right now. Give me the key," demanded E.J. in his sternest voice.

"I'm telling you. Somebody overdid it. They changed the plan without including me. There wasn't supposed to be a bomb," she screamed.

The dramatic artist threw her head back, slinging her perspiration-soaked blonde locks. "I see the message. The perfect imagery. The perfect message. We're all facing the ticking time bomb of climate change." A strange laughter exhaled from the woman. "It's genius. Total genius, but I wasn't in on it. I swear, no one told me."

E.J. saw no intelligent thought in any of it. Was she talking out of her head? More than once, he had witnessed the moment people came to terms with their own mortality. The experience taught him there was no one-size-fits-all response.

The fact she hadn't panicked to this point didn't mean she wouldn't lose it, making a difficult situation impossible. Panic equaled death. Such was the only mathematical certainty universally true in crisis management. Her mind shouldn't focus on imminent death. "You sound like my daughter," said E.J.

"And any other rational human being," snapped the thespian.

So odd, how she prided herself on her rationalism. However, she obviously put herself in an absurd situation, even if she didn't know about the explosives. What thinking person would chain herself to an enormous excavator without a way out? It was worth one more shot. "Give me the key." E.J. barked the words at the top of his lungs.

The woman's responding shriek rivaled in volume any screech of victim or monster ever appearing on the silver screen. "I threw the key away at the hotel."

"Kind of dramatic, isn't it?"

She rolled her eyes.

It hit him. A celebrity christened a modern-day saint by her Hollywood peers wouldn't have a good understanding of how strange she seemed to a group of Texas pipeliners. "You see that gaggle of welders and dirt movers about a half mile down the line? Tried convincing one of them to drive a welding truck down here and cut you out with a torch," said E.J.

"Cowards."

E.J. shook his head. "Ordinarily pretty brave lot. Suppose they think this is poetic justice. Tree hugger trying to take their livelihood does herself in."

"Shut up and come up with something." The sharp tone rose to an even higher level.

"Seems like dynamite would be like gunpowder. We get it wet, and it won't go off. Makes sense, right?" said E.J.

She stared at her phone, thumbs oscillating.

"I told you I'm worried phone signals will set it off," said E.J.

She shook her head in disgust mixed with fear. "Yous people know nothing."

"Yous people, like New York or New Jersey?" E.J. grinned, emphasizing the last syllable in jersey.

"Cincinnati by way of Philly parents. Congratulations, one trip to hick-land has undone thirty years of speech classes. Nitroglycerin can build up and explode unexpectedly when dynamite gets wet according to Wikipedia," she said.

"Wikipedia can be wrong," said E.J.

Waving her head in disbelief, the movie star screamed at him. "Wikipedia wrong? It's a better gamble than some cowboy flunky for big oil."

The only other person capable of dressing him down in such a witty fashion had been his ex-wife, Rebecca. E.J. looked at the ring he couldn't bring himself to keep off his finger. The celebrity's gaze jerked him back to the explosive device. Why did his mind wander?

He fumbled thumb to index finger on his phone's screen, sending a photo and calling the contact. Locking gazes with the actor, E.J. nodded to her, attempting to express assurance in the latest plan. "Calling the best munitions guy there is. Fellow was a firearms analyst for the DPS lab. Jay? Jay?"

The voice came through the speakerphone feature. "Ranger Kane?"

"I need some help. Did you get the picture I just texted?"

"This is real?" asked Jay.

"What I'm asking you?"

"Drop me a pin and get out of there. I'll have a bomb squad en route."

"Not an option. I'm on a pipeline location in the middle of nowhere. Crazy situation. Movie star has chained herself to a huge track hoe trying to stop a big pipeline project. Chain thicker than a set of bolt cutters can cut." E.J. waited out an uncomfortable pause.

"You know people in the FBI. Why call me and not Quantico? I'm just an old toolmark analyst."

"Not gonna trust our lives to a stranger. You know more about munitions than anybody. Might soak it with water, right?"

"No. Go with diesel, but I wouldn't touch it. Probably a hoax. The bomb has more of a Wile E. Coyote look to it, though I wouldn't touch it. Get your movie star out of there," pleaded Jay.

E.J. looked downcast at the woman, then spoke into his phone. "Not gonna happen."

"Figure it out. Send me a pin. I'm estimating a bomb squad is two hours out, but I'm going to get one your way."

E.J. ended the call. He had smelled diesel and the lesser odor of hydraulic fluid since he got there. A bucket of diesel wouldn't be hard to find.

"Two hours. I need to call my kids and tell them I died in Ignorantville, Texas, killed by an incompetent, inbred buffoon."

E.J. pointed along the massive thoroughfare, holding back both sides of a piney wood to a group of pipeline constructors. "Welding trucks have oxyacetylene cutting rigs and diesel tanks. I'll be back."

Her tears streamed dirty checks. "Really? Really?"

"Really," said E.J.

"You're not coming back."

E.J. turned back. He saw what must have been a daughter on the lady's phone screen. Every moment he wasted might make the difference. He looked deep into her dark orbs until, satisfied she had provided her full attention. "Lady, I don't lie."

Chapter Two

The Actor

E.J. reached his truck, spinning the tires before he shut the door. No longer would he make a request for suitable equipment. Making fun of a person in dire straits instead of offering a helping hand disgusted him, regardless of whether she placed herself in jeopardy. They had declined to choose to do the right thing. This time, he would choose for them.

The environmental zealot held no animosity toward these folks, though her actions amounted to taking food off the worker's tables. Likely she had no thought about them at all.

A welder's helper smarted off on E.J.'s arrival. "Can't get the old bossy cow untied?"

Another popped off. "Maybe the talkin' fish gal can swim through the air with the explosion."

The punch jutted out in front of E.J. as if someone else threw it. His fist connected under the younger man's jaw. A line of bone forced E.J.'s knuckles to rebound, stinging as he pulled back the hand.

Stumbling onto his heels, the man struggled to find balance. He fell to a knee, looking upward, registering shock on his face.

In an involuntary fashion, E.J. stepped closer. He towered over the fallen youth. "Not a talking fish."

Kneeling, the youngster covered his head. The entire company of men laughed the great cackling laughter of good old boys accustomed to ridicule from each other.

E.J. threw open the door on a one-ton flatbed. The big diesel motor stood idling a fierce hum.

A flurry of expletives filled the burning, hot air followed by an arm garbed in flame retardant beige. E.J. slid under the grab. He caught the hand with his own swinging upward. The twisted appendage made the fellow yell in agony, dropping him to the ground.

E.J. raised his leg. Stepping hard, he drove a boot through the side of the man's knee.

No longer encumbered by the owner, the big Cummins diesel roared when his foot crashed down on the accelerator. Careful to avoid running over the welder with his own truck, E.J. swung the wheel hard.

The heavy flatbed sported a boom and a full complement of metal working gear. Launching through the rough construction easement made the weighty vehicle over travel vertically nearly as much as horizontally. An unexpected dip caused E.J.'s head to bounce to the roof of the cab. Dazed, he bounded nearly over the wheel. His toes struggled to push the brakes. Gradually, he gained traction over the pedal. The Dodge Mega Cab came to a stop nearly touching the starlet.

Her head jerked up to the same height as the grill and what must have been a million-dollar smile broke the tears and terror of the actress's sad countenance. She mouthed a minuscule thank-you in a state of both fear and joy. The driver's door swung open while E.J. ground the manual transmission. He popped the clutch, letting the behemoth lurch backward and die while he stepped forward.

As he transferred the diesel into a green bucket, the liquid splashed all over his hands while using the pump attached to a large white fuel container. The fuel odor irritated E.J.'s nostrils.

She lurched forward against the bonds. "I was certain you were a real cowboy."

E.J.'s arm lifted the heavy pail, moving it closer to the cab of the monstrous dirt mover. The enormous, tracked vehicle seemingly held the woman like King Kong clutching Fay Wray.

He needed to take her mind off what might happen. The bomb could erupt the moment he lifted it. Even if they survived, then it could still detonate the minute he placed it in the fuel.

E.J. turned his head, trying to breathe fresh air. Fumes from the yellow tinged propellent burned his lungs like a torch. "Why am I a real cowboy?"

She struggled to speak between tears. "You came back to save the damsel in distress."

The action of moving the explosives into the five-gallon bucket of liquid compelled him to confront her mortality. His life hadn't held value since Konner's death. Despite remaining nameless, he was aware that she would be missed. How great would the loss affect her children?

Would their suffering be compounded by the absurd and needless way she died? Her wealth and fame would only assure her of greater ridicule if she met her end in such an ignominious fashion.

In his career, he had seen many people panic when confronted by death. The woman's commitment to battling climate change rivaled religious martyrdom, forcing a heartfelt respect for such an absolute commitment. "Damsels don't try to save the planet by chaining themselves to giant diggers."

She raised her hand, leaning forward in the chains and filling her nose and mouth with air. Then she exhaled a nervous giggle. "It all made sense on the plane ride out here from LA. Don't move it yet. I don't want this to be the end. Not yet."

There was no point in the torture. He dunked the device in the lemony hued liquid sloshing over the crude bomb.

She forced out all the air she had held. "Might be a dud."

"I expect it is." He smiled and the corners of the tearful celebrity's mouth turned upward. E.J. thought about running with the device. Perhaps if it activated, he could get far enough away from her before it detonated. No, the smarter play was to set aside the diesel container and cut her free.

After unrolling the dull red-and-green rubber tubing off a wheel on the rear of the flatbed truck, he turned the knob to fuel the torch.

She spit away the hair sticking to the perspiration on her face. "You've used one before?"

"No." E.J. found the striker. A thought reproached him. She must be fearful he would burn her. "It's easy. You turn it on and light it."

"It's not," she snarked. "My father was an ironworker."

E.J. tried to hand her the torch and lighter.

She shook her head. "I can't get the angle tied up like this. Turn the red one on a little to get a flame, then add the green knob until you get a blue cone. You'll see what I mean."

E.J. snapped the striker in front of the torch. Light and a loud boom all in one moment left him holding a still, dark torch. The acetylene odor settled over them. E.J. tried again after additional instruction.

This time the boom continued, and he adjusted the wide flame as directed from sun like orange to a narrow sky-blue blaze, giving off the illusion of coolness.

The torch heated the steel links to a bright orange as she had directed him. He depressed the oxygen, painting the flame a brighter blue. The blue cone bit into the metal. Sparks flew, dancing toward the movie star, despite E.J.'s best efforts to cut the chain behind the track.

Twice he moved too close to the thick chain link, causing the conflagration to pop and end. Ablaze again, the torch sprung to life. The link transformed from chrome to a brilliant cherry, then burst into liquid. Gases from the torch blew away the molten semisolid orange gel.

She leaped forward, dropping to her knees before scampering for balance. From there, her movement morphed into a dead sprint.

Turning the knob to put out the flame, E.J. tossed the wand from his hand. He chased the woman, fearing he had burned her. His knee turned and snapped against the bone, inflicting mind-numbing pain. The heel of his boot on the other leg twisted on the packed soil. His teeth gritted back the pain and E.J. closed the distance.

They slid across a carpet of copper-colored spindly needles under a thick canopy of planted pine. E.J. pushed back the narrow branches ending in long green needles. Despite dragging the clanging chains, the actor shimmied down a gulley, sliding against the clay bank before nearly folding over backward.

The tips of E.J.'s boots stumbled over the backs of her feet, colliding into the small of her back when she fell backward. There was nowhere to go. He couldn't move out of her way.

She collapsed over him, twisting and looking sideways, her aspect facing his own. Warm breath flooded over his mouth and nose. Her dark eyes projected a magnetism. He leaned back to escape. Strawberry perfume added to his clouded mind.

"You're on my gun," E.J. said.

She released a hearty laugh. "I'm not complaining." Relief exploded across her face.

"My boss's lawyer insists we never risk a lawsuit. Don't want to be improper." E.J. looked down and away. "Lawyer is going to insist on charging you with criminal trespass."

She continued cackling, tearstained cheeks beaming. Retreating, he pulled his head back until it pressed to the ground. Vibrant full lips parted, drawing him closer.

The smile morphed into a mischievous beam. Her eyes searched for his as her cadence and tone slowed to a whisper. "Who is this big, bad lawyer who is supposed to scare me?"

E.J. found the performance over the top, yet effective. How could such conflicting results be correct? "My ex-wife."

Moist air enveloped him. Her fingers and long nails wrapped around his wedding ring. "Ex-wife?"

Even invoking Rebecca's memory did nothing to release him from the power of the celebrity's appeal. Where was the formerly abrasive and disagreeable person who couldn't mask her opinion of him as a fool?

The polarity now fully reversed, E.J. witnessed the magnetism the woman conveyed in her profession. Why invest her time mocking him? Did she want to determine if he was susceptible to her charms? His feet sunk deeper every moment.

Why did Hollywood people do anything? Her demeanor conveyed sincerity. Immersing herself in the dramatic arts likely taught her how to express anything with compelling persuasion. He craved a release from her eyes. Rolling upward, his view caught a high cloud floating over a clear sky above the pine canopy.

"Call me if your lawyer is ever not your lawyer anymore."

Chapter Three

The Writ Begins

S hort, prickly brown grass snapped under E.J.'s boots like shards of glass. How could a drought be strong enough to curdle bottomland yet leave the air so thick with humidity it poured more than stirred?

His nostrils filled with the musty odor of the brindle-faced longhorn laying in the dead grass. E.J. gingerly made his way around to the back of the bovine. "Easy, old girl," he whispered.

Through the darkness of placenta and birthing fluid, E.J. spied legs and a cherry red head splattered with white splotches. No matter how dark, how ugly the world turned, creation kept pushing through.

The phone's speaker screeched the song "Black Betty." E.J. jumped, then gritted his teeth. The ringtone denoted his ex-wife, Rebecca. He pushed the button, knowing she would inundate him with a cascade of expletives.

"Calm down." As fast as he said the words, he realized such would only aggravate her. He chided himself for his stupidity, vainly trying to remember the strategies Sharla's therapist had suggested to facilitate communication with Rebecca.

"You're telling me to calm down? You're not the one going to change diapers and be up all night. And since when does our daughter share anything with you—"

"I swear, one minute we're riding through Big Bend, the next minute she drops a bomb on me." The therapist hadn't appreciated that communication strategies were worthless when arguing against a world-class trial lawyer.

"You shamed her into wanting to keep it," said Rebecca.

"No. I swear I—"

"Don't lie to me. More Baptist ignorance," yelled Rebecca.

E.J. saw no point in further defending himself. He hadn't been Baptist anything since before their son, Konner, died. E.J. couldn't remember ever winning an argument against Rebecca.

Her forceful demeanor came across despite being limited to the phone. The same presence had drawn him to her over thirty years ago when he first witnessed a young assistant district attorney commanding the courtroom. He looked over his shoulder at the bovine birth. The windstorm of arguing with Rebecca had swept him some distance away.

First the pink nose, then the entire bundle of wet fur pushed into the world. E.J. drew a deep breath. "I know it's rape. Remember, I'm the one who killed the traffickers."

Rebecca gasped and then the phone went silent. Had the line gone dead? Perhaps he shouldn't have said it, but Rebecca was aware. She had to have known.

He had often looked down his long driveway, picturing federal officers just out of sight staging to knock him down. A euphemism for throwing him to the ground and putting a gun to his head to execute a murder warrant.

"You brought our baby home." Rebecca's tone softened. "Never say more."

"Lost track of where wrong ends and right starts a long time ago, especially when it comes to Sharla," said E.J.

"She can't have this baby." Rebecca's tone switched back to terse.

"Best I can tell, neither one of us has a say. I don't know what more to add," said E.J.

"G.H. Burton," said Rebecca.

"Burton? Stacked life sentences, Burton?"

Rebecca exhaled through the phone in a burst. "He filed a writ."

"For a trial thirty years ago?" asked E.J.

"Twenty-five. Actual innocence. DNA exoneration. Wrongfully convicted, dirty cops, what they do in all the TV shows these days. I only got wind of it from a bailiff who knew it was my case." Rebecca's voice had the same lilt she used to highlight a phrase for the jury.

E.J.'s teeth clenched. Of all his cases, the one most certainly guilty was Burton, yet DNA didn't lie. It held the title as the gold standard of evidence. Immediately, his mind flashed back in time to an image of a cramped interview room. Burton's thick body odor infected the air. E.J. witnessed the glee, the knowing smirk of a man sanctimonious enough to justify the most horrid abuses of humanity, like some holy warrior. "DA fighting it, isn't he?"

"No, hearing the fool is rolling over. You know, be the big man who corrects the excesses of renegade police and prosecutors. Makes him a hero," said Rebecca.

E.J.'s shoulders slumped, weighed down by the overwhelming sense of powerlessness pouring over his body. He suspected having a disgraced former ranger as a lead investigator made an already salacious case irresistible to the media. Pity tried to course through him from the unfairness of life. He fought the emotion, lest it consume him.

Then his mind fired. Something akin to a match struck through the darkness. Rebecca never stopped persuading. She had formed a plan or she wouldn't have called. Of course, her primary purpose, their daughter, remained foremost, but they had this out twice already.

She'd prosecuted Burton with the old district attorney, Norton. The art of silence was one of the advocacy techniques that she had mastered. He was aware she patiently awaited the only proper response.

He had nearly died the first time he tangled with Burton. Why couldn't he pass on one? Wasn't his career over? Rebecca would never quit on justice.

Since their son's death, the law was her life. She would never willingly let someone like Burton make a mockery of everything she held sacred, even to the point of risking her career or her life. Rebecca needed him, though admitting it was impossible.

"What do you want me to do?" asked E.J.

"Courthouse now. Hearing is in a few hours. Got it from bailiff who overheard the DA bragging about turning Burton loose." Rebecca ended the call.

E.J. looked back again. Another shaky-legged, silly-looking longhorn calf in this world normally wouldn't be noteworthy. Welcome to the jungle, little one.

Scrambling back toward the barn in a long stepping attempt at a run, his bad knee stabbed him with pain. Showering, shaving, and dressing in record time, E.J. stepped out of his travel trailer and jumped into the new pickup furnished by his employer, Rex Ashe, founder of Devekon Energy.

If he weren't in such a hurry, he would call Rex Ashe to tell him about the calf. Rex insisted on keeping the big pets in old age to the point of feeding sugar cubes, because they had worn their teeth too much to chew. The image of old Rex petting on those nine-foot-wide horned critters brought a chuckle.

The momentary brevity didn't last. As he swung the big truck onto the highway, Rebecca's words pierced him again. Was the father a john, a pimp, a dealer, another user?

Sharla hadn't completed inpatient treatment. A career in law enforcement convinced E.J. there would be a lot of backsliding on the road to true recovery. The odds were against Sharla. Add the stress of single motherhood and her chances of remaining drug-free were near nil.

An army of people waving signs demanded E.J.'s full attention on the road. The Irish castle-style courthouse rose two bricked stories normally overlooking a town square reminiscent of a Norman Rockwell painting contrasted today by national news trucks sporting colorful logos and modern equipment.

He parked some distance away and came in through a rear entrance, typically reserved for law enforcement and transporting inmates. E.J. took the steps double-time, gritting his teeth from crunching bone on bone. Fighting an imaginary clock, he bounded onto the second floor, taking the briefest of moments before reaching a tall oak door with a white glass pane reading *District Attorney* in black letters.

The perfume he and Rebecca picked out on their honeymoon filled his nostrils. E.J. smiled, though Rebecca's dire expression ended any further nostalgia.

She rose from a wingback chair and stepped toward the inner office door. "We'll see the DA now."

Chapter Four

Rebecca's Plan

An older lady seated behind a desk raised her hand. Her face contorted into an aspect only practiced by the sternest of parents. "He's meeting with the speaker."

"The judge from Burton's trial?" E.J. acknowledged her nod. He knew Larence Kutnick had been elected to the legislature, but the speaker of the house seemed too much. In Texas, the speaker overshadowed the governor. He couldn't process Kutnick as the most powerful man in Texas.

Listening to Rebecca revealed she hadn't been living under a rock or a travel trailer watching old Westerns instead of news. Her eyes flashed a greater note of determination. "Good. I need to talk to him too."

Before the downcast-looking lady could rise, Rebecca had swung the next door open, surprising not two but three men. A tailored three-piece suit and striped tie matched Larence Kutnick's gray hair. He swung around and up from a short-backed leather chair. "Rebecca Johnson, how have you failed to age?"

E.J. stopped midstep. How did Kutnick pull a line like that off without sounding cheesy? Despite the man's sincere and warm expression, E.J. couldn't shake off the uneasiness. The involuntary twitch between his shoulder blades paled compared to the disgust at seeing Fenton's thick handlebar mustache leading down to the badge glinting on his chest.

Kutnick opened his arms, leaning toward Rebecca, and she shifted to take a side hug. E.J. shook Kutnick's hand, then the DA before looking at the third man's outstretched paw. "Fenton?"

"You haven't changed. Still not professional enough to understand I had my duty," said Fenton.

E.J. grunted something indecipherable, and Rebecca stepped in front of him, extending her palm to Fenton's. The man wore too much aftershave, soaking the air in Aqua Velva.

University of Texas football memorabilia filled every corner of the office. A white football embossed with a rose and final score decorated the desk while white wainscoting met burnt orange paint halfway up the walls, drawing E.J.'s attention.

"Permit me to present your newly elected DA, Robert Barton," said Kutnick.

"Went to the University of Texas?" asked E.J.

"No, just a fan. Community college then attended a low residency law school in Arizona. Had to keep the family business going. We couldn't all be homecoming queens and cattle barons."

A loose-fitting seersucker suit hung from the DA's narrow form as he motioned for Rebecca and E.J. to join the other two men in a row of chairs across the desk. "Please take a seat. We were just discussing the exoneration," said the DA.

"It's a writ. There has been no finding," said Rebecca.

The DA and Kutnick looked at each other in a knowing smile. "Tunnel vision," said Kutnick.

For a moment Rebecca's stoic trial-lawyer cast registered irritation before she buried it.

"The speaker had just addressed how hard it would be for some to accept the truth. Evidently, the human mind forces even contrary information into the tunnel toward the theory supporting the guilt of the victim," said the DA.

"Victim?" asked E.J.

The two gently made brief, awkward chuckles together. The fingernails on E.J.'s right hand pressed into the leather covered arm of the chair until he found the brass tacks on the underside. He wanted to touch the Sig Sauer pistol he carried in his pocket, though he didn't.

"You should not have a sense of embarrassment. The literature tells us this tunnel vision phenomena makes otherwise ethical professionals do some questionable things to impose their version of justice. I've sat through several hearings on the subject," said Kutnick.

E.J. pushed through gritted teeth. "A jury found him guilty—"

"Twelve people too stupid to formulate an excuse to go home driven into a rage by tainted and false evidence. All the while, old Norton hopped around like a wild Indian," said the DA.

Kutnick raised his arms, showing some effort to diffuse any possible insult.

Rebecca shifted in the seat to mirror Kutnick's posture. "I thought maybe you had Major Fenton here because you would have the rangers investigate the allegations."

"Nothing to investigate. DNA on the knife doesn't match Burton. I'm here to make sure the ranger service doesn't get drug through the mud," said Fenton.

"Rangers not going to investigate? Who is your superior?" asked Rebecca.

E.J. answered, "He is the major."

"Lieutenant colonel now. Technically, rangers are under the DPS umbrella so the colonel can overrule me, but as a practical matter, you need to direct your correspondence to the Almighty." Fenton snarled at E.J.

"When I saw your hat on the desk, I figured this thing was saucered and blown," said E.J.

Kutnick leaned forward onto the edge of the upholstered oak chair. "I have no authority even being the original judge. However, a certain morality compels me to urge Robert to agree to the writ."

"Thinking of your image too, Mr. Speaker?" asked Rebecca.

The DA's torso leaped forward in his chair. "D-N-A on the hunting knife, the murder weapon. I mean, come on. You argued racial motivation on Burton's supposedly Aryan Triangle and the DNA belongs to an unknown seventy percent sub-Saharan African descendant. It's over," said the DA.

E.J. caught himself after balling his fist. "Burton's Aryan Triangle. I've seen the tats."

"Maybe, but he's not sub-Saharan African and science doesn't lie," said the DA.

"We have to overcome our biases to get to the truth, right?" said Kutnick.

Rebecca turned in her chair. Her posture issued a challenge to Kutnick. "You've convinced the DA quitting gets votes," asked Rebecca.

"I know all these new developments. To be so wrong for so long, it's a shock. Can't you see how we all need to get out in front of this thing? We're preserving the legitimacy of the system. The wrong side of an actual innocence claim is like being stuck on the tracks with the train coming. You're not stopping it, so best to lie back and go with it," said Kutnick.

"Like rape?" said Rebecca.

The question hit Kutnick with the jolt of a cattle prod. "I didn't say that. I did not. I'm trying to help you. You can salvage all this.

A member of the original prosecution team with the courage to do God's work releasing an innocent man. Every innocence project in this nation will honor you with awards and banquets. You'll be at the top of the profession," said Kutnick.

The red-faced DA erupted, "Like the last time she climbed the ladder convicting an innocent man while bedding the lead detective."

E.J. shook his head. The only thing worse than a sanctimonious political opportunist was a jealous one. He had to rub the outside of his pocket over the top of the pistol. Years ago, rage would have fueled his decisions. Now, he took comfort in knowing Rebecca always gave better than she got.

"Let's not question each other's motivations. We're here to work together. All Robert is trying to say is the evidence compels granting the writ. Of course, Robert wants votes like you want the monied interest you've built your law practice on. And you, Ranger Kane—" Turning to stare at E.J. stopped Kutnick midsentence. He closed his arms over his chest.

"Not a ranger anymore." E.J. spit the words at Kutnick.

"No, you're not." Fenton smiled.

"You earned the title. I always liked you." Kutnick swung his arms back open. "You may not know I called Rex Ashe to let him know you needed a soft landing when you were getting drummed out of the ranger service."

The DA raised a hand. "Wait, we hold some terrible cards here. Some big-time actors and media influencers, along with several innocence projects, and major law professors, flew in for the hearing. We're talking about an assemblage with enough cash to elect a senator. After they get through wiping the courtroom floor with us, they're going for disbarment. You hear me, disbarment."

"There is no place for integrity?" asked Rebecca.

"You can have integrity flipping burgers. Frank Malgrone, the big-time thriller writer, with all the movies, is down here. How many Fortune 500 corporate clients are going to stay with you when a court rules you conspired with a crooked cop to frame some innocent guy?" asked Kutnick.

"You want to watch it on Netflix? Producer has already interviewed me. The story is written, only the facts need adding. What possible difference if Burton dies in jail or gets released? For Jesus's sake, the man turns sixty next month," said the DA.

Rebecca's head turned from partially facing Kutnick to concentrating her gaze on the DA. Like so many times during her and E.J.'s married life, Rebecca had made a plan. She had mastered putting people where she needed them to be like actors on a stage. E.J. took comfort in the fact, though unaware of the details.

"Kutnick is taking care of Kutnick. He is pushing the best option, parachuting him out of this mess. But you'll get crushed in the rubble. A horrible white supremacist crime becomes just more Black-on-Black violence 'the man' doesn't care to solve. A case this heinous can't remain open. When we unwrap this little care package of DNA results, there won't be a tidy CODIS hit connecting John Doe. It's unknown DNA. No one to convict. Nobody to blame." She turned to Kutnick. "Think your new Hollywood friends are going to tell the thirty percent of this electorate that is African-American how hard you're trying? No, they're gone to find some other poor sucker selling out his constituents to promote their cause."

She paused, her voice dropping to a whisper. "How many folks did Kutnick dip in the grease to get the speakership? You know the stories, selling the chairmanships, easy PAC money, the kickbacks. Nearly one hundred fifty billion dollars and not one nickel moves except through him. Think he'll hesitate to grind you into the dirt to protect his kingdom?"

The puzzled look on the DA's face acknowledged suspicions about why the most powerful man in Texas made an unannounced visit under the guise of seeing justice done. The DA released a long exhale, followed by one of the few curse words still capable of raising eyebrows.

Did Rebecca lead him to an epiphany? The look in his dim gray eyes was something akin to a kid who finally figured out the coin wasn't in either hand.

Kutnick pointed to Rebecca, drawing the eyes of all in the room. He shook his head, then displayed a scowl before straightening his tie to the point it rolled under the vest. "Thought you were smarter, Mr. DA."

"You leaving?" asked the DA.

"Potty training the grandson. Only person in the world whose backside I'll wipe. The worst is letting him clean himself. I still smell the mess and it gets everywhere." Kutnick stormed out, then turned and gently closed the door with a final menacing look around the room. "Getting an odor in here, might want to have the next DA clear it out."

Those last words floated in the stale air of the room. The DA turned his attention from the door to Rebecca, then he raised both hands toward his chest as if she missed the cue. "Ideas?"

"Your predecessor never revoked my deputation," said Rebecca.

E.J. observed her pause, as if someone had interrupted her. He softly shook his head before catching himself rubbing his knuckles across the top of the leather armrest. Was it a technique for drawing her audience's complete interest or did she think everyone put two and two together as fast as her?

The DA leaned forward in his chair, touching the desk with his torso. "Sooo?"

"Make me a special prosecutor. If I'm right, I prove this actual innocence claim amounts to a scam, then I'll step aside and you bask in the glory," said Rebecca.

"It's not a scam. I get stuck looking like a crook persecuting an innocent man." The chair creaked as the DA reclined. "Best you got? I should have chased after Kutnick."

"The selling point is I take this tar baby. If the judge approves my appointment, then I own an unsolvable, heinous murder cold case with racial overtones. You blame me. You sell it as you thought one of the original prosecutors would be most familiar with the witnesses and facts. If I lose, then you say I betrayed your trust by going rogue to fight an actual innocence writ. I'm giving you permission to sell me out," said Rebecca.

This time Rebecca leaned forward in her chair and E.J. mirrored her posture. "You're either the hero who uncovered a scam or you're the betrayed hero misled by the now rogue soon to be disbarred lawyer. You can't lose."

"Are you crazy? Can't you see she is playing you?" asked Fenton.

"You and the speaker weren't? Why he left you in here to report back, right?" asked the DA.

"You're crazy. We're trying to help you," said Fenton.

"Then go report I'm crazy," said the DA.

A tightness gripped E.J.'s chest. She was risking her law license? If they couldn't prove the writ false, then she faces disbarment, even jail.

With a direct gaze into the DA's pale gunmetal eyes, E.J. saw this man held the flare to Rebecca's gasoline doused career. The sight of Fenton triggered memories of his departure from law enforcement. It had devastated E.J. in a way he didn't fully appreciate at the time. He had remembered the rough peaks and valleys of the elaborate scroll on his badge, heated by his trembling hand. Even now, he nearly saw Fenton's desk before him. He'd rather have taken a bullet than drop the *cinco peso*.

Rebecca was tougher than he in many ways, though she wouldn't survive the loss of her dream. The great legal career and the powerful trial lawyer persona defined her and sustained her through the death of their son.

Tearing into opposing lawyers, the only respite from endless conjecture concerning why her son, her freedom of information request, and worst of all a mind forced to come to terms with the cosmic unfairness that the baby she carried, she bore, she loved, suffered what she thought a meaningless death on the other side of the Earth. Died trying to emulate the glory of his father, the famed Texas Ranger E.J. Kane, in whose heroism the child had basked.

E.J. placed his palm over her hand on the arm rest while his stomach knifed him like the day it all had ended. Stepping back in time, he watched a Marine give her a flag honoring Konner's "faithful and honorable service." She had passed it to E.J. The cloth had a thick, solid feel, especially the raised embroidery of the white stars.

The DA's voice pierced E.J.'s suffering with a shrill tone. "When I choose, I burn you down and you don't retaliate?"

"Everyone knows I take all the heat no matter how hot. My name settles cases," said Rebecca.

The DA nodded, setting his jaw. He stood up from his desk and shook her hand. "You keep junior ranger boy here away until I'm out of this and you're appointed. None of us can carry his baggage." The DA walked past them, ignoring E.J.'s partially extended hand.

"We're going to get the judge to make it official." Her eyes lowered and her raspy voice softened. So many compared her distinctive timbre to the singer, Stevie Nicks. "You can sit in the courtroom, but it's probably best to keep in the back."

Her eyes softened the command. E.J. had felt a tiny tremble in her hand. The slight shake was mere momentary evidence the super lawyer, beloved mother, and the best friend he had ever known still suffered the limitations placed on the rest of us mortals. The brief quiver in her fingers had been enough to pull him to the image of the flag at the funeral. Tears had streamed from the woman he had sworn to love, honor, and cherish for all of his life.

Each droplet served as a vicious indictment proclaiming her husband's failure. She was right. Konner had grown up hearing exploits of his heroic father. Every son needed to best his father. An image flashed of the beaming smile from Konner the first time he outshot his father in a pistol match. Why hadn't he talked his son out of the military?

Despite the fear he felt for his son, a great pride had consumed E.J. seeing his son in the magnificent dress uniform. "Faithful and honorable service," the words echoed through his mind, falling like the *cinco peso* badge he'd dropped on his major's desk.

An edict akin to a commandment from the recesses of his mind catapulted to the fore demanding, not this time. He twisted the wedding ring he'd never been able to truly put aside. This time, he wouldn't fail Rebecca. His legs seemed rubbery, yet he rose and kept moving, wishing to put emotion behind him like a foul stench he could walk past.

E.J. looked up into the busy hallway. His thoughts had consumed him. Evidently Rebecca had followed the DA out while E.J. had wandered aimlessly through the hallway.

Rebecca wouldn't suffer even if he had to kill G.H. Burton. Better to spend life in a cage than cause her more grief. E.J. looked for a corner to compose himself. He recognized a rarely used back entrance to the law library and stepped toward it.

The heavy door swung open, releasing a musty, foul odor akin to unsealing a tomb. A surprised bearded face turned to a self-satisfied smirk. Mr. G.H. Burton sat clothed in a new white suit behind a table between bookshelves. Bright light from a magnificent, refurbished chandelier illuminated him so his gray stood out in the hair and beard, yet the eyes evoked the same unmistakable chill along E.J.'s spine.

"Shalom, dear friend. Do come in."

Chapter Five

Meeting a Murderer

"**P**retending to be Jewish too?" asked E.J.

A swastika moved into view tattooed on the back of Burton's left hand. "Did study the kike's kabbalah, though. I've dedicated my life to the pursuit of knowledge. You look confused, dear friend."

E.J.'s mind struggled to process how G.H. Burton sat before him when yesterday he had been certain Burton would die in prison. There were no handcuffs, no leg cuffs, and no guard. In his era, a capital murder defendant would have been restrained by all such devices and likely a belt capable of delivering a jolt equal to a stun gun.

Burton laughed. "Dear friend, I feared you would decline my invitation." G.H. Burton raised his arms like a minister making an altar call.

Though startled by Burton, E.J. surveyed the room. Dark wood bookcases, chairs, and a pair of tables outfitted with computers. "Invitation."

"I told the bailiff I was trying to keep the hearing from being completed before your little strumpet found out. Why, I might as well have called her myself. Always wanted to visit with her, anyway."

"Where's your lawyer?" asked E.J.

"Lawyer? Lawyer? Dear friend, why would the judge need a lawyer?" Burton turned his outstretched palms open.

"Drop the bull. I'm not wearing a wire," said E.J.

Burton smiled, then looked around the room. "I'm so happy to see the dear friend. Dinner tonight? They tell me I'll make bond. I want to thank you and the strumpet personally. It has been a constant dream of mine all these years."

"Really believe you can pull this off. You got classified intellectual disabled the first time you went down. Heard you ran the ID section of the Grissom Unit like some kind of mafia godfather," said E.J.

"Retardland. Little tards called me their tard king. A whole army of mud people, mongoloids, at my command," said Burton.

"You always gaming the system, aren't you?" asked E.J.

"I had difficulty getting news about your trial. Why when you get your men killed it is criminally negligent homicide, but I kill my own darkies and it's capital murder?"

Rage extended through E.J.'s torso, radiating down his arms. He glared through Burton.

"Because right is made by who wears the badges. You'll find out," said Burton.

"Always manipulating. Last time you pulled me into an argument, you shot me." E.J. leaned against one of the neat shelves of leather-bound volumes.

"Shame junior weren't bulletproof too, dear friend," said G.H. Burton.

The matter-of-fact tone and the glee in Burton's countenance made the comment unbearable. E.J. touched the outside of his pants pocket, comforting his stifled rage.

G.H. Burton flung his arms wide. "God sent you to release me from this material state. Your destiny, dear friend. Don't fail again."

Did Burton want to die? Did he have some plan to get E.J. in prison for killing him? Nothing else made sense. Over Burton's shoulder, a sliver of light expanded to a halo. The inflating, glimmering crevasse froze E.J., preventing him from reaching the subcompact semiautomatic in his pants.

A familiar monster stood in the doorway wearing a badge on his chest. The man drew a large frame semiautomatic weapon, smooth and fast. E.J. witnessed the wide bore of what looked like a forty-five. E.J. knew the true caliber of the pistol from experience. Sheriff B.B. carried the rarer ten millimeter. The man had despised E.J. since they were kids, for reasons he never shared with E.J.

From under a palm leaf cowboy hat, Sheriff B.B.'s customary crooked grin shone. E.J.'s attention switched back to the pistol pointed at his gut before Sheriff B.B. yelled at him. "Pretender, got you good. Trying to draw down on the law."

E.J. pulled his hand away from his thigh, well aware he looked guilty.

"Draw, pretender. Not like you to hold back. Must be getting more cowardly in your old age," said Sheriff B.B.

"Stepped through the wrong door is all. Lots of folks here today. Didn't know he was in here," said E.J.

"The dear friend came to see me," said G.H. Burton.

Sheriff B.B. snapped back at E.J. "This old boy's not your friend. He's the crooked cop who put you here. I'd do us both a good here, pluggin' him. Self-defense n' all."

"Think about it. You've never got the drop on me, even once in a thousand times when we were kids playing fast draw. What if I'm really unarmed? People all around us. Fire and you won't have time to drop a throw-down piece on me," said E.J.

The look in Sheriff B.B.'s dark eyes caused an uneasiness all the way up E.J.'s spine before cresting on his shoulders. The white-hot fire of B.B.'s hatred had always taken E.J. aback. Why the animosity? What had he ever done to B.B. to rate murder? Could he bluff B.B. one more time?

Burton yelled, "Don't shoot the dear friend."

Sheriff B.B. beamed like a kid finding a bicycle under the tree on Christmas morning. "Pretender, rent a cop, came to kill you. Wanting to cover up for his crimes. Would've got away with it, too, but for me interrupting him. You get set free and old Matthew McConaughey plays me in the movie."

Burton yelled, locking eyes with B.B. and breaking into a tirade, slapping his arms on the tabletop. "No. Leave dear friend alone."

Chapter Six

The Farce Begins

"Get out of here," Sheriff B.B. yelled in a guttural chant, motioning with his pistol toward E.J.

E.J. walked out the door he had entered. He had forgotten the moniker G.H. Burton had tagged him with, "dear friend." How could he have ever forgotten? Cold sweat beaded his forehead. Had he nearly died by opening the wrong door?

Walking a few feet, E.J. leaned against the wall, his shoulders shuddered. Why did B.B. let him go? When would he accept the truth? B.B. really wanted to kill him. What did this guy hold against him?

E.J. slid his hands over his pants, letting his fingertips ride over the rail of his pocket gun. Had he bluffed B.B.? No, at least not entirely because everyone knew he carried a pocket pistol. There he had stood with the man he despised having the drop on him. B.B.'s analysis had most probably been correct as to how the press would write the story. What a headline—hero sheriff kills rogue cop. His death would have affirmed everything Burton's defense team had claimed.

Courthouse security fell within the authority of sheriffs. Texas law only prohibited weapons in the actual courtrooms and judges' chambers. Still, why else would a disgraced officer end up armed and alone with the murderer who claimed the officer wrongfully convicted him if not to silence the inmate?

After surviving a night "off the books" in Sheriff B.B.'s jail, the memories flooded back to him like a thick liquid, leaving E.J. gasping for air. Several weeks went by before he was able to breathe without his ribs causing pain. The force of B.B.'s steel-toed boot slamming him in the kidneys made him buckle from recall alone.

E.J. carried his Sig Sauer 938 in his pocket, walking down the stairs through the mass of people and locked it in the glovebox of his truck. The decision proved more providential than he had expected. Upon his return, E.J. saw deputies had set up a metal detector at the courtroom entrance. He had never previously seen a metal detector in this courthouse.

Navigating through the crowd of more than a hundred people, E.J. successfully reached the back of the room. Images of the victims' family sprung through his thoughts. Nothing struck him as so insensitive as failing to recognize a victim's kinfolks he should know.

Young people composed most of the gallery adorned in "Free G.H. Burton" written in dark ink on red tee shirts. Half a dozen lawyers in suits took a seat around a far too small counsel table featuring G.H. Burton at the end. The DA stopped and shook hands with each attorney.

Rebecca made a faint nod at an older lawyer wearing a blue three-piece. She took a position alone behind the table closest to the empty jury box.

An overwhelming desire washed over E.J., the need to go to Rebecca. She looked alone on her side of the courtroom, awash on a stormy sea, yet the baggage he carried most certainly would sink her. His shoulders and arms shuddered from the sudden feeling of powerlessness like a dream where he lay paralyzed.

The doorway drew his attention. What fool wears his hat in the courtroom? Sheriff Benjamin Berryhill walked in under a flat-brimmed, short, crowned Stetson.

A straw stuck E.J.'s thick-skinned fingertips. He realized he had pressed the wire brim of his straw hat until the thick weave bent into the flesh of his finger pad. E.J. had grown up with B.B. Plenty of older men and women would have knocked the hat off B.B.'s head as a youth. The door opened from the judge's chamber and Sheriff B.B. called the court to attention, still wearing the headgear.

Why had B.B. let him go after catching him in Burton's holding room? The former lead investigator, armed, alone with the man he supposedly railroaded on the eve of the hearing to free Burton and prove E.J. further disgraced his badge. It amounted to plenty of motive and opportunity, perhaps even probable cause for an attempted murder charge.

Motive, opportunity, and he had been armed. B.B. wasn't known for patience or calm reflection. For that matter, rational decision making wasn't B.B.'s strong suit either. Why didn't he shoot? Whatever shortcoming B.B. suffered, cowardice wasn't one of them.

The judge ascended the bench, gracefully befitting her demeanor. Long dark hair matching her robe appeared too uniform not to be dyed. The confident gait reassured E.J. she possessed a wealth of experience. "Be seated. I'm Judge Rhonda Simon, sitting by assignment. Counsel, are we ready?"

Three-piece blue suit stood and said, "Your Honor, Ray Weatherstine, for your applicant, G.H. Burton. Who has spent near twenty-five years wrongfully incarcerated in the foulest prisons on Earth. As set forth in the writ, testing has confirmed DNA from a different person on the murder weapon."

Three-piece blue suit extended an open hand toward Burton. "Despite the egregious misconduct my client suffered, he has requested in exchange for his freedom waiving any monetary actual innocence claims as well as bar discipline complaints for the prosecutorial misconduct putting him here."

A small spattering of boos splashed through the courtroom until the judge spoke. "I'll tolerate no outburst. That's an incredibly gracious offer. I'm not certain some of these matters can be waived. Counsel, are you satisfied your client is mentally competent to proceed?"

"Yes, Your Honor. Despite his obvious intellectual disability. He has a present understanding of what is occurring and can assist his counsel."

"Mr. Burton, do you understand what is taking place?"

"Yes, Judge."

"You understand you don't have to give up any compensation you're entitled to?" asked the judge.

"Justice. Only justice." Burton fumbled past the words.

The judge smiled. "Commendable."

Rebecca's harsh tone shredded the emotional blanket wrapping around the room. "Your Honor, Rebecca Johnson. My former deputation remains on file as a state's attorney and the Honorable District Attorney Robert Barton has approved. In fact, he has requested I represent the State as special prosecutor because I am well versed in the issues surrounding the case. I've already taken and filed the oath. I only lack your signature on the order before you, Your Honor."

"All true, Mr. DA?" asked the judge.

"Ms. Johnson has won acclaim for her skill and integrity. No one could doubt she will do the right thing. It is only proper she remedies any mistakes she made long prior to my taking office. Your Honor," said the DA.

From E.J.'s seat in the back of the courtroom, the DA's voice cracked and sounded weak.

"What says the State, Ms. Johnson?"

"The order, Your Honor," said Rebecca.

"Of course." The judge signed the document and handed it down to a clerk.

"Your Honor, may I be excused?" The DA turned on his heel before the response.

"Yes. Now, what says the State?" asked the judge.

Rebecca delivered her response in a deadpan tone. "The State announces not ready. I need time to investigate the claims." A brief clamor broke out and ended in the audience.

"The murder weapon matches someone else's DNA. Not only is Burton excluded, he shares no demographic characteristics with the person. You either have the integrity to dismiss and I release this man or you don't," said the judge.

"For twenty-five years, America believed G.H. Burton perpetrated a racially motivated, heinous multiple murder. The crime captured the news cycles for months. Doesn't the collective wisdom of a generation and a jury verdict upheld by appellate courts, including the U.S. Supreme Court, merit one month?" said Rebecca.

E.J. drew deeply, drawing air into his lungs, surprising himself that he had been holding his breath. Go Rebecca.

Three-piece blue suit chimed in. "Not one more day. Before we could feign ignorance, Your Honor. Now we all hold the truth hostage to the failed tunnel vision of an overzealous prosecutor. Parties to it. A month seems small, seems prudent. It's not. Even a day, an hour, is enormous. As massive a chasm as the abyss between right and wrong.

In your own words, Your Honor, 'You either have integrity or you don't.' She is not even offering bail while the State investigates the results of its own laboratory system."

G.H. Burton locked eyes with E.J. Evidently, he had been looking for him. Meanwhile, E.J. had watched G.H. Burton from the start of the hearing. Burton had alternated between smiling and shaking his head at inappropriate times. The defendant had to remain in character, maintaining his own imitation of the intellectually disabled. When Burton caught E.J.'s eyes, he winked.

E.J. looked away. The sham, the total mockery G.H. Burton made of man's greatest attempt at justice was unfathomable. This farcical hearing only proved its own absurdity. John Wayne's voice recited the lines from the movie of Charles Portis's *True Grit* on the service of a rat writ, writ for a rat. "You can't serve papers on a rat, baby sister. You gotta kill him or let him be."

E.J. turned his head back to the icy stare of G.H. Burton and mouthed "You gotta kill him or let him be." Regretting having stashed his pocket pistol in the truck, he slid his hand across the cotton pleat of his trousers. The thing spoke for itself; this rat gamed the system. E.J. rejected the actual innocence conclusion of Burton. Further, an Aryan Triangle leader partnering with a Black man seemed implausible. Therefore, logic dictated the results were erroneous.

No one made DNA, yet one could transfer it from one item to another and it bore no time stamp. Somehow, Burton used his Aryan Triangle brethren to contaminate the evidence. How? Didn't the lab store the knife all these years? The lab evidence storage bested Fort Knox for security.

E.J.'s gaze shifted to Rebecca. She addressed the court in a technical argument about the actual innocence writ procedure. What would happen to her career if he couldn't prove the writ bogus, disbarment? What a horrible disgrace might await her.

The families of the victims' suffering had been horrendous, transporting his thoughts to their small family cemetery. At the time, death hadn't eclipsed hope in his life, so there had been an abstract quality in witnessing their grief. The grief of others, the poor unfortunates upon whom evil had been visited. Only years later, when Konner died in the war, did grief materialize in a tangible and debilitating form.

The pit of E.J.'s stomach twisted. Every time he heard a new report on Afghanistan, Konner's death materialized from a dull pain, sometimes leaving him alone to a sharp burning throughout his heart. He couldn't let the families suffer the murders all over again. Killing Burton would end so much harm.

His training convicted him with the knowledge any killing outside the penal code justifications amounted to murder. Admittedly a wrong, still a wrong restoring order to the mockery of justice playing out before him. He could protect Rebecca from further pain and bring closure to the victims' families. There had been half a dozen times since Old Sheriff Wharton tossed a badge at E.J. when his life had been forfeit. A marker fate might call at any time. Shouldn't a person choose what he died over? Why not a time and place of his own choosing? Wouldn't him trading his life be a fair bargain if he made the world a little more just?

What would Konner think of him? The thought startled him into looking toward the door where his former pupil walked into the courtroom. She wore a black Western string bow tied against a white starched button-down shirt accenting a silver *cinco peso* badge. He knew what Cooper would think and what she would do.

She never understood the greater good. For her, right and wrong were not abstract ideas based on the notions of justice, rather, they were concepts defined by the Texas Penal Code and Texas Department of Public Safety policy. Her actions implied such bright-line rules took precedence regardless of whether the portrait they painted looked like justice. Were an inmate's life in danger no matter how depraved the fiend, she would eliminate the threat or, worse, protect him with her own life.

He couldn't be responsible for hurting Cooper. She was more like a daughter than a trainee.

The formerly hushed gallery erupted in noise and the judge snapped the gavel against the pedestal. The action made virtually no sound, yet the movement resulted in immediate quiet. "I'm prepared to rule."

Chapter Seven

Ruling

"Mr. Burton, please stand. Sir, you may have suffered the worst indignation our society can perpetrate on a citizen. I am concerned from reading the reports and your demeanor here today about how much of these proceedings you fully appreciate. Do you understand me, sir?"

Burton smiled. Three-piece blue suit spoke under his breath. "Answer her."

Burton smiled broader.

The judge leaned forward. "Do you know what you are doing here today?"

"I saw dear friend." Burton pointed to the back of the courtroom, and everyone turned.

E.J. wanted to hide. The alleged dirty cop the entire proceeding had vilified was now called out and laid bare before the world. The stares radiated through him. E.J.'s shoulders pulled back. He had to remain stoic.

The judge looked at E.J. then ignored him and continued her pronouncement. "Mr. Burton, the Court is appointing Dr. Robert Dirne, the foremost authority on intellectual disability. The sheriff

shall transport you to Beaumont for evaluation. We'll reconvene in
fifteen days to review the findings. Which means you have fifteen days
to explain the exculpatory DNA findings, Ms. Johnson."

"Your Honor, not enough time. I need to comb the case file, interview everyone connected with the investigation to—"

"Fourteen days." The judge flashed a stern countenance to Rebecca. "Fourteen days and if you have made this court a party to extending
this man's unjust confinement, then I will personally file the state bar
complaint against you. Do you understand me, Counselor?"

"Yes, Your Honor."

Three-piece blue suit rose, and the judge turned her head toward
him.

"You want to except to the ruling, Mr. Weatherstine."

"Your Honor, you gave the State a two-week continuance without
even taking testimony about whether the State has a hypothesis to
explain the exculpatory DNA. My client has been in jail for decades.
The public outrage is so powerful the elected DA quits the case. I suspect you can't find him in the courthouse. He has left an illegitimate
substitute who doesn't even express conjecture on how the results are
anything but divine truth. Meanwhile, my client suffers irreparable
injury every day, every minute, every second he sits wrongfully incarcerated by a corrupt system and respectfully, Your Honor, you are
making us all a part of the disgrace. I demand a bill of exceptions."

The judge peered down over her blue reading glasses, then she
nodded. "Make your bill, Counselor."

Three-piece blue suit called another attorney from his team as a
witness. Testimony revealed this more junior attorney held a master's
degree in biology. However, she explained the DNA testing like a
child's science television personality. Sprinkling four and five-syllable
words into her plain-speaking answers to highlight the integrity of

DNA testing. Matches are never matches. Rather, we use statistical modeling formulas to provide context for DNA results by exclusion.

An impressive animation, including a graph showing two alleles assigned numerical variables at thirteen different locations, appeared on monitors at the counsel tables and a big screen to the judge's right. In this instance, the odds of anyone other than the unknown person sourcing the DNA are computed to one in eight quintillion. Then she tried to put the number in context by estimating how many people may have lived in the planet's history, evidencing the truly staggering nature of the number and concept.

"So even though the science doesn't recognize the term match. Common sense tells us it's a match on the most epic scale fathomable in the universe," said three-piece blue suit.

Without waiting for the witness to answer, three-piece blue suit passed the witness.

E.J. scanned Rebecca's direction. Three-piece blue suit had reached his crescendo and no one could deny him the drama of the moment. The courtroom leaned forward in collective pause.

The judge turned to Rebecca. "Ms. Johnson?"

"Tell the judge about the National Forensic Science Commission and their report."

The puzzled witness turned toward the bench. "It's an attempt to end the junk science obscuring the truth. We all know our nation stands plagued with an epidemic of wrongful convictions. Unsupported scientific theory presents a critical factor."

"Suffice to say much of what the criminal justice system formerly held as the quote gold standard at some point in time had now been proven false, right?" Rebecca made air quotes as she spoke the words gold standard.

"I wouldn't phrase it that way, but yes," said the young lawyer.

"Why wouldn't you? I mean, it is how you're employed. Innocence projects exonerate people often convicted by purported junk science, right?" asked Rebecca.

"In general terms," said the young lawyer.

"You would point to bite marks, gunshot residue testing, blood spatter, fingernail striations, and we go back far enough, truth serum and polygraphs, correct?" asked Rebecca.

"Yes," said the young lawyer.

"Yet each such forensic discipline at one time was considered the gold standard of its era, right?" asked Rebecca.

"Bad science and prosecutorial misconduct." The young attorney smiled, looking at three-piece blue suit for encouragement.

"Bad science like DNA?" Rebecca had a lift in her voice, mirroring the surprise she had exploded with the assertion.

The attorney's head snapped toward Rebecca. "No, DNA truly is the gold standard. It's the real deal." Suddenly looking self-conscience, she added, "So to speak."

"Then why have the FBI and all state crime labs changed the manner of reporting the results?" asked Rebecca.

"I don't understand. What are you asking?" said the young lawyer.

"Like, for example, in Texas we had to create a commission of lawyers to review cases because the statistical models proved erroneous, correct?" asked Rebecca.

"Not the way I would phrase it?"

Rebecca swung her hand toward the judge. "Then please tell us how you would phrase it?"

"The DNA science never changed. Mathematicians discovered some statistical models were imprecise dependent upon certain demographic population groups—"

Rebecca cut her off. "Why in the modern era are we even still comparing people by demographic groups like race? Strike that."

E.J. knew Rebecca didn't start then withdraw questions without a purpose. He concluded the question made her argument much better than the answer.

"Isn't the truth that science discovered some of these assertions about the odds of finding another quote, a match, proved false and misleading in terms of common sense? For example, some of those results where one in more than all the people who science tells us ever lived on the Earth corrected to one in fifty, right?"

"The models appeared inexact in certain circumstances," said the young lawyer.

"Quite the understatement, isn't it?" asked Rebecca.

"No," said the young lawyer.

"Inexact enough, your organization was able to get some people released from prison based on errors in your purported gold standard, DNA itself, right?" asked Rebecca.

The young attorney exhaled like a bellow. "I wouldn't phrase it that way."

"You didn't have a problem phrasing it that way when you were getting people released or grant applications and fundraising literature, did you?" Rebecca didn't provide an opportunity to answer the question. "You called the inexact results erroneous in cases where it suited your purposes, right?" asked Rebecca.

"We reviewed discrepancies—"

Rebecca raised her hand, halting the witness. "Like maybe instead of from a one in six quintillion number to a one in ten thousand number. Meaning there are more than half a million people on the planet who are a match? And this example isn't near as bad as some of the matches, right? Strike that last part because we certainly don't have matches in this scientific discipline, do we?"

"We found some models less discriminating than originally calculated?" answered the young lawyer.

"Models based on race, right?" asked Rebecca.

"Not based on race. Race serves as a discriminating factor in the analysis."

"But you break each statistic down based on racial groups. One in so many Blacks or whites and so forth, correct?" asked Rebecca.

"Yes but—"

"Pass the witness." Rebecca's voice boomed like an exclamation point ending a paragraph.

E.J. couldn't suppress a smile forming at the corners of his mouth. Minutes before, this entire room had believed the truth of DNA compared to the certainty the sun rose every day in the East. Nothing had ever showed the contrary.

Three-piece blue suit performed a lengthy redirect explaining the science never changed rather only the interpretation of the results through the statistical models. He took great lengths to crush any suggestion there was an improper racial element. Though pressed into areas of first impression, the witness took his hints and ran with them.

She identified her preteen daughters before explaining how she articulated the science into understandable terms the girls could follow. The anecdotal explanation made for an effective presentation. However, to E.J.'s mind, the well-executed routine raised the truism which had helped earn Ronald Reagan the title great communicator, "If you're explaining, you're losing."

Rebecca declined further questioning. An obvious sign she had won this skirmish, causing E.J.'s shoulders to relax and release a deep breath.

Three-piece blue suit turned to face the back of the courtroom. E.J. grinned when three-piece blue suit's gaze locked on to his.

"Call Elliott Kane, Your Honor."

E.J.'s mind sprung to an expletive while Rebecca leaped to her feet.

Chapter Eight

Elliott Takes the Stand

"Objection, Your Honor. We've exceeded the scope of the bill. Counsel's exceptions to the court's ruling can't possibly encompass calling a private citizen."

Three-piece blue suit grinned. "Your Honor. Unlike the DA, Ms. Johnson, as the purported special prosecutor, commands no resources. Rather, what she can bring to bear amounts to the same misconduct, bringing us before the court today. Her original investigator and..." He took a long pause. "Her original husband."

"Call your witness, Counselor," said the judge.

"My colleague, Mr. Gresham, calls E.J. Kane."

E.J. stepped inside the rail, stopping before the judge in the well of the courtroom. Why did he smile at three-piece blue suit? Perhaps, especially given the different attorney, three-piece blue suit had always intended to call him to the witness stand. An uneasy pull in his back made him aware of the room full of people staring at him. During the oath and the few steps to the witness stand, E.J. forced himself to pull the thick, stale air of the courtroom into his lungs.

Three-piece blue suit nodded to a twenty-something lawyer who asked his question in a tone heavy with disdain. "You are the E.J. Kane who originally arrested my client?"

G.H. Burton nodded, adding, "The dear friend."

"Please, Mr. Burton. Your lawyer will speak," said the judge.

"Yes." E.J. fought back a rage at the smugness and Burton's show. From the sarcastic tone, it was apparent the kid had reached the conclusion that E.J. had behaved like Dirty Harry on steroids, yet the attorney probably hadn't had a single adult tooth in his head at the time of the murders.

"At the time of this case, you were a Texas Ranger, were you not?"

"Yes," said E.J.

"However, you are no longer associated with the rangers because of a scandal, correct?" asked the attorney.

E.J. shifted and shrugged in the witness chair. "I don't know about 'scandal.'"

"Rangers fired you, correct?" asked the attorney.

"I resigned—"

"Resigned while the subject of an internal investigation, correct?" asked the attorney.

"That is correct," said E.J.

"It's also correct to say the investigation never concluded?"

"Pointless after I resigned," said E.J.

"Among the matters investigated were allegations you took a bribe from a member of Zarcata cartel, correct?" asked the attorney.

"No," said E.J.

"No? I have Sheriff Benjamin Berryhill's letter to the Department of Public Safety's colonel stating he believed you took a bribe—"

"I expect you do." E.J. surveyed the room. Sheriff B.B.'s egotistical grin jumped out at him under a straw cowboy hat near the entrance of the crowded courtroom.

"Ultimately you were charged, correct?" said the lawyer.

"Not with bribery," said E.J.

"Charged nonetheless, correct?" asked the attorney.

"Criminal negligence for the death of the officers under my command, but a jury acquitted me."

"Let's return to the bribery allegations. Would you describe bribery as honest or dishonest?" asked the lawyer.

"Dishonest," said E.J.

"And what would you say about the character of one who takes bribes, moral or immoral?" The young person made a check mark on a paper and looked for approval from three-piece blue suit.

They had always intended to call him. His reputation was toxic, and the taint spilled over to everything before or after his disgrace. Not guilty by a jury of his peers made no difference in his case.

"Immoral." E.J. nearly spat the word, fuming in a stew of indignation. He pressed his fingers into the wood rail around the witness stand. He had to resist playing into the kid's trap. Losing his cool would only make him look exactly like what they claimed, a dirty police. He had to admit to himself their strategy was working and formulate a plan to keep his cool. No wonder three-piece blue suit had looked at him. E.J. served as an ace in the hole.

Three-piece blue suit spun the web using the petulant lawyer precisely because the counselor couldn't control his contempt for a crooked cop and likely in this young man's estimation all police fell into such a category.

Calling E.J. served as an opportunity to provoke a rage. The court of public opinion presented a far more expedient trial than a writ moving through the system. After all, the governor might issue a pardon to end the total fiasco.

The strategy couldn't fail. Even if E.J. didn't lose his temper, then they still taint the lead detective with ignominy.

"Because of the alleged bribery, two officers murdered—"

Rebecca jumped to her feet. "Objection, it exceeds the scope of the writ?"

E.J. lifted his head and leaned back. Did Rebecca fear he couldn't appreciate the true intent of the examination? Regardless, he welcomed the respite, though he knew the same odd objection had failed earlier. No doubt Rebecca had tried to protect him. Maybe she didn't think the questioning had unraveled him. Perhaps she still loved him. Could the cunning trial lawyer's true motivation be a desire to protect him because she still loved him?

The young lawyer didn't rise. Three-piece blue suit rose. "Your Honor, the U.S. Supreme Court has placed a continuing duty upon the state to advise of exculpatory and mitigating information. The lead investigator took bribes, leading to the deaths of his own troops. Granted, it's a different case, though otherwise how could it be more exculpatory? Who knows what he did to my client? Who paid him off? Given his disgraceful service, we must presume he planted evidence and framed my client to exact revenge for some unknown slight."

Three-pieced blue suit pressed G.H. Burton's shoulder, then raised his arms in a flourish. Burton responded with a near whisper, "The dear friend."

"Rank innuendo and rumor unworthy of a court of law, Your Honor." Rebecca's words erupted through the courtroom.

"The ranger who beat a confession out of an innocent man gets accused by the high sheriff of taking bribes and being party to a capital murder. And they don't tell us. This is an independent ground for the writ and even without the DNA, evidence entitles us to a finding of prosecutorial misconduct and reversal on such grounds."

E.J. stared hard at G.H. Burton. G.H. Burton extended full lips, grinning back.

Why shouldn't G.H. Burton smile? E.J. had lost his cool, though not completely succumbing. Did he look and sound like the dirty cop obsessed with his own version of justice, as the defense had portrayed him? After all these years, had he come unglued, not the psychopath? In his periphery, he saw Rebecca rise, arguing a point, though he listened to none of it.

E.J. ran his fingers along the silhouette of where he normally concealed his compact pistol. Muscle memory caused his mind to remember the touch of the slick steel and rough-textured grip of his compact, then his full-sized 1911 pistol. The feel on his fingertips pulled him into the past, filling his nose with the sweet-and-sour smell of early stages of human decay.

E.J. looked down at the young couple. They had a mannequin-like quality with elbows flared and hands folded under their foreheads. Humanity demanded one nudge them, wake them from a slumber, yet even in E.J.'s early career witnessing man's innate inhumanity had instilled in E.J. the desire to maintain the fragile illusion of serenity for even one more second.

The young attorney's shrill replacing Rebecca's strong, raspy voice jarred E.J. from the grisly scene back into the courtroom. A brief observation of the elderly bailiff stationed on his left demonstrated that the geriatric guard was incapable of capturing a dream. E.J. could draw the deputy's duty weapon, fire a bullet through G.H. Burton's skull, and surrender the gun onto the judge's bench all before the old-timer would look up. The exchange of spending the rest of his life in custody seemed justifiable if only one of the young individuals would raise their head from their wrist as they had evidently intended and take a breath.

E.J. stared at the flag next to the judge's bench, finding the magnificent vision of the corpse's reanimation had escaped into the fog of his imagination. A soft, burning sensation behind his eyes forced him to lift his head and swing it back to deny the hot tears forming behind his eyelids. What was wrong with him? He knew better than to succumb to emotion. Three-piece blue suit had succeeded at unraveling him.

Three-piece blue suit said, "That concludes our bill, Your Honor."

"My original ruling stands. Fourteen days, Ms. Johnson."

Rebecca nodded.

Three-piece blue suit turned to the gallery, rising to a theatrical voice. "Your Honor, I'm formally offering the bill of exception because the nation demands justice. A formal ruling, if you please."

"Overruled, Mr. Weatherstine. Unless there are additional demands, parties and counsel are excused." The judge rose, moving quickly into chambers.

E.J. stepped down from the witness stand as the onlookers shuffled out. Burton had years to weave this web while he and Rebecca had two weeks to cut through the morass of falsities.

Within moments, he and Rebecca stood in an empty cathedral of justice. "Can he win?" E.J. whispered.

"What hearing did you watch?" she asked. "He reached the pinnacle by implying if only they only caught you lying and destroying evidence sooner, the officers under your command would be alive today."

E.J. turned his face toward the back of the courtroom. "Not fair."

"No, it's not fair. It's effective. Lawyers call it prejudicial," said Rebecca.

"He's sharp," said E.J.

"Sharper than we are."

The lilt in her voice pierced E.J. She hurt too. He wanted his arms around her. These days, all he ever brought her was suffering.

Rebecca moved her hand from her side to in front of her chest. Like examples from so many interviewing courses, he knew she had closed herself off. She would hide the chinks in her armor. Did her law partner, Stuart, comfort her now? How does a man who wears loafers without socks comfort anyone? Jealous fire burned through the sorrow in his heart.

"E.J." The shout rang out from the hallway. E.J. stepped to the door. A young man whose biceps stretched his knit shirt stepped around the hallway. When the speaker saw Rebecca, his hand swung down the large-brimmed straw hat from his head.

Chapter Nine

You're That Ranger

It wasn't the first time E.J. had asked himself how this deputy rose, so much in the shadow of his father that everyone had called him Son, and distinguished himself in every meaningful manner from his father, Sheriff B.B.

"Do you need me?" Rebecca asked.

Son nodded. He did not.

"Then I should go," said Rebecca.

"Detective?" asked E.J.

"Move up quick when your dad is the sheriff. People assume I'm a putz."

"You've earned every break you ever got. I'll tell anybody." E.J. looked curious, unable to determine the emergency causing Son's fast pace.

"The Blakes are in the county clerk's office. Their daughter got murdered a year ago tomorrow," said Son.

E.J. recognized Son's expression from his own years of working investigations. "No suspects?"

Son shook his head.

"Why doesn't your father talk to them?" The process of hearing the words out loud answered the question. B.B. had acted like a jerk since E.J. and he were kids. The man's rudeness made E.J. question how he ever got anyone to vote for him. All politics must be crooked because B.B. kept winning sheriff elections.

Son told him what he had suspected. "Dad said they shouldn't try to tell him how to investigate his cases. Said he'd charge them with criminal trespass if they ever stepped foot in the sheriff's department again."

"Why the county clerk?" asked E.J.

"I got them out of the hallway. They heard about Burton and knew Dad and the media would be here. I'm guessing they figure they can embarrass him into working on their daughter's case, but you—"

"Yeah, I know." E.J. followed Son downstairs and across the hall. The musty odor of old leather-bound volumes identified the room as a records vault.

A middle-aged man in a dark suit stepped aggressively toward both of them. "We want to see Sheriff Berryhill. What we come for."

"No, you didn't," said E.J. He put up his hands to signal the man to stop the advance.

A woman in a dark dress said, "Yes, we do. We demand to see the sheriff."

"No, you want peace with your daughter's death. And I promise peace is the one thing you'll never find in a courtroom," said E.J.

She poured tears and her husband sunk his head before turning back to E.J.

"I've buried a son. I've also worked a lot of murders." E.J. extended his hand. "You don't want B.B. Son cares and he has already made a better lawman than his father. So, we'll let Son find us some chairs while we talk about it. Hoping I can find another stone to turn over."

"You're that ranger?" The woman in the dark dress asked through gritted teeth, fighting the tears streaming through her makeup.

"I'm him, ma'am." How else should she sum up thirty years of public service? He was diminished. No, not diminished, disgraced by some moments of grand failure? He would forever be that ranger. "Still, want my help, ma'am?"

Her husband answered. "I'd sell the devil my soul to kill the man who murdered my baby girl."

The woman in the dark dress looked at her husband, expressing her shock. Whether the remark or the public pronouncement shocked her, E.J. wasn't sure.

"I'm Ellie Ruth Blake and my husband, Steven."

Son stepped out. E.J. and the Blakes performed the Southern ritual of explaining what Blakes they were, or in the vernacular, explaining who their people are. The tension in the victims' faces eased.

E.J. took it as a sign they hadn't really wanted to deal with Sheriff B.B. today. Who would ever want to deal with B.B.? In contrast to the neat appearing Ellie Ruth Blake, Steven Blake had pulled at his collar until his tie looked askew.

Ellie Ruth Blake told the tale of a good, albeit an unusual youth. Like most teenagers, she found rural Texas too constricting. The mother's perfume overcame the stale condensate of musty of old books.

They had named their daughter Melinda. E.J. recognized the expression on Steven's face as Ellie described Melinda's early years. It was inevitable for him to compare Melinda to Sharla. E.J. listened intently about a little girl who represented the entire world to her parents. A sensitive, special soul who focused on the needs of others, even at an early age.

Ellie Ruth Blake described a high school junior who spent too much time on social media. What child didn't? "We caught her talking to men, but it didn't go anywhere—"

Steven interrupted, pumping his fist. "We didn't think so, anyway. I used to say I was going to wall her window up. If I'd have done it, then I would still have a daughter."

"We now think she was sneaking out, a lot," said Ellie Ruth Blake.

"Really don't know if she slipped out or if someone took her. Her friends told me she climbed out the window quite a bit." Son had rejoined them.

"She had seemed like a typical girl—honor society, key club, band. She loved Taylor Swift and spent hours listening to music. Then slowly the music changed. She began dressing in all black, dyed her hair, dark eyeliner," said Ellie Ruth Blake.

Steven added, "The kids call it emo because they listen to screaming music. It's crazy, and we couldn't see—"

"We had shielded her from the world. She had no idea there were people out there who would harm her. All this was just a phase, right? What we assumed anyway," said Ellie Ruth.

"I have to ask if she had a young man in her life because boyfriends and husbands are the number one suspect to eliminate," said E.J.

"Right, path I've been trying to go down. She had someone new, according to her friend Elizabeth, Lizzy," said Son.

"Melinda shared little with me, though I suspected she was seeing someone. A mother just knows. She had moved from sullen to smitten," said Ellie Ruth.

"Never told me anything. Emo, right here in rural East Texas. I'd never heard of emo. It's not like we're New York." Steven pulled at the tie, shaking the knot loose.

E.J. looked at Son. The father must have felt like he should have foreseen these events, and the guilt must be unbearable.

"I didn't want to believe it. My baby girl was sick, and I couldn't see it. Catting around on the Internet." Steven looked as if he would vomit at any moment.

E.J. searched for some comment to ease the man's suffering. "It's a different world than when you and I were young." He wanted to ask where her body was found but dared not.

Ellie Ruth Blake leaned forward as if she read his mind. "They found her in a bar ditch off the county road three twenty-three, the old Hays Cemetery Road."

"Naked." Steven's voice buckled on the emotion.

"No computer, no tablet, and she was never without technology. I was unable to find her cell phone, so it seems likely that the killer took it all. Tried air tags and locator app the family used, nothing. So, I started hounding her friends. They're not talkative outside of themselves," said Son.

"These emos?" asked E.J.

"Kids aren't bad or even really suicidal. They are dark and sarcastic. Took forever to get one to open up to me. Lizzy told me Melinda had a boyfriend. She saw a picture online but never met him. The name Melinda used for him was Brokheedron Michelle," said Son.

"Find anything in her social media?" asked E.J.

"No, but Lizzy was unaware of the app Melinda met him on. Lizzy and I went through everything on her phone and some apps she guessed Melinda's password. Led nowhere, so finally I sent search warrants off to social media companies, but they're out in California—"

E.J. read Son's face. "Being horsey about it? How did you get the warrants?"

Son motioned to the Blakes, shaking his head. "Some software people in California versus a local family with a murdered daughter. Judge signed anything I wanted but told me it would never stick if the warrants were challenged."

"Not sure I can help. Sounds like Son has spent a lot of time on the case and unfortunately, these things take time, a lot of time," said E.J.

"Nobody else helps him. No one believes him or us," said Steven.

Steven's shaking hands and tear-filled eyes made it clear to E.J. that he wasn't getting the complete story. Ellie Ruth Blake stared at her feet. No one spoke, yet Son would tell him if he pressed him enough.

Son spoke in a soft voice. "Fentanyl in her system, enough to kill thirty people. Supposed to look like a weird suicidal kid finally over-dosed—"

"Why do you say, 'supposed to'?" asked E.J.

Ellie Ruth's head tilted up. Her voice turned assertive. "How did she get out in the middle of nowhere? Naked? In a bar ditch? No vehicle? No ride? And my baby never did drugs."

Steven added, "I know what you're thinking. We just don't want to see the truth, but Son knows. Son believes."

"I believe Lizzy. She tells me Melinda never used drugs. She didn't even drink," said Son.

"You will help, won't you? I feel so much better knowing you're helping. You are helping?" Ellie Ruth's soft, dark eyes pleaded.

What could he possibly say? Her eyes looked like they would drop tears at any minute. He hated when women cried. E.J. wanted to say no.

His mind ran with thoughts of how massive an undertaking it would be to foil Burton's plan and help Rebecca in fourteen days. The most plausible explanations were usually true. Maybe she had accidentally overdosed and her friends dumped her, or she killed herself and some guy she was with dumped her. "Yes, ma'am, I'll do all I can."

Chapter Ten

Call Hall

Promises E.J. hadn't kept over a long career hounded him all the way out of the courthouse. Son moved much faster across the street and up the stairs of the sheriff's office. Ultimately, it didn't matter because the case file added nothing to the working knowledge of the murder E.J. operated under.

E.J. lifted a stack of grand jury subpoenas and warrants, dropping them onto the desk. "These California outfits always fight us just to fight us. They take pride in not revealing anything."

"It's like they are trying to attract drug dealers and perverts to their platforms," said Son.

"DA says I would have to take my warrant and get a prosecutor in California. Then hope the prosecutor out there gets a warrant based on it. He says I can't because of no probable cause. Besides, where would we send it? She never confided in her mom and you met her dad."

"Perhaps why he is falling apart now. He knows he wasn't accessible to her. In his mind, he thinks he failed when it counted. He can't let it go," said E.J.

"Maybe somebody should tell the guy his daughter's problems aren't his fault. There was nothing he could do. You know, tell him to let himself off the hook," said Son.

E.J. knew the remark was meant about him and Sharla. He pondered over the fact that it wasn't any of Son's concern, then he realized it. Without Son partnering with him to rescue Sharla from sex traffickers, she would still be laying in a prostitute's crib full of dope or dead. Let him say whatever he wanted. Moreover, the young man was unable to comprehend the guilt of both himself and Melinda's father. Guilty of something they should have done, whether they had the ability to perceive it.

"We got lucky she mentioned to Lizzy this Brokheedron Michelle, which I'm pretty certain isn't a real name. Ran it blind through everywhere. Nothing," said Son.

"How did she leave the house with all her electronics? No phone recovered, no devices?" asked E.J.

"Carried a backpack, little black one, held a little laptop, tablet, and a school tablet. She never went anywhere without all of it and her phone," said Son.

"School might get you an image of what was on the tablet," said E.J.

"Nothing on it not supposed to be there," said Son.

E.J. held up a stack of subpoenas. "You guessed at what she might use for social networking?" asked E.J.

"Some I found out from Lizzy, but nothing there. It had to be something new. I'd call app providers wading through automated systems to learn how to send preservation letters. If I got lucky and spoke to a human, I begged for help throwing around the phrase murder investigation and claiming I was the sheriff."

"How'd that work?" asked E.J.

"Like you'd figure," said Son.

E.J. reached for his cell phone. He hoped pushing a button would connect him to all the resources of the Federal Bureau of Investigation. "Hall." Over the years, Hall had saved E.J.'s backside more than once.

"How's Sharla?"

"Fight's all uphill," reported E.J.

"Amy and I pray for her every night," said Hall.

"Thanks…"

"You didn't call to catch up," said Hall.

"How do you know?" asked E.J.

"You only call when you want something. What is it?" asked Hall.

E.J. considered defending himself. Then he conceded his social skills, cultivating and maintaining relationships, left something to be desired. They were friends because Hall worked at it. Seems like Hall liked helping charity cases, he thought. "Cold case murder. New boyfriend she met on the Internet, but we don't know what app because killer took her phone and whatever else."

"God bless America, you drinking the Kool-Aid about Big Brother reading every email," said Hall.

"You intercept them all and store 'em all out in the desert in Utah, right? Got storage buildings size of football fields full of mainframes and artificial intelligence spying on all of us," said E.J.

Hall laughed. "Tell me you got an email address."

Son evidently overheard some of the call, writing Melinda's email address on the outside of a file folder. E.J. read it to Hall.

"Not promising anything."

"You've seen this show. Parents begging. Good people. I'll email you what we've tried," said Hall.

"How's Rebecca?" asked Hall.

"Mean as ever."

"I'll call you if I can find something out in Utah." Hall laughed, then ended the call.

E.J. shuffled more papers. "Crime scene photos?"

"You mean where the body was dumped?" asked Son.

E.J. nodded. "Who found her?"

Son clicked his cursor onto a folder and his computer displayed a slideshow of predictably awful scenes. Awful, not from blood or gore, rather because of her youthful and pudgy childlike face. Her lifeless form was tinged with blue, yet otherwise the photos captured a surreal quality.

"Guy running a rural trash route." Son shrugged. "More rich folks in the country, they'd rather pay somebody than burn trash," said Son.

E.J. studied the photos. "No defensive wounds like somebody fought her to inject her?"

"Figure she knew the killer?" asked Son.

"Or she overdosed. Son, it might well be true. No parent thinks their child would take their own life or become addicted. They tell themselves they would have acted had there been any signs. And we want to let them off the hook because we're human too," said E.J.

"Three hundred kids in her high school. I interviewed everyone. Stared each one down. She had grown darkly sarcastic and liked weird music true enough, though I'm convinced she didn't use drugs and wasn't suicidal. Besides, the most likely explanation is she overdosed and one of those kids dumped her. I'm certain I would have picked up on it if one of them did it," said Son.

E.J. lifted a picture. "This one little puncture is all?"

"No needle tracks. Autopsy pics made it clear," said Son.

"Nacogdoches for the autopsy?" asked E.J.

"New guy you like, Meecum," said Son.

"Sexually assaulted?" asked E.J.

"Autopsy combined with toxicology and forensics, it gets complicated," said Son.

"I don't understand," said E.J.

"You should talk to Dr. Meecum," said Son.

Chapter Eleven

Right with God

"Are you going with me?" asked E.J.

"Probably should make sure the Blakes really left and didn't try to find Dad," said Son.

"Want a little advice?" asked E.J.

"Lawman lessons from Wyatt Earp. Are you kidding?" quipped Son.

E.J. stood. "Don't let it eat you up inside. People like the Blakes lose you. They got nothing. Nothing, you understand?"

Son had earned the compliment, to the extent it was a compliment. His investigation hadn't been shoddy. The onetime arrogant kid wearing a badge had made a detective. Such forced E.J. to ignore a terrible jealousy and the guilt gnawing at him while he studied Highway 59 to Nacogdoches. By any standard Sheriff B.B. amounted to a disgrace, yet his child lived, more than lived, Son made a difference in the world. Konner was dead, Rebecca facing the end of her career, and Sharla battling the demon of methamphetamine addiction while facing unplanned pregnancy, begged the question. What had he done to merit such?

He tried to not question how a just God might inflict such misery upon him. The arrogance of such self-pity struck him. Who was he to merit divine attention of any kind?

Still, it seemed unlikely that a giant unintelligent mistaken big bang forming the universe had the ability to heap such a massive amount of misery on one person. What were the odds of such cosmic unfairness happening randomly?

He pulled into the parking lot of the pathologist building. The meaning of life would have to wait for further contemplation. In a way, he envied how Dr. Meecum, a devout Christian, didn't suffer these debates warring within himself. E.J. had shared the same resolute faith prior to Konner's death. Had the need to have faith in his life drawn him to Meecum? Can this resolute certitude beyond our senses be genuine?

E.J. studied his phone, looking up *Walker, Texas Ranger* on Wikipedia. Chuck Norris solving homicides in an hour had been an inside joke for E.J. and Cooper, resulting in mocking Dr. Meecum's childhood idol. Who would figure a kid growing up in Ghana watched a pretend Texas lawman kick guns out of murderers' hands? Now that he focused on it, how different from a kid who grew up in Texas watching a masked man shoot guns out of a killer's hands with silver bullets? Could anything be sillier? Grown men building their lives on the simplistic moral codes of *Don Quixote*-style heroes.

Dr. Meecum's adherence to correctly pronouncing each syllable distinguished him from everyone else.

"How is your daughter?" asked Dr. Meecum.

E.J. looked away from the picture of Dr. Meecum's family dressed in their finery, standing in the sanctuary of a church. Instead, he met the doctor's dark eyes. "What?"

"When we last spoke. You asked me to pray for your daughter, Sharla," said Dr. Meecum.

"She is not doing well."

"I'm sorry," said Dr. Meecum.

E.J. shifted in his chair, concerned he'd been too short. "Your prayers helped. She escaped some human traffickers. The way I see it, you're right with God."

"You do realize, you can pray too." Dr. Meecum winced, then titled his head. "We can pray together."

"Let's not dilute a powerful thing." E.J. read the name of the file on the pathologist's desk. "Son call you?"

"It's an unusual case. The case raised so many questions. Likewise, the forensics left us puzzled. I'm preparing a paper, a journal article," said Dr. Meecum.

"Before I ask about Melinda Blake, let me ask you a religious question," said E.J.

Dr. Meecum leaned forward, putting his hands together over his desk.

"Are Jews the only people who use shalom as a greeting?" asked E.J.

"I can only guess. Probably the most common, though I suspect not," said Dr. Meecum.

"What religion talks about God releasing them from the material state? Is that Jewish?" asked E.J.

"Like a Gnostic?" asked Dr. Meecum.

E.J. shrugged. Curiosity had overwhelmed him, yet not enough to concede he was ignorant of the term, having previously concluded it had something to do with Greek history, not theology.

"Attractive to the inherent human nature, isn't it? By our wits and reason, we can uncover some secret knowledge to unlock our own divinity or, as they refer to it, the divine spark within ourselves," said Dr. Meecum.

"Ancient Greeks or something, right?" asked E.J.

"Each generation reinvents hearsay. Look at all the books and movies like *The Da Vinci Code*. It's too simple to have faith that God gave us the Bible. No, some top-secret information exclusively revealed to the special people has to exist to justify their view of themselves." Dr. Meecum leaned back.

"One person's heresy is another's gospel, isn't it?" asked E.J.

Dr. Meecum dismissed the remark with a flat, "No." The word hung in the air for a moment and then the doctor added, "Why?"

"I'm getting us sidetracked. Let me take you back to young Ms. Blake," said E.J.

"Where to start." Dr. Meecum opened the file.

"She raped?" asked E.J.

"Complicated question," said Dr. Meecum.

"Way I'm phrasing it wrong? I've listened to enough sexual assault nurse examiners and pathologists testify to know trauma to the genitals isn't dispositive either way, right?" E.J. turned his head toward the open door to the examining room. The burning aroma of bleach assaulted his nostrils.

"Correct. As I tell juries, God designed the human body for reproduction. Therefore, signs of trauma are rare even in known sexual assault cases. One can't always determine when the person last had sex, nor even whether it was consensual sex. Regardless of whether the person was sexually active or even had their virginity," said Dr. Meecum.

"I've dealt with all this a little from child molester cases and delayed outcries. Science doesn't support all these notions people have developed over physical signs of sexual assault. So, let's act like I asked the right question. Did you see any tearing or other damage?" said E.J.

"Yes, however, it was perplexing," said Dr. Meecum.

"Perplexing?"

Dr. Meecum leaned forward, placing his elbows on the desk. "We start with the significant damage to the genitals. Not life threatening and not necessarily inconsistent with what some might refer to as rough sex. However, in such consensual though 'rough' cases, there is generally other trauma to the body. None here."

E.J. nodded, reckoning the remark made sense. Then a peculiar notion came to him. "Damage inflicted after death?"

"No. Perimortem, all I can say. At or near death. Yet odd for what the justice of the peace assumed was a teenager overly sensitive and emotional, committing suicide," said Dr. Meecum.

"But you did a rape kit, right?" said E.J.

"Yes, and in this case, toxicology," said Dr. Meecum.

"I've heard about the fentanyl," said E.J.

"More," said Dr. Meecum.

"Date rape drug?" asked E.J.

"Ketamine."

"Son didn't tell me about the ketamine," said E.J.

Dr. Meecum nodded. "He called, but we haven't discussed the case in detail since the results came back. You know how slow the labs work. Ketamine is not on the normal screen like fentanyl. I discussed the case with my peers for the article and described the rape kit results. The consensus was I should request a specific screening for date rape drugs."

"Pretty sharp, Doc. The killer sexually assaulted her," said E.J.

"Certainly, there is evidence to support the conclusion. Yet so often our only indication of sexual assault is DNA from the rape kit, much less immediately obvious than physical signs visible to the naked eye," said Dr. Meecum.

"Are you saying someone staged a rape? Makes no sense. What did the rape kit show?" asked E.J.

"When I told my colleagues the DPS lab report found spermatozoa on the vulva swabs, they immediately suggested the more intensive drug screening." Dr. Meecum pushed the rape kit report across the desk.

"Here it is. We need to find this male contributor. He raped and killed her," said E.J.

"Look closer, Ranger," said Dr. Meecum.

"I've told you, I'm no ranger," said E.J.

"Lab identified three profiles—"

E.J. interrupted him. "Three?"

"Three." Dr. Meecum held three fingers aloft.

Chapter Twelve

The Conundrum

"Three?" E.J. said. His repeating the number didn't make it sound right out loud or in his head, nor did it matter which one of them said the word. E.J.'s mind fumbled through the possibilities.

She must have had sex with someone else during the hours preceding her death. How many hours? Perhaps she had a sexual relationship and then, sometime later, the killer raped her. In such a case, the killer wasn't necessarily the new man, Brokheedron Michelle.

As if Dr. Meecum saw the wheels turning in E.J.'s mind, he added a further complication. "Spermatozoa revealed only one profile. Amelogenin tells us the third component of the mixture is female epithelial cells."

"Female, skin cells?"

"I've spoken many times with the chief of the DNA section about all the possible scenarios. Son interviewed people in college and high school who knew the victim to make some speculation even if the basis rings of gossip. Nothing." Dr. Meecum shrugged.

Did Son ever make an understatement by saying "It's complicated." E.J. asked, "I take it you eliminated every hypothesis as implausible?"

Dr. Meecum nodded in the affirmative. "Quite the conundrum."

"I know there is some question on DNA science, so are these results sure?" asked E.J.

"These profiles are complete, not partial. The scientific community has a well-settled understanding of the identification of peaks, profiles, completeness, and mixtures. Only the statistical models have ever been controversial and it's not an issue here because we have no one to compare anyway," said Dr. Meecum.

"Can I make a copy of the autopsy and lab reports?" asked E.J.

Dr. Meecum pulled a stack of papers from under the file and handed them to E.J. "Son and I expected you to ask."

E.J. rose to leave. Another picture of Dr. Meecum's family standing outside a church caught his eye. Was it taken on an Easter Sunday or at some family member's wedding? For a moment, he lost himself in the nostalgia of recalling his own such family events.

E.J. looked down before meeting Dr. Meecum's eyes. "I'm driving to San Antonio. Appointment with my daughter." E.J. stopped. Appointment must sound odd, yet it wasn't really a visit. "Doc, you stand right with the Lord."

"You believe God hears my prayers because you say I stand right with God?" asked Dr. Meecum.

E.J. nodded. "We've had a development with Sharla. I can't tell you what's going except—"

"You believe in me. You believe I believe in God. Odd way to have faith in God without admitting to faith in the Almighty, isn't it?" asked Dr. Meecum.

"Quite the conundrum," said E.J.

As he drove north, E.J.'s mind twisted, analyzing the DNA results. DNA testing had moved during his career from nonexistent to a not very discriminating tool needing a stain of blood or fluid the size of a half-dollar to the advent of PCR technology. Modern lab work replicates small amounts of DNA to reveal profiles from the most minor biological material, even skin cells. Forever increasing sensitivity now demands investigators provide known profiles for elimination, no matter how carefully they handle evidence.

As the science attained magical attributes, the volume and meaning of the results moved toward the realm of inscrutability. Investigators opined the ever-increasing sensitivity would reveal the profile of an employee who stocked the item on a shelf or a manufacturing employee long before the item became probative to some investigation. No chart revealed the correlation between scientific results and materiality to the case. Ironically, the reliance on science only increases the necessity of the subjective thought process by investigators determining the probative value of the evidence.

What if it was possible for an investigator, a sexual assault examiner nurse, or any number of people to have come in contact with the sample? He stopped. There was the answer. No one came in contact with these actual swabs. These were rape kit swabs, not swabbing from physical items like a weapon. There wouldn't be any human contact other than the victim, Melinda.

No explanation presented itself, despite E.J.'s best efforts.

The baffling problem had crowded out Sharla from her permanent place at the fore of his thoughts. For over a decade, DNA results dominated forensic science no less than if Moses had brought test results down from Mount Sinai written by the hand of God on tablets. Then today two complex unrelated puzzles confronted him. DNA on the Burton murder case blade and the additional DNA in Melinda Blake's rape kit.

He microwaved a can of soup upon return to his travel trailer, and Sharla resumed her place at the center of his thoughts. Thinking of how it should have been to have Sharla tell him she was expecting eroded the logic he attempted to apply to the DNA testing. The joyous spin on becoming a grandfather that other father daughters had shared.

She would have already built a good marriage, career, and home. He imagined the sun reflecting off a glimmering green sport-utility vehicle parked in the driveway of an expensive subdivision somewhere. One of those places featuring luxury houses lined up in rows marked by cement streets leading nowhere.

The fantasy came unraveled when he saw his son, Konner, in the picture. Konner's death pulled the thread, unraveling his quilt of a perfect family. Konner's memory inevitably led to Rebecca's insistence on Konner's military commitment, amounted to a boy's desperate desire to live up to his larger-than-life hero father.

Images of Konner's casket, the honor guard, and the boom of the guns flooded his mind. He inhaled the sulfur odor from the twenty-one-gun salute as it washed past him. Grief had filled his heart, rendering it a bucket of painful muck.

Suddenly, the plastic laminate paneling of the travel trailer spun around him and narrowed. E.J. drew air into his lungs, yet the more oxygen he ingested, the less his body benefited. His throat tightened and face grew flush with heat and sweat. He fumbled through the sheet metal framed screen door, gasping in the darkness.

No need of a psychiatrist telling him it was a panic attack. Nor did he want one to prescribe him some dope. Drugs wouldn't work, anyway, and he would lose his edge. If he saw a shrink, wouldn't it be the final nail in his professional coffin? People should have to buy a ticket to see the onetime exalted ranger, now a broken-minded crazy fool blathering to horses high on prescription smack.

While forcing himself to reject the physical symptoms, he sat stoic in his circa 1970s latticework lawn chair bathed in moonlight, certain he would overcome anything by forcing himself not to dwell on what should have been. To discipline his mind would prove to be the key, not some headshrinker. Though every thought denigrating mental health providers collided with the need to believe the profession could restore his daughter, Sharla.

He located his cell phone on the charger and returned to the folding chair. Did the IT department at Devekon get his music transferred? The mellow tones from Patsy Cline's cover of Bob Wills's "San Antonio Rose" filled the empty night.

E.J. lurched forward, shocked he had fallen asleep and groggily pulling the phone off his chest.

"Where you at? We're late."

"What?" asked E.J.

"You were supposed to get me a half hour ago."

"What?" asked E.J.

The speaker's voice rose into a parade of curse words and the identity dawned on E.J. His old boss and friend, Rex Ashe, continued his tirade. A onetime captain of industry, Rex now suffered from Alzheimer's.

"Rex, where's Kevin?"

"We should be in the spread already?"

E.J. stood trying to organize his day once he pacified Rex, then he could get an early start for San Antonio. Spread sounded like a goose shoot. E.J. hoped Rex hadn't got a hold of a shotgun. He needed to call Kevin. Rebecca had hired the male nurse, who stayed in the condo next door to Rex Ashe.

The wealthy oil man annually hunted greater Canadian geese in early season with a group of businessmen. In later years, E.J. had taken part. Experience had taught E.J. to make conversation long enough to calm Rex.

Once Rex sounded semipacified, E.J. ended the call, then dialed Kevin. After dressing, E.J. started his second cup of pleasantly aromatic coffee. Kevin called, reporting the all clear.

E.J. drove south to Highway 21 following the old El Camino Real. The monotony of the road allowed his mind to drift under a sky dark with geese. He wasn't really missing the hunting. For all his eccentricities, Rex Ashe had befriended him and stood with him when few would do so. The man gave him the opportunity to earn a livelihood when no one would hire him.

Despite being his boss, Rex had served as a confidant. Rex's constant wisecracking style made it easier to share personal concerns, like Sharla, with him than Hall or Cooper.

Rex's progression under current medical technology could only be slowed. Despite the lifelong battle addiction presented, Sharla's prospects appeared brighter.

Even when sex traffickers abducted her, E.J. never gave up. In hindsight, Son had shown great promise as a detective finding Sharla's specific location, then backing E.J.'s play to steal her home.

This time, true helplessness overcame E.J. He couldn't defeat the devil of meth addiction for his daughter, nor could he undo the consequences of the sexual abuse she had endured. What would become of her and the unborn child, or would Rebecca call it a fetus? Either way, it was growing, developing more each day.

Chapter Thirteen

Is Sharla Using, Again?

E.J. remembered Sharla's ratty haired, unkept appearance, and the mix of urine and body odor from when he rescued her. He tried to force the image out with better mental pictures from better times to no avail.

The traffic of Loop 410 around San Antonio demanded his full attention before exiting off Walnut Drive. E.J. navigated the long, private, landscaped driveway. Dated buildings covered in cream-colored brick comprised a compound akin to a small college, complete with dormitories.

The noon sun felt warm on his face after so many hours in the air-conditioned truck, and he basked in it for a moment. Interactions with Sharla rarely went well these days, causing him to approach the door filled with dread. Then he chided himself for being reluctant.

The brown metal door flew open, and Sharla leaped into his arms. Her strawberry blonde hair was as fragrant as a garden in full bloom.

Her warm arm clung to his neck, reminding him of all those hugs his little munchkin gave him before bed each night.

"I keep having a nightmare. A massive cat attacked Sunshine and there was no saving him," said Sharla.

"Old horse misses you, like me," said E.J. taking a step back.

"Thank you for saving me. I need to go home to my bed, my room, my things." Sharla's voice reached a pleading tone, though she removed the shrill quality by the end of the request.

"You look so good." E.J. took in the entire view of his daughter. She progressively improved with each visit. The open sores healed, the pale deathlike quality of her skin gained color, and her formerly hollowed and dulled eyes now caught the light and shone bright.

"I'll be better at home," said Sharla.

E.J.'s arms dropped the tension from the hug. He opened the back door of his truck cab and lifted a white cardboard box, handing it to Sharla. "Your mom here?"

"You know how she gets. The same way she does you. I can't even talk to her." Sharla lifted the lid, releasing the freshly baked aroma of her favorite cookies. The treat from her childhood resembled a Danish wedding cookie except larger, more like a sugar cookie covered in white powder, created in a specialty shop in Medina called Jolly's.

E.J. watched her bite into the cake-like pastries. Sharla's smile beamed so genuine, it infected E.J. with the recollection of a little girl pulling herself onto a stool in front of the pastry counter at Jolly's Bakery.

They made their way into the closest building of the compound. A structure identifiable by architecture and decor inside as 1970s chic.

A tall African-American woman rose to greet him from a green couch. "I'm Sharla's counselor, Lucretia Wagoner. Call me Doctor Lucy."

"Where is Dr. Grayson?" asked E.J.

"He assigned me."

"Are you a psychologist or an LPC?" asked E.J.

"I'm a substance abuse counselor under the supervision of an LPC," said Dr. Lucy.

E.J. nodded to Rebecca. "Rebecca." The gesture seemed so stupid, so poor to acknowledge the woman with whom he had previously built a life, though her response didn't evidence any better grip on the circumstance. No one ever contemplates they would one day be visiting their daughter in a drug treatment center.

"E.J.," said Rebecca.

"Have a seat, Dad." Sharla guided them to the couch while Dr. Lucy moved to a nearby armchair. An institutional odor like a nursing home assaulted E.J.'s nose, causing him to add the hypothesis to his conjecture on the former purpose of the compound.

"We were talking about how much you and I want Sharla home, but it was counterproductive without a plan." Rebecca projected the comments at Sharla.

E.J. understood now. No wonder Sharla greeted him so warmly on his arrival. She was playing dad against mom to get him in her corner.

"No, you were telling me I needed to stay because you can't take off work to watch me so I don't kill myself." Sharla's features turned pale as she lifted her head. "You just want me to kill my baby—"

Her comment crashed into the room like a rodeo bull. E.J. raised his hands like he was trying to quell the dispute. "Your mother wants the best for you, like I do." He pointed to the counselor. "Why Ms. Lucy is here to help us figure out how we move forward." E.J. looked at the ceiling, already awkwardly regretting his attempt at making peace.

"I should be grateful Mother is not just here by video like normal." Sharla hesitated, then added in a sharp whine, "I wanted to see you, Daddy."

E.J. let Sharla lift his hand into her own. The act of contrasting the two brought back memories of how her small fingers fit perfectly in his hand when she was a baby.

"We're all here for family counseling?" asked E.J.

"Planning strategies for the next step in the recovery plan," said Dr. Lucy.

A series of questions revealed E.J. didn't put enough thought into Sharla's homecoming. He had never progressed past the joyful celebration the fantasy held in his mind. Clearly, fantasy or dreams better described the endeavor than plan.

Every time E.J. articulated an idea, Rebecca or Dr. Lucy revealed the inadequacy of the proposal. Each time Sharla waded into the discussion defending her father or deftly changing the subject to some pleasant memory or childhood vacation. The paradigm continued for over forty minutes until the exchanges grew sharper between Sharla and her mother.

"You need time to transition. An opportunity to get on your feet," said Rebecca.

"Say it. Say I'm a junkie and I'll go back to the dope the first chance I get," said Sharla.

"Sharla—"

"Tell Daddy, you want to lock me away and kill my baby 'cause this is all my fault. Rebecca Johnson's perfect little daughter failed her momma and the universe—"

"We should return to the subject," said Dr. Lucy in an odd-sounding, calm timbre.

An unnatural smirk passed onto Sharla's face, disquieting E.J. "Tell Dr. Lucy how you think Daddy killed my brother," yelled Sharla.

E.J. recoiled on the couch, finding no comfort. He experienced bile rising from his stomach. His efforts to mediate nearly depleted him. The attempt to prevent the mother and daughter from exchanging verbal insults proved more frustrating than hard labor.

"Sharla—" Rebecca yelled, rising to her feet.

"Tell everyone how the perfect momma did nothing wrong." Sharla screamed and ran past Rebecca.

"Sharla..." Rebecca leaned forward, then raised her leg, launching into a run. She chased her daughter. They both plowed through the exit door.

E.J. considered trying to catch his wife and daughter. A question in his mind kept him from chasing them. What if he caught them? Refereeing the verbal onslaught wearied him. His knee folded up under the best of circumstances, so what use was he? Instead, he walked outside the great room and stood in the foyer looking for a break. Drama made him anxious and being anxious made him more anxious. Above him, a large picture window framed a huge live oak made of wide horizontal branches. A flush overtook him. Please don't have a panic attack or whatever it was.

In the back of his mind, a thought sprung. What if he still had the ability to piece life back together? Sharla hadn't really hugged him in years. The warmth, the vibrancy of his daughter's touch, conveyed love. Love, he hadn't realized how much he missed.

Sharla might yet put the pieces of her life together. Some people overcame drug abuse. There were some recovered addicts, right? They were always being congratulated in celebrity interviews. Psychologists developed new theories circumventing triggers and developing new behaviors instead of feeding the addictions.

The dualism reared itself again in the back of his mind. What was he defending? Maybe Rebecca overreacted and Sharla had improved enough to come back, back to his Sharla. One couldn't deny the evidence, the improvement.

Dr. Lucy, standing to his left, startled him. "Aren't you going to follow them?" asked E.J.

Dr. Lucy shook her head. "Sharla will come back. She has to," said Dr. Lucy.

"I don't understand," said E.J.

Dr. Lucy pursed her lips in a smug gesture. "How long has it been since she called you 'Daddy' and held your hand? Told stories about Disney World?"

E.J. moved a step away from the counselor. The woman hadn't told him anything he shouldn't have picked up on. All the clues he had suppressed leaped forward in unison. Battling the sting of tears in the back of his eyes, E.J. realized the immense enjoyment and captivation that the illusion Sharla spun brought. Just like the gas the dentist administered, there was no way to avoid the consequences.

He'd fallen into an abyss of delusive hope. The same void he had witnessed snare so many countless victim families bold enough to hope their lives might be reconstructed.

An addict was capable of telling any lie, spinning any story, to get back to her dope. How had he forced himself to forget it, to disregard such truth?

E.J. turned his back to her. "Don't you think I see it?" The pain had to end. Why couldn't it be true? Why couldn't this two-bit counselor, want-to-be doctor let him enjoy the lie for a moment? A chance to draw a full breath and hold the child she had once been. The gift from the merciful God he had studied in his youth before the heavens had opened and revealed a capricious deity, or whatever random design, guiding the universe, pouring misery into his life.

"Dr. Grayson asked me to talk to you," said Dr. Lucy.

"Wasn't he supposed to fix her? Supposed to be here." E.J. saw the faces of the thugs he had killed in Shreveport to get Sharla back. The urine-soaked hallway of his recollection overcoming the pine air freshener in the foyer of the drug treatment center. He would kill two more, or two dozen more, if he could truly save Sharla.

How could a child conceived in the horror of rape and sex trafficking while exposed to crack, heroin, and methamphetamine in the womb ever survive? Wouldn't it be premature and require massive medical intervention? Thereafter, how could such a baby ever hope to develop normally? What if the child required constant care? Who would take care of it?

Was Sharla considered mentally competent at this point in her treatment? Where would she live? How would she provide for the baby?

Dr. Lucy stepped around to face him. She stood close enough he suspected he smelled the Dial soap she used to bathe. He had permitted her to trap him near the wall. "Didn't she say what you wanted to hear? Even without prompting, she reads your gestures, your posture, your expressions."

"Is it possible for a child to recover from the mother's drug use?" asked E.J.

"Were you aware this complex started as an adoption agency? Old style. The girls stayed here, had their babies, and went back home." Dr. Lucy looked out a vast picture window. "Never designed to hold anyone against their will. We test, even hair follicle test, but it's so hard to establish a baseline. A whole industry has sprung up in beating tests and getting drugs into the most secure places."

The explanation for the compound made more sense than his speculation about a nursing home. As if a light flipped on, he saw the buildings in the correct context. A place where in a different era, young women had left their homes under many rouses and excuses to have their children, place them with adoptive families, and return to their lives. All to avoid the stigma once associated with an unwed pregnancy. How archaic an idea it all seemed. And yet at least on the surface there was a wholesome quality to the era no one could deny.

How many babies had been carried to term in these facilities? How many adoptive couples had received the unfathomable gift of parenthood? E.J. wanted to dwell on the pleasant images, yet he couldn't. The counselor's comments begged a question even when one wanted to ignore it.

He summoned his courage to the sticking point and asked what he didn't want to ask. "Is she using?"

Dr. Lucy's brown eyes locked on E.J. "I don't know for sure."

E.J. wanted to argue about how Sharla had more sense, more honor, more of everything than to bring harm to her unborn baby. Instead, he studied the leafless live oak, feeling a pull in his throat, and choosing not to speak. "But you think she is."

After a long pause, Dr. Lucy said, "She keeps trying to take you into her denial. Encourage her to work the program. She has to learn her triggers and strategies to address them in a healthy manner or…"

E.J. watched a cat squirrel scamper up the live oak tree before returning to the parched lawn. The creature repeated the action twice more before E.J. noticed Dr. Lucy had stopped talking and started staring at him.

"I arrested this old man one time. Game wardens had a big operation catching duck hunters hunting illegally in a park. Old inbred outlaw lived back in there somewhere. He'd hunted those sloughs all his life. This man looked a hundred, stares all around at park police, wardens, deputies, troopers, constables, rangers and tells me, 'We got more law and less justice than we've ever had.'"

Dr. Lucy stepped back, raising her eyebrows.

"We got more doctors, counselors, and psychiatrists than ever but fewer healthy people," said E.J.

"You find it ironic?" asked Dr. Lucy.

"I find it something, Doc. I'm begging you to fix what matters most in this world to me."

Chapter Fourteen

Taking the Bait

E.J. took Hill Country highways more or less paralleling Interstate 35. He stopped along the scenic Medina River, a favored riding destination where he took his family on mini vacations. Sharla and Konner took to the horses, while Rebecca proved neither a horsewoman nor a camper.

The long summer hadn't given way, so leaves weren't turning the fall colors he enjoyed, nor did the vegetation hold the bluebonnets and Indian paintbrushes of springtime. Rather, the bland, khaki shades of drought punished the landscape. The view presented no comfort. Likewise, his recollection seemed forced and artificial.

The mental images of the family trail rides had lost detail with time. Terror engulfed him in a manner that facing no danger that threatened his own life was capable of causing in his heart. Were his memories of Konner no longer vivid? Was he losing what was left of his son? Would Sharla ever be anything more than the husk of his daughter? Would she ever show him affection without attempting to manipulate him so she could obtain more drugs? What a fool to let his heart soar even for a moment.

As he navigated Waco moving onto Highway 84, the phone rang and Son's voice exploded through the radio, relegating a favorite Ernest Tubb recording to standby in some digital wasteland.

"Wanna help take G.H. Burton to Beaumont for the evaluation?" asked Son.

"I'm sure your dad claims I'd kill Burton if I got near him," said E.J.

"Dad's the one who suggested you," said Son.

The answer bewildered E.J. At first, he wasn't sure he heard the response correctly. Sheriff B.B. specifically asked for him, especially after their recent showdown in the courthouse. He pulled over to finish the call.

"Why would your father ask for me?"

"Figured he thinks there'll be trouble. He wouldn't let me go. Even Dad knows you're almost as good as me." Son chuckled at his quip. The two both enjoyed competitive shooting and shared a good-natured rivalry.

"Your father once threatened to tie me to a tree and feed me dog food for two weeks until I behaved." He emphasized all the syllables of behave as Sheriff B.B. had done when he made the original threat. "Were B.B. burning in hell, he wouldn't take a glass of ice water from me."

"I keep telling you. He's not as bad as you've decided. Kind of the Doc Holliday to your Wyatt Earp." Son's second hushed giggle conveyed an artificial quality.

E.J. couldn't determine if Son was proud of his remarks or was trying to make light because he knew the offer posed a danger. Son's natural state was light-hearted, anyway. It was difficult to watch the young man carry Melinda Blake's murder on his shoulders like the weight of the world.

Sheriff B.B. never asked E.J. for help. The refusal denoted more than pride, rather E.J. knew the man held him in low regard since high school. The pause lingered.

"Dad said meet him before five a.m. at the jail," said Son.

"No, he didn't. Tell me what he said?" asked E.J.

"He said tell the mall cop to be here at five if he wants to be real police," said Son.

There was no arguing with the authenticity. B.B. spoke in the exact manner, but why ask for his help? E.J. had no official capacity. His reputation in and of itself endangered any official law enforcement endeavor.

Further grilling Son didn't reveal B.B.'s motive, so after a few more exchanges, E.J. ended the call. Why did B.B. want him to help take Burton? Did B.B. want to kill Burton? E.J. would look good for it.

Burton probably already told his lawyers or some cellmate about E.J. confronting him, surely spinning E.J. as an attempted murderer. They had him, right? Armed in a place he shouldn't be, with all the motive in the world to kill Burton. Why had Burton asked B.B. to let him go? The question presented one of those mysteries which only grew greater the more one studied it. Like why would Sheriff B.B. follow Burton's instructions and let him go?

Whatever the reasons, he couldn't resist escorting Burton. Sometimes even mice could tell the cheese baited a trap, yet the knowledge didn't keep an inquisitive rodent from tripping the mechanism snapping his spine. Perhaps the trap was too well baited. Sometimes saying no to certain doom wasn't an option.

He had gotten back underway when a buzzing shocked him. Speed had gotten away from him and the driver's assistant activated, slowing him from nearing an eighteen-wheeler's bumper.

It wasn't enough to see a wreck ahead. E.J. needed leverage. Leverage strong enough to bend the trap spring before it could snap closed. Some special advantage to keep B.B. from releasing whatever lay in wait.

"Call Cooper." B.B. wouldn't try anything with a Texas Ranger watching him. The rangers amounted to the internal affairs department for all sheriffs. A fine chaperone for the trip. The added advantage of Cooper's absolute integrity and competence would make escorting Burton into an old-fashioned Sunday drive. He had mentored Cooper and took a special pride in knowing she would jump at the opportunity. She even thanked E.J. for including her.

After arriving at home and feeding Sunshine, Hall came to mind. Cooper had been a good call, yet one couldn't be too careful with B.B. Surely B.B. wouldn't risk anything with the FBI watching, even from a distance. Perhaps a phone call from Hall offering federal assistance would send a message to B.B.

Hall crashed the grand façade E.J. had created. "No."

"What do you mean, no?" asked E.J.

"Both of us know a setup. The worst imaginable kind of setup. You don't know what you're getting set up for. Absolutely asinine," said Hall.

"Didn't you give up cussing?"

"Asinine means stupid, stupid. How's Sharla going to handle you dying on her? Pregnant and stuck in recovery. Stupid." Hall's volume had risen to match the insistence of his tone.

Arguing with Hall when he had decided was akin to having a discussion with Rebecca. E.J. let the conversation lag into silence.

"I smoked ribs—dry rub—and Amy got the last of the purple hulls from the garden 'fore they burned up. Come on over," said Hall.

"Been driving all day. I'll lay up, but thanks." The idea of Hall further pointing out the stupidity of the venture didn't appeal to E.J. primarily because it was stupid.

"Everything about this is wrong. Can't you see? You're risking Cooper's life too. Did you think about that? Husband and two daughters. Better decide how you're going to tell those precious angels you got their momma killed," said Hall.

"I know you've come through for me. More, more, more than any friend should—"

"Then shut up and don't go, stupid." Hall had ended the call.

Was it really as bad as he made out? E.J. walked through the drought-afflicted pasture to his stock pond. The edges of the tank revealed the toll summer had taken on the water level.

He stood on the dam trying to construct reasons Hall exaggerated the risk. The special agent neared mandatory retirement. Hall's actual fieldwork had been many years prior. E.J. added rationales why Sheriff B.B. would never harm him or Cooper.

A pesky recollection came to the fore of his mind. The FBI had assigned Hall to interrogate some high value terrorists all over the world since 9/11. Uncle Sam considered Hall among the best. Ignoring Hall's counsel wasn't prudent.

Moments later he stared at a dollar store wall clock leaning on his travel trailer kitchen counter, mentally chiding himself for how logic had never swayed him. Duty, loyalty, family, and other concepts moved him. He dozed off, telling himself one way or the other B.B.'s trap would spring soon.

Chapter Fifteen

The Thicket Closes Around Them

Sheriff B.B. possessed a colossal frame, though age now sagged the formerly lean muscle. He stood in the vehicle entrance to the jail, by tradition called the sally port. Sheriff B.B. held a black mug. Gold "Reelect B.B." lettering and a fake pistol handle decorated the coffee cup. "Lookin' peaked, old pretender, scared of real work."

"Trying to figure out how I came by the invite," said E.J.

"Well, pretender, it's your party, isn't it? You bankrupted this county trying an innocent man. Then want my deputies hauling him all over creation. Can't afford you, pretender," said Sheriff B.B.

He had always wanted to ask Sheriff B.B. if he spelled pretender with an *i* like he sounded it out. E.J. looked past Sheriff B.B. at the sport-utility vehicle behind him. "Should have at least two vehicles and four deputies."

Sheriff B.B. pointed at E.J.'s holstered Colt 1911. "Big iron to be so afraid. You know, we never have four deputies on duty. I'm supposed to use more deputies to protect the guy you're trying to kill than all thirty thousand folks in this county. That's ignorant, pretender."

E.J. spoke through gritted teeth. "He's Aryan Triangle. A nationwide security threat group. Cooper can get highway patrol units to trade out following us. Even get a DPS helicopter up."

Sheriff B.B. folded his one free arm under his shoulder in a mock chicken dance. *"Baaak, baaak."*

The buffoonery stopped when an oversized metal door to the right opened wide, flooding the big bay with cooler air. E.J.'s locked jaw tightened at a smiling G.H. Burton. Accompanied by the high-crowned, short-brimmed silverbelly hat and black bolo tie of Cooper pushing the tension out of the moment. Cooper pointed and Sheriff B.B. opened the Suburban's door.

Stuffy, hot air once again overcame the brief relief from the now closed door. "Cooper, you'd wear a felt hat in hell, wouldn't you?" asked E.J.

"Hoping you don't rope me into that duty," said Cooper.

Sheriff B.B. snapped a rude comment about E.J. finding them some female help. Cooper ignored the remark. Did Sheriff B.B.'s opposition to Cooper arise from her association with E.J. or did he really hold a low opinion of women in law enforcement?

Jailers checked the handcuffs and leg cuffs restraining Burton after seat belting him in the Suburban. Sheriff B.B. oversaw securing the prisoner, making a production out of assuring the cuffs and seat belt were secure.

E.J. whispered to Cooper, "Thanks."

She nodded.

E.J. moved toward Sheriff B.B. then stepped into a cloud of musky cologne. Why wouldn't B.B. assign his best deputy, Son? Should he ask? The young man had proven himself a powerful force and further insurance Sheriff B.B. would remain on the up and up. "Can't you spare Son?"

Sheriff B.B. swung his arm to project the star on his chest. "Gettin' all in my business, aren't you, pretender? Nobody elected you to decide. They elected me to clean up your messes, pretender."

E.J. clamped his jaws onto each other for fear a response would provoke a confrontation. B.B. wouldn't even provide an excuse for refusing any reasonable precaution.

The pause in their discussion appeared to annoy B.B. "Been meaning to talk to you 'bout Son. You got the boy's head full of foolery. Wasting time on suicides for sad sack parents who didn't understand their kid was an emu. Gonna get my boy killed like you did your son?"

Did he know the term was emo not emu, or was he mocking the whole thing, including a child's death and her parents' grief? E.J. balled a fist, then swung his head toward laughter emanating from the third-row seat of the Suburban. G.H. Burton cackled like canned audience laughter on a television show before adding his designation for E.J. "The dear friend."

Cooper stuck her head in the vehicle, staring at Burton.

E.J. figured further comment would only land him stuck alone smelling car exhaust in the sally port. He assumed that Sheriff B.B. had taken the new Suburban as a forfeiture from a drug dealer or borrowed it from a dealership in debt to the sheriff for purchasing fleet vehicles.

Why was B.B. mad about Son helping the Blakes? Arguably, it helped B.B. by taking the ire out of his constituents. Had B.B. found out about E.J. recruiting Son to rescue Sharla in Shreveport? Sheriffs had all kinds of snitches. The FBI and Cooper required evidence, but not the dopers and meth heads out there on the street dropping a dime on anyone, especially current and former law enforcement.

Didn't putting two and two together seem easy? One morning Sharla's back and there are two sex trafficking pimps dead in a rough Shreveport neighborhood, but how would he discover Son's involvement? Someone might have seen them coming back with Sharla in Son's distinctive old GMC Jimmy? Did B.B. know or not?

E.J. looked to the dash, then exchanged a glance with Cooper.

"We should check out a couple of body cameras since we don't have a unit cam," said Cooper.

"Sheriff's unit exempt from all the profiling stats bull," said Sheriff B.B.

"Kind of insurance in case something goes wrong. Burton's pack of lawyers couldn't blame us if we had to subdue the prisoner. If you don't have a spare body cam. I can get a couple, probably even a trooper escort part of the way," said Cooper.

E.J. wanted to emphasize once more how DPS had the ability to put a helicopter above them, but with B.B. already rejecting Cooper's suggestion, he suspected the helicopter idea was dead on arrival.

"You sheriffing now too, Ranger?" asked Sheriff B.B.

"No, sir," said Cooper.

Sheriff B.B. spun the wheel and stomped on the accelerator. In an unmarked vehicle without lights or sirens, they sped in a southeast direction, hugging the Louisiana border. Sheriff B.B. kept the air conditioning fan on low.

The silence stiffened further into the stale air. Was this some kind of ruse? Why use one unmarked vehicle? There had to be some kind of plan beyond E.J.'s knowledge.

Beaumont lay hours to the south. E.J. assumed they would house Burton in the Jefferson County Jail. E.J. weighed the advantage of traveling off the main highways. They would pass through mostly rural communities, including national forest country. He saw a certain advantage in stealth, though there would be few law enforcement resources in a pinch.

Wouldn't it make more sense to pass closer to larger communities with full police departments? Rebecca had often accused E.J. of preferring silence to conversation, yet after nearly an hour he wanted someone to speak so badly his skin itched. Instead, he heard the rhythmic clatter of G.H. Burton's snoring, making E.J. appreciate the old clichés about a freight train.

Huge pin oak and red oak trees lined the road. Their gigantic limbs interlaced across the top of the thoroughfare, forming a shroud. What light penetrated the canopy of leviathans cast dim and sullen shadows like a movie based on a Jules Verne novel.

Cooper's shoulders shuddered. E.J. recognized a kind of claustrophobia common to westerners. Raised in the Panhandle of Texas, she had moved to East Texas upon graduating from the Department of Public Safety Academy.

Likely Cooper had spent no time off the main thoroughfares south. Her exposure to the Big Thicket National Preserve would have been a national forest sign.

"Big Thicket?" asked Cooper.

"You wanna ask if we're there yet?" Sheriff B.B. laughed. E.J. caught sight of G.H. Burton jostling awake in the back.

"Odd path?" Cooper obviously tried to work the comment into a question without antagonizing Sheriff B.B.

Another awkward pause passed between them all before Sheriff B.B. broke the silence. "Odd path is why I let y'all come along."

E.J. leaned forward in his seat, making eye contact with Sheriff B.B. through the rearview mirror. Sheriff B.B. wasn't making sense.

"Scared, wannabe law, afraid?" asked Sheriff B.B.

Further unease settled over E.J. from the nape of his neck through his shoulders. He slid his thumb over the hammer of the Colt holstered on his waist.

Sheriff B.B.'s face grinned framed in the mirror, obviously pleased with himself. "Word on the street."

E.J. drew a deep breath of warm, static air.

"What word on the street?" Cooper asked.

"Old meth cook turned snitch told my interdiction guy. Some skinheads were planning to waylay us when we got on U.S. sixty-nine."

"So, instead of asking for troopers, federal marshals, or eyes in the air, you decide to go an obscure, longer route in a civilian vehicle because no one would ever expect it," said E.J.

G.H. Burton piped up from the back. "Dear friend, scared."

If Sheriff B.B. noticed E.J.'s sarcastic tone, he didn't acknowledge it. "Bet some thugs gonna be sitting on the road a long time."

Cooper turned to E.J., her eyes widening. The band Ram Jam's "Black Betty" blared from E.J.'s phone.

"I'm tied up, Rebecca."

"Not calling to talk. I didn't want you to say we didn't tell you." Rebecca stomped the words out in a harsh tone.

E.J. whispered, "Can I call you back? I'm in a car with a bunch of people."

"Sharla finally came to her senses. I'm driving her to the abortion clinic," said Rebecca.

"You sure it's what she wants?" E.J. didn't know whether the call had dropped or Rebecca had finished it. "Rebecca. Rebecca."

"Dear friend, sad."

Rebecca had spoken like a roaring jury argument filling the cavern of the automobile. Was she trying to convince him or herself? Maybe

Sharla had been sitting close, and she needed more convincing, or perhaps Rebecca had worked herself into what she believed was righteous anger? They had been apart too long for E.J. to know her mind from the inflection in her voice, if he had ever been so privy to her thoughts.

Cooper lifted her phone, then looked at E.J. He assumed she had no service. E.J. took some small comfort that Rebecca hadn't hung up on him, but Cooper's dark countenance woke E.J. from his misery to the danger confronting them. Cooper put her hand on the hilt of the semiauto on her hip.

"Well, I've lost a C-note. Now we'll never know what color your grandbaby was gonna be." Sheriff B.B. boomed laughter through the truck.

E.J. clenched his fist, making his fingernails stab into his palm. His shoulders tensed. He wanted to go at B.B. through the front seat when a vehicle sitting at the start of a bridge caught his attention.

Chapter Sixteen

The Bridge

C ooper drew her pistol. E.J. dropped his hand to his own pistol. Before them stood four men pointing AR-style carbines. Though clad in black, they didn't wear masks over their skin heads and faces. Bile rose in the back of E.J.'s mouth. The assailants weren't concerned with being identified because no one would survive.

These men must have been G.H. Burton's handpicked soldiers. E.J. assumed it was a show of force. They wouldn't fire for risking their leader's life.

E.J. leaned forward enough that the seat belt caught him. Despite the restraint, he reached for the steering wheel, yanking it hard right. The Suburban careened off the road. Sheriff B.B. struggled against E.J.'s left hand, retaking the wheel only to overcorrect, swinging the car further out of control.

With a strong rebound, the Suburban quickly descended, causing the heavy automobile to crash into the ground with force. E.J. fought to keep his head from jerking off his neck. First one, then all four tires left the roadway. The wheels stuck in the loosed gravel, then caught traction.

Now airborne again, the SUV flew over the precipice to the right of the bridge, angling downstream of the creek. The waterway itself measured fairly narrow, yet a substantial depression bowled under the roadway, necessitating the bridge.

The steel coach leaped back into the air. Cooper's cell phone flew past E.J.'s head. Her hand wielding her pistol plunged into the air like a professional bull rider after the gate opened. A loud boom briefly overcame the calliope of crashing and shearing noises, formerly filling the cab. The steering wheel exploded, forcing an airbag to cram Sheriff B.B.'s skull backward.

Wheels crashed into the dirt. Momentum swept the vehicle along the crest of the creek bank. A back tire caught traction, twisting the auto into a spin, slowing only from vegetation acting as netting. E.J. raised his weapon to cover his face with his hands. He saw little over the crumpled hood, though he gained an awareness the world spun nearly upside down, then righted itself.

Impacting vertically into the other side of the cut bank and bringing the flight to an end, the Chevrolet slid down farther along its hood. A rock shelf capable of holding the automobile's weight ended the slide with a sudden stop.

The seat belt button likely wouldn't release with E.J.'s weight against it. He slipped his pocketknife out with his left hand while holding the forty-five in his right.

From his periphery he saw Cooper free herself, rolling toward the glassless door window. "No. No," screamed E.J.

Rat-a-tat-tat. The riflemen finally achieved a clear target away from Burton. E.J. exhaled in relief at hearing Cooper's nine-millimeter firing in response. Though outnumbered and outgunned, Cooper would pin the attackers down.

E.J. pushed the sharp blade through the seat belt, catching himself for balance. He saw B.B. half conscious, covered in powder from the air bag.

"Git, pretender."

"I'll cut you out—"

"Go, take care of Cooper," said Sheriff B.B.

E.J. lifted the blade across the seat belt, freeing Sheriff B.B.

A gruff voice erupted behind them between gunshots. "B.B. kill him and get me free."

"He's got the drop on me," Sheriff B.B. hollered back to G.H. Burton in the third row. "Pretender grabbed the wheel; near killed all of us."

E.J. stabbed the barrel of the forty-five into B.B.'s temple. A seasoned shooter, well aware where the trigger would break, he drew his finger taut.

The realization crushed him like the sun rising over a hungover drunk, coming to terms with the delusions he had labored under. If he hadn't grabbed the wheel, then B.B. would have stopped at the bridge, allowing G.H. Burton's cohorts to take him.

B.B. deserved to die. A bullet through the head. Then he could turn and kill Burton, but Cooper wouldn't approve. Had he heard a help during the exchange with Burton? "Cooper," yelled E.J.

"I'm hit." The urgency in Cooper's voice confirmed the statement.

E.J. lifted the barrel, shifting the butt of the gun into B.B.'s temple with a hard thump. He maneuvered toward Cooper's window.

Burton shouted, "Did you kill him?"

E.J. ignored the question, sliding through the open window. Much as he expected, she had the superior gunmen taking cover behind the guardrails of the bridge. She had moved from the back of the Suburban to a nearby oak tree.

The attackers were carefully working their way down the bridge toward her end. Such explained why she moved to the tree trying the circumvent the maneuver. She would eventually be flanked if she didn't run out of ammo first. Her belt contained two magazine pouches. Combined with what she had loaded in the weapon, probably gave her close to fifty rounds.

He caught movement nearing the edge of the bridge. E.J. lifted his pistol, finding the post and squeezing off three rounds. The first two struck the rail. The third connected with one of the Aryans. He couldn't tell where or how badly the man was hit, but he caught a glimpse of the man rolling away. She had removed one from the fight. Four had been at the bridge, there were at least three more and who knew how many reinforcements had or might soon arrive if not already on scene.

E.J. scrambled, leaping through the creek bed reeds and brush to Cooper. The ever-dapper Cooper, reduced to a disheveled wreck covered in sweat while crimson spurted from her thigh. He knew the femoral artery could bleed her out in short order.

From the bridge, a machine gun erupted, bullets pressing them deep into the tree's trunk. Projectile bits skirted through the air by E.J.'s head, pressing him lower. "We got to go."

Cooper nodded, dropping her service arm. "I'm out."

E.J. handed her his pistol. "Five left." He lifted her over his shoulder, swinging into a mad retreat.

Cooper fired until the final round kicked the slide back, evidencing an empty gun. She threw it in a useless act of defiance. E.J. made it over the creek's tall flood bank nearly toppling over. He regained his footing. He carried her like a sack of feed swinging wildly between trees.

His lungs burned in agony and his back and legs spasmed with pain, yet he didn't stop. Death didn't hold the abhorrence it once did for him, but his mind raced with Cooper. Images of her girls from their early years to high schoolers. Would he tell those athletes their mother died because he quit running?

Her husband begged her not to take the ranger appointment. He wanted her to work license and weight or a desk job somewhere. Cooper asked E.J. to assure him of her safety. E.J. remembered shaking the man's hand on a promise he would do all he could to protect Cooper.

Would he tell the father of Cooper's children the promise had been too hard to keep? Would he tell champion volleyball and softball players that their mother had been too heavy?

A chuckle crested his mind. He wouldn't live to tell anybody anything. They might even shoot him before Cooper. The absurdity of the amusement caused his mind to laugh all the more.

His boot hit a log. Cooper flew from his grasp. As he got onto his knees, E.J. extended his hand toward her. He ripped his shirt off, pressing it hard against the wound. Satisfied himself as she drew breath, E.J. found a stick for a tourniquet while Cooper moved in and out of consciousness.

There were no options. Cooper needed medical attention. They couldn't fight machine guns with rocks and sticks. For all he knew they could have recovered their leader, Burton added an army to their ranks.

E.J. forced himself to lift Cooper again. Thirst choked his dry throat. One foot in front of the other, he had to keep moving.

Cooper's weight forced E.J. forward, nearly toppling over coming down a hill through a pine grove. He stumbled, stepping into a dry branch. Would it lead him to water? Sweat stung his eyes, irritating him to the point of tears.

Stepping on the uneven ground twisted his leg, toppling E.J. forward. His face smacked branches. Aware he had fallen into a morass of tree roots like netting, E.J. struggled to break free. He snapped through the webbing, resulting in the brief exhilaration of a free fall.

He heard Cooper splash, then his face hit the gritty water. The murky liquid had appeared so dark that he had assumed it was the bottom of the hole. Striving to touch the bottom with his feet and falling short, E.J. remembered he had longed for water. This viscous filth bore little relation to the drinkable fluid. It would certainly make him sick if it didn't kill him.

E.J. pushed his head through the gelatinous mixture of decaying plant material and mud to draw air into his exhausted, burning lungs. His mind raced to Cooper. She had tumbled past the deepest part of the sinkhole, laying near the edge. Wouldn't this mire infect her wound with bacteria? The army of machine-gun-wielding thugs chasing them rendered the question moot.

The sinkhole stretched longer than a truck and wider than his height. A putrid smell lifted his nose before completely pervading it. What kind of critters had fallen into the quagmire, unable to extricate themselves? Would he and Cooper join them?

He slapped Cooper's face with the gentle touch of a father prayerfully, searching for signs of life. Mosquitos buzzed into his ear, reactively snapping his hand to his head. The brown goo coating his hand curtailed the insects for the moment. A thick ball of tree roots formed a canopy nearly eliminating the sun's rays. What light passed the porous dark roof showed the mud-cloaked wall, slick and insurmountable.

E.J. suppressed the desire to cry out, to surrender to his fate. Cooper lived and concentrating on returning her to her family consumed him.

"R-A-N-G-E-R," sounded over some distance denoted by an artificial quality. Perhaps help had found them, searching while using a
bullhorn. Who could be searching?

Could Cooper have managed a phone call? No, she had no signal,
and he had seen her phone fly across the Suburban cab. An image of
his own cell phone last seen on the seat of the vehicle flooded his mind.

The second time confirmed in E.J.'s mind the speaker had to be
Burton. Of course, his partners in crime had brought a bullhorn.
White supremacists committed acts of racism and bragged on bull-
horns at public gatherings about themselves and their repugnant phi-
losophy.

"Ranger Kane."

Chapter Seventeen

Every Angle

"Dear friend."

The phrase eliminated any doubt owing to the amplified quality of the voice. How close was he? Where was he?

"Dear friend, I know you can hear me."

E.J. checked the tourniquet. How had it held? Cooper drifted into consciousness, looking up at him. How surreal the scene must appear covered in foul-smelling goo in an underground compartment. E.J. whispered, "It's Burton. Don't cry out."

"Dear friend, I'm certain we hit your baby girl. She is bleeding like a stuck hog or a piglet. I'll go have some coffee, get a change of clothes, and come back with bloodhounds and a half dozen search parties."

If Cooper bled like he claimed, then Burton didn't really need bloodhounds to follow their bloody trail. Likely, he wanted to toy with his prey. Either way, time worked against them.

"Better for you to die now. Perhaps I'll spare your new strumpet. You brought her to your party. I didn't send her an invitation. The trap was for you. I didn't want her to get hurt. B.B. couldn't turn her down without arousing suspicion and if she got suspicious. We

didn't need a troop of highway patrol and rangers in our business."
The megaphone blared like he was right there in the putrid-smelling
sinkhole, yet E.J. suspected more than likely a substantial distance
separated them. Otherwise, it was unlikely Burton would try calling
out for fear of giving away his position, not knowing for sure he and
Cooper were unarmed.

"Not so intellectually disabled," whispered E.J.

"I thought you would have killed him after the wreck," whispered
Cooper.

E.J. spit silt past his lip. "What Texas Ranger Sergeant Elizabeth
Cooper would have done? Gunned a handcuffed prisoner down. Even
one who needed killing."

"Walk toward the sound of my voice and I'll let your little chippie
go. Even get her medical attention." The echo resonated through the
primordial wilderness.

"No. Yet, you can argue that it serves to prevent him from engaging
in future acts of murder. Like the time the schizophrenic stole a trac-
tor-trailer rig and we couldn't stop him with spike strips. Forty-thou-
sand-pound weapon weaving in and out of traffic," said Cooper.

"Got lucky, just had to wound him. Think Burton's gone?" asked
E.J.

"He'll keep walking around a while. Likely broadcast another
threat before he leaves. Hates you. You'll regret not killing him," said
Cooper.

E.J. nodded.

"Wasn't luck on that truck either. Best shot I've ever seen." Cooper
closed her eyes.

"You've had the badge on so long you're getting gray." E.J. stared
past Cooper at the wall of sludge encasing them. "In truth, another
half second and I might have shot. Not certain myself. Got concerned

about getting to you, especially when I found out B.B. was in on it. Became obvious no help was coming."

"Surprised me, too, shouldn't have, though we were both well aware that B.B. was crooked," said Cooper.

"Suppose I never really saw how bad." E.J. scratched a handful of soft mud and placed it on Cooper's face, trying to paint it like his own. The decaying muck offered the only possibility to dissuading the army of mosquitos buzzing and snapping at the flesh of both.

"I had to work with him. People kept electing him, and I never could get enough for the DA to put him away. I thought you were blinded from growing up with him. We cut people slack who are familiar," said Cooper.

"Suppose you're right. His kid and wife are good people?" E.J. phrased the comment as a question.

Cooper nodded. "Yes."

"I'll scratch my way to the top, then I'll give myself up. If he convinces me, he'll keep his word, then I'll tell him where you are. If not, then surely somebody will come by," said E.J.

"You'll never scale the wall. Besides, we're not leaving here alive. He can't let me testify. I'd ruin the whole intellectual disability rouse. And if you don't tell him where I'm at, then I'll die slow in a pile of muck, unless a water moccasin finds me and ends my suffering," said Cooper.

"Made your decision?" blared the amplified voice of G.H. Burton.

"It's our only chance," whispered E.J.

"You're my only chance. The only chance for my girls. You give up and I die."

"Girls" hit a chord. He had failed her daughters by leading their mother into a trap. E.J. couldn't fail them again.

He wiped some of the sweat and goop off his face. Grit covered his lips, and he tried spitting some out, only to increase the volume.

Despite the moisture, the grime stole E.J.'s last traces of saliva. Ironic how dehydrated he remained in a pool of liquid. Even if he choked down some of the filth-ridden slime, it certainly would gag him to death.

"Time's up." The phrase echoed across hollers and hills through the boggy terrain before descending into the sinkhole. "Don't be getting hopeful while I'm gathering hounds and troops. B.B.'s on his way to the main highway where he'll report you went nuts trying to kill me. Why he took us down these pig trails?"

"Got us good," said Cooper.

"He'll say I had to run to keep from being murdered, or maybe he'll say you killed me. I'm still writing his story." The echo hung over the swamp like fog. "Whatever the story, he will have figured every angle," said E.J.

"Dear friend. Oh, dear friend. Stop hiding out with your little girlfriend. She'll be stiff before we get back with the bloodhounds. Sit there smelling her decay knowing your cowardice killed her. 'Course her kids will think momma's lover conned her into helping him try to murder me."

Chapter Eighteen

Rebecca

"Sharla finally came to her senses. I'm driving her to the abortion clinic." Rebecca pulled the phone away from her ear, looking at the screen. "I've lost your father."

She placed the phone back in the charging cradle of her Maserati. "Call E.J." The call failed. "We'll keep trying. We'll get him before we get to New Mexico."

"He won't understand. For him, it's killing a baby," said Sharla.

"He told you so?" asked Rebecca.

"You know Dad doesn't talk. Sort of broods," said Sharla.

"Your father and I don't always agree, but he loves you. He'll come around because he knows you can't care for a baby right now. We have to concentrate on saving your life."

The silver coupe glided over the open space of U.S. 87. She had recently traded her Mercedes for the GranTurismo. Rebecca enjoyed the smell of leather and sports cars, rarely keeping an automobile for a full two years. It still had its new-car smell.

The pause became more awkward as each moment passed. E.J. had shared with Rebecca the suspicions Dr. Lucy had held. How to bring it up? Should she bring it up? If Sharla were using, she would lie. Of course, she would lie until caught, then Rebecca risked poisoning their relationship exactly when Sharla needed her.

Rebecca glanced at her daughter. She didn't present like the addict anymore. When E.J. had spirited her away from sex traffickers in Shreveport, she looked terrible compared to the honor student who fastidiously kept her appearance.

The old Sharla never would have been seen in public wearing a jogging suit and tennis shoes. Would she never revert to her old self? Perhaps they would both have to settle for less in life. It was possible success looked like Sharla alive. Rebecca turned back to her daughter.

She could ask by throwing E.J. under the bus, blaming him for her suspicions. After all, he had raised the issue with her. But it might drive a wedge between father and daughter. E.J. didn't deserve that. He had literally killed to find and save their daughter. If only he could have saved their son instead of inspiring him to join the Marines.

"I will get a debit card?" Sharla rolled her hair on her finger.

"What?"

"With the apartment."

"A debit card?" asked Rebecca.

"You promised after the procedure you would get me an apartment and a debit card," said Sharla.

"Certainly, when the doctor says you're ready." Rebecca suffered a pang through her stomach, confronting the truth. Sharla was still trying to get to drugs. Her acquiescence had been purchased with the promise of independence and money.

"The abortion doctor," said Sharla.

"No, your therapist, the clinic, like Dr. Lucy. It must be part of the treatment plan," said Rebecca.

Sharla's countenance fell, making a production of exhaling air through the automobile before moving into a shriek. "You lied to me."

Rebecca mouthed the word, then yelled, "No."

"You lied to me." Sharla slapped her window with her hand, causing a thunderclap inside the cab of the sports car. Sharla continued her ear-piercing hysterics while she grabbed the door handle.

Rebecca reached for her own door panel to control the lock, but was too late. She stomped on the brakes, swinging the automobile crossways into the center of the highway's dividing line.

Sharla leaped out the door before the car completely stopped. Harsh Texas heat pulled the air-conditioned air from the car. She ran toward a barbed wire fence separating her from a field of leafless mesquite brush, prickly pear cactus, and tan-and-red dry earth.

Rebecca screamed, chasing her daughter until they reached the fence. Sharla lay on her knees, violently ill to her stomach. Her mother held her hair back.

After exhausting the meager contents of her belly, Sharla continued to heave in her mother's arms.

Rebecca held Sharla, placing a hand on Sharla's back. "I've got some wipes in the car. Let's get you cleaned up," said Rebecca.

"I felt sick," said Sharla.

Rebecca saw the miniature dark colorations around Sharla's eyes, how the tiny blood vessels had broken in her self-induced distress. She had been prone to throwing these fits since early childhood, though Rebecca hadn't witnessed one in years.

Sharla tilted her head and shook it side to side. "I'm clean. I'm clean."

Rebecca wrapped her arms around the girl. "You didn't really change your mind about the procedure, did you?"

Sharla swung her head back. Tears poured down her cheeks, blotted by her long hair. "I did. I did."

The next line came to Rebecca like the muscle memory of a superb athlete. "Tell me about the moment you changed your mind?" She invoked the question after establishing a flip-flopping witness with the old standby "Were you lying then, or are you lying now?"

"I don't know," said Sharla.

"Tell me about the moment you told your father you were pregnant?" asked Rebecca.

Sharla wailed louder.

"You were riding through Big Bend. As scared as you were to tell your dad, you needed to tell him because you were happy," said Rebecca.

The tears eased and Sharla looked into her mother's eyes. Rebecca recognized the glare. Like so many times growing up, Sharla had been transparent, but when Rebecca read her, it was as if the girl thought her heart had been unlocked.

"You don't know when you changed your mind because you never changed your mind." Rebecca rocked her daughter back and forth. "You saw a chance to get out, get an apartment, and a debit card where you could do what you wanted to do, didn't you? Freedom is what resonated with you?"

"I don't know," said Sharla.

"We're going back. You will come clean with your counselor about everything. I will talk to her with you. Then you and her will consider all the consequences. I will support your decision, and you will continue your recovery setbacks and all. I will be with you." She interlaced fingers with her daughter, making a solid fist.

"We're going back?" asked Sharla.

"Not yet. We are going to the hospital. I'm getting you checked out, and drug tested—hair, blood, and urine," said Rebecca.

"What?" Tears had matted Sharla's locks around her face.

"I've been too lenient since your brother died. You will not play your parents against each other any longer. Your father and I shall find a way to present one united front. In fact, let's try him again." Rebecca lifted Sharla's shoulders, guiding her to the sports car.

Once seated in the soft leather, Rebecca said, "Call E.J." The call failed again, prompting Rebecca to lift the phone to view the display. "I got a text from an unknown number. What if it's your father on a different phone? No."

Check Burton's jail email.

Chapter Nineteen

Check Burton's Email

"**S**tuart, I'm holding for Jacobs," said Rebecca.

"He's probably out detecting something," said Stuart.

"Clever. I called for Jacobs because I need Jacobs," said Rebecca.

"You have to tell me what happened between us? One minute we were headed to a wedding chapel in Vegas and the next, you drop me." The nasal quality to Stuart's voice sounded more pronounced.

Rebecca rolled her eyes. Likely Stuart had been crying. "I am a little too busy to explore your feelings today. Call your life coach."

"He says I need closure."

She had no time for Stuart's theatrics. E.J. had been right. Stuart was a miserable fop of a man. Why had she ever taken up with the fool? Because he wasn't Elliott. She considered it odd, the strange appeal he had, without even reminding her of E.J. "I'm still on the road. Get me Jacobs?"

"I will instruct Meredith to transfer you," said Stuart.

Rebecca exhaled in relief. The formal tone indicated she had emotionally crushed Stuart. There was no time for sensitivity. She needed Jacobs to work his magic one more time. Anything to get Stuart off the phone and get her to the firm's investigator.

"Jacobs."

"Any luck running down the text I sent you?" asked Rebecca.

"Impossible," said Jacobs.

Did he need more time? Surely he was still trying, she told herself. "For lesser detectives."

"No. Really impossible. How is Sharla?" asked Jacobs.

"Stuart tell you?" asked Rebecca.

"One, her being in drug treatment is not a secret. Two, I'm an investigator. I battle some of the same demons. Every day is a gift. Many people in this office care about Sharla," said Jacobs.

Rebecca eased. "I'm sorry. Yesterday was a long day. I planned on being back today, but I'm still on the road. Probably better if we meet in person? I'll see you tomorrow."

"Don't you want to find out what I discovered?" asked Jacobs.

"You told me, impossible," said Rebecca.

"To trace your text is impossible. But I found Burton's prison emails like the text said."

Rebecca's throat tightened. "They actually have email privileges."

"He's gen pop," said Jacobs.

"I thought all Aryans were in administrative segregation. Isn't AT still a security threat group?" asked Rebecca.

"General population. This whole intellectual disability label keeps him out of ad seg. Figure it is why he first started it. They put him out of the ID ward because he had all the poor folks toting and fetching like slaves," said Jacobs.

"Tell me? What were his emails?" asked Rebecca.

"None, not one, which I thought odd, so I went through everybody in his pod's codes—"

"How did you..." Rebecca thought better of the question. She did not need to know.

"Wasn't the hard part. Anyway, I figured it out because he uses the same PIN for his phone calls to his AT bros. Our intellectually disabled G.H. Burton has a profile on a dating site posing as both women and men. Something heartstrings. I'll send you the link," said Jacobs.

"Pretending to be both men and women? You're sure we're talking about Mr. White Supremacist. Aren't they chauvinist?" asked Rebecca.

"'Tis a mystery. But he also calls himself the intellectual heir to his hero, whom he calls the genius Joseph Goebbels, all while he masquerades as intellectually disabled. I'll email you what I've got," said Jacobs.

"Thanks again," said Rebecca.

"You da boss lady. Anything else?"

"Shouldn't we run down everyone who connected with him online?" asked Rebecca.

"In the process now. If I don't sleep, I can have it for you in the morning," said Jacobs.

"Good."

"Sarcasm, boss lady. Stuart is counting on me to find a witness for his patent case," said Jacobs.

Rebecca quipped, "Sincerity is not required—"

Jacobs joined her in completing her mantra, "Just get with the program."

Rebecca grabbed her mail out of the box, then pushed the gate opener to her lakeside home. She threw the bills in a stack on an elegant baroque dining room table. She used to pay bills immediately and never needed to make a stack. They now piled up because she took so much time off for Sharla, compounded by taking on the Burton case.

The poor publicity from standing in the way of Burton's actual innocence claim mortified her law partners. No doubt they were likely joining Stuart in reviewing the partnership agreement for a way to send her packing. Get all this behind her and return to corporate litigation in federal court and all would be forgiven. The Eastern District of Texas still served as a favorite venue for the gladiators of Fortune 500 companies. Bad press or not, she spoke the language of corporate America and legal partnerships—money.

Her other three partners would fall in line once she made the money rain. If Stuart failed to mature, then she would have the ability to compel him to leave. She had found his compliant puppy-dog nature a refreshing change from E.J. Over time, Stuart had proven needy. Even with the backing of his life coach, therapist, and astrologist, the man was never capable of aspiring to match her.

Rebecca called E.J. again, to no avail. She left a voice mail. "I've tried all day. Clearly you are ignoring me because I told you what you didn't want to hear. Grow up, Elliott."

Disappointment in her ex-husband smothered her. She would have expected it twenty years ago. She never won a fight with Elliott. Her arguments could easily carry the day, except Elliott walked away and did whatever he deemed proper.

She carried the children to practices, took off from working when they were sick, and supported them through perceived crises. E.J. chased outlaws, provided security for state officials, and worked on his family farm. She made the excuses to Konner and Sharla explaining why he had to miss holidays, and the importance of Texas Rangers. In a way, she blamed herself as much as E.J., because she had contributed to the admiration she thought inspired Konner to volunteer for war.

Reason told her she struggled against herself to set forth in her mind all the arguments necessary to form a hard shell prohibiting her from running into E.J.'s arms. He made no pretense of accepting the divorce. The man even continued wearing the wedding ring.

To see him lifted her heart, then some gesture would remind her of their son like a razor slicing through her nucleus. He couldn't see the hurt he caused by being near. The big lug didn't process his own grief, much less understand her emotions. Now, she no longer had the distraction of Stuart to push E.J. from her mind.

She poured a glass of sweet red wine, taking a seat on her white leather couch and dropping her red soled shoes on the plush white carpet. Before searching her tablet for the website, she looked through the enormous bank of windows at the lake shrouded in darkness. Only the lights from the other large homes punctuated the panorama of the private lake.

Jacobs emailed his results as the night passed, providing Rebecca the opportunity to ask questions in real time. She woke to a mix of oranges, yellows, purples, and blues comprising the divine palette of the sunrise.

Her phone vibrated and blared on the top of her refrigerated wine cabinet.

"Mom, turn on the TV."

"Sharla?"

"Fast, Mom, turn it on."

"What?"

"Your television, channel three. It's about Dad."

"What about your father?" asked Rebecca.

"A guy I knew from college called me, said they would have an update on the search." Sharla's exasperation reached a crescendo.

"What search?" She yelled over a distraught Sharla.

Rebecca reached the remote control and turned to face the television, raising the volume as the screen illuminated. Her life-sized television displayed an image of Sheriff Benjamin Berryhill sitting at a table with a hospital system logo behind him. Next to him sat a middle-aged man in a lab coat and Son seated on the other side.

A reporter asked, "Doctor, can we ask Sheriff Berryhill where Ranger Cooper is?"

"As I stated, we treated the sheriff for a mild concussion and will release him later today. The sheriff wanted the opportunity to take questions after he makes a statement updating you on the whereabouts of the ranger."

A pale Sherriff B.B. leaned forward. "I've given a statement to Colonel Fenton of the rangers and just got off the phone with Ranger Cooper's husband. There's no good way to say this. Ranger Cooper has gone rogue. Led astray by her old supervisor and trusted instructor, E.J. Kane."

Chapter Twenty

Liar

"Cooper. But where is your father?" asked Rebecca.

Sharla spoke fast before abruptly stopping. "They told me he was missing wit—"

Sheriff B.B. continued the interview. "Cooper demanded I take her and Kane with us. I knew better, but she was a ranger throwing her weight around. I'm glad for 'em, but they think they're God on Earth. We were transporting G.H. Burton down to Beaumont for evaluation by an expert on ID per the judge's order. I didn't have enough deputies to cover the county and take the prisoner. Cooper figured the bind I was in and volunteered to help me. She insisted on E.J. Kane. I was skeptical because of Kane's reputation, what I had seen, and his history with Burton."

Rebecca thought the cadence and pauses strange. Had B.B. memorized this speech?

Sheriff B.B. turned to Son, then back to the camera. "I suppose I need to blame myself. I keep kicking myself. Cooper couldn't see Kane's true colors because he brought her up through the highway patrol. She owed him for her quick rise. He took advantage of her loyalty, especially after he got her the ranger position.

"I had caught E.J. Kane alone with Burton the day before when the judge had the writ hearing. But I couldn't prove for sure he intended Burton harm, though we all were aware he had plenty of motive for having framed the poor slow fella, like he did. Man has the mind of an innocent child." Sheriff B.B. paused, shaking his head from left to right.

Rebecca looked at the phone in her hand. "Let me call you after it's over." She ended the call before launching several curse words at the television, critical of Sheriff B.B.'s poor acting skills. People who hadn't dealt with the sheriff might buy all of it. The thought gripped her into an icy chill.

"So, we took off, taking to highway fifty-nine, then sixty-nine. All going well till we got down there somewhere south of Woodville. I can't get it all straight in my head now." Sheriff B.B. stopped and pressed his lips for a moment.

"Did they overpower you?" asked a reporter.

Son looked away.

The doctor interjected, "Please be patient. He is trying to tell you."

"I'm driving. Ranger Cooper and E.J. Kane are in the back seat while I had Burton secured in the third row. Kane fired at Burton. He was quick." Sheriff B.B. lowered his head and covered his eyes like emotion overcame him. "I half expected it from Kane, but Cooper..."

"Liar." Rebecca lifted a lamp to hit the televised image. The heavy ceramic lamp slid out of her hand, falling to the carpet, making only a deadened thud.

"How did you get away?" a reporter asked.

"I didn't get away. After, after, well, Kane put the gun to my head. He forced me to pull over. Then he smacked my skull. I literally saw stars. Everything went black." Sheriff B.B. reached to the back of his head.

Sheriff B.B. lifted his arm, placing it on Son's shoulder. "I came to several hours later hid by the trees off the highway. No cell phone. No gun. I staggered into Woodville after dark."

Rebecca watched Son turn further away. Even the man's child couldn't buy this bull, yet how many others were familiar enough to recognize he lied? Sheriff B.B. played the part of the wounded hero. A powerful image selling a story of intrigue, treachery, actual innocence, crooked police, and murder.

"Is there a manhunt underway for E.J. Kane and Ranger Cooper?" asked a reporter.

"Should be a warrant for Burton's murder. For some reason, the DA and judge wanted to wait. I'm not familiar with their system down here. Guess since Burton didn't live long enough to get officially cleared, his life don't matter," said Sheriff B.B.

"Why didn't you report your suspicions about E.J. Kane earlier?" the same reporter asked as a follow-up.

"Never actually drew his gun or hit Burton. Has to be a huge amount of stress getting called out for a false confession. Look, I've known E.J. Kane all my life. I won't say anything bad about him. Not gonna do it. Even when we were growing up, we all saw the boy had problems. Surprised me when he even made ranger. Go back to when he got them other folks kilt on his little raid. I didn't believe he got paid off by the cartel, even though the department fired him. I'm sorry I won't say anything bad about him."

"What raid? Who got killed?" yelled the reporters.

"Didn't you hear me? I said I'm not saying anything. Lot to deal with. Guy's daughter in rehab. Pregnant with her pimp's baby—"

Son grabbed his father's arm. "The sheriff is tired. We've gone on longer than anyone expected. Thank you for coming. No more questions today."

Rebecca grabbed the wine bottle from the counter launching it by the neck into the flat-screen TV. The screen cracked in jagged sections yet continued the picture. She walked onto a sweeping veranda overlooking the lake, screaming with so much might she had to grab the rail for balance. The mother within told her Sharla must be in pieces.

Rebecca walked back through the doorway finding the cell phone. She steeled herself as she had so many times when a legal strategy blew up in the courtroom the jury could never find out. She slowed her breathing, then saw from her phone Sharla had already called.

Soothing her daughter took longer than Rebecca hoped. The girl had worked herself into a frenzy. Rebecca sympathized with her, because were it not for Sharla, she would still be cursing. Maybe firing the J-Frame revolver she carried in her purse across the lake.

Rebecca pointed out how entirely false the story sounded. Everyone was aware Sheriff B.B. hated E.J. The obvious fabrication hadn't even fooled B.B.'s son. Nearly a half hour later, the conversation ended with a promise Rebecca would phone her again later.

Rebecca poured herself another glass of wine, then stepped onto the huge patio next to the lake. Participating in a discussion with Sharla gave her the opportunity to develop a plan. She settled on the one person E.J. had completely trusted, even more than Cooper.

"Bec. I'm sorry things are moving so quick I couldn't call you," yelled Hall.

"I can barely hear you. Where are you?" asked Rebecca.

"It's the copter. Let it take off." Hall paused and the rotor noise faded. "Can you hear me now?"

"Where is E.J.?"

"We've got teams up and down the highway," said Hall.

"Probably took a lesser route. When has B.B. ever told the truth? He is a racist, misogynist swine..." Rebecca's language grew ranker and more descriptive. She could tell Hall had moved the phone from his ear, yet she continued for the moment.

"I know. Whatever you think I need to know, I know. The story makes no sense. E.J. wouldn't and he would never ask Cooper to do anything improper. E.J. loved her like a daughter," said Hall.

"Loved?" asked Rebecca.

Hall paused, then added, "We got a massive net looping a grid up and down sixty-nine from Houston to Lufkin."

"You won't find him." Rebecca leaned back against the kitchen counter. "You won't find him," said Rebecca.

"Burton would have him in the hinterland, likely deep in the Big Thicket. Problem is, no one listens to me," said Hall.

"I'm satisfied someone contaminated evidence in the Burton case with newer DNA," said Rebecca.

"What?" yelled Hall.

"We can't date DNA or say how long or when it was deposited on an object. Even if an item was previously tested, the science is so much better at picking up material and replicating it," said Rebecca.

Hall raised his voice. "I have to go. I'm at the command tent."

"Listen to me. B.B. is a pawn of somebody huge. Somebody capable of accessing a secure laboratory's evidence locker. They don't want you to find E.J. then he won't be found."

Hall swallowed, then blasted the words out. "I pray you're wrong."

Chapter Twenty-One

Into the Abyss

"Leave me. You have to live for Sharla and Rebecca." Even Cooper's whisper had lost its timbre.

"Rebecca hates me and Sharla..."

The thermal response radiated from the thick subtropical jungle, meeting the sun at its low point in the sky, broadcasting heat back onto the morass of monstrous trees and dense wild vegetation.

"Sharla is pregnant, or she was."

"Was?" asked Cooper.

"Rebecca. When she called. She was taking her to get an abortion," said E.J.

Cooper looked away.

E.J. studied the muddy walls, their muck caked his fingers. His mind failed to fathom a plan as he sat in murky goo.

"Probably for the best. You know she can't beat meth and raise a baby. Rape baby. She'd see whatever scum pimped her every time she looked into the kid's eyes. Nobody can think that's right. Nobody should make somebody suffer forever. Plus, she'll die if she gets strung out again." E.J. looked down before continuing. "Baby wouldn't have a chance, no way. What kind of life would a kid have? Probably malformed from drugs. Might even be born addicted. The counselor thinks Sharla is still using. You know how they can always get to it. Crack baby is no life for a human being."

Cooper's soft voice reached him in the near darkness. "Good speech. Got yourself convinced yet?"

"I thought you were realizing there's no certitude in this world. I'm being practical. Would you have shot Burton?" E.J. knew the answer yet wanted to hear her say it. He wanted to confirm what was right.

"No," said Cooper.

"No? Because it's the law?" asked E.J.

"But I would live with it if you killed him," said Cooper.

"A little gray. Careful, a little gray might take you down my road." E.J. laughed.

"You're the most honorable man I know." She looked at him resolutely. Cooper had found a second wind.

"Fever making you crazy?" asked E.J.

"You never break the law. Maybe bend it considerable. You apply it to take justice for people who can't get justice for themselves. Always have. Why you can't take a life without sufficient justification? I want my girls to grow up like you," said Cooper.

E.J. touched her forehead with the back of his hand. "You're burning alive." He got to his feet, lifting the only thing left on him, a small pocketknife. He fashioned a hole, though the silty nature of the wall made it difficult because the opening kept collapsing.

"What are you doing?" asked Cooper. Her voice stuttered into a tremble.

E.J. dug out another hand holt above the first one. His mind played a series of images of Cooper's children from the photos she had shown him over the years. Despite the veneer of a tough, no-nonsense peace officer, many times over the years she shared the trophies of a proud mother, photographs of birthdays and Christmases, videos of piano recitals, and softball at bats.

Occasionally, the mire of the wall supported short hairlike moss, filling his nostrils with the odor of moldy bread. He pressed his face deeper as his entire body tensed, pushing against a slick reverse incline. E.J. wanted to quit. Even if he got out, how would he ever get Cooper up the side of the crevasse?

His fingernails had broken and chiseled from the sludge gumbo pressed under them. Once more, he lifted his hand over his head to dig another hold while his body held tight. Cooper's baby daughter's image in his head turned to Sharla, silently urging him forward. This time, the hand grabbed emptiness.

He looked up, seeing the world above the sinkhole. A victory dash of breath from above filled his lungs. Struggling to get his elbow over the rim, E.J. swung himself up, hopeful the side didn't collapse. What if the entire lip of the chasm collapsed, swallowing Cooper?

E.J. looked down at a hole which had seemed an abyss from below. Tears of pain blurred his vision and blood drained from his fingers into his hands.

"Cooper? Cooper?" He yelled.

E.J. wiped his bloody, dirt-coated hands on a clump of long, leafy grass. In the near darkness, he saw the drought draining green from the rest of Texas only removed a shade of brilliance from the emerald of the great jungle. He caught a hint of dark shadow inconsistent with the surrounding darkness. "Cooper?"

E.J. saw her grime-covered face. "I'll find a rope or something, somewhere." As he said it, the absurdity struck him. What if he cut one of the many rattan vines hanging from the big pin and water oaks?

His pocketknife wouldn't cut one of these thick runners. Cooper lacked any means to tie it around herself anyway, nor did he envision a way to get it securely enough around a tree to climb up and down.

What if he made it back to B.B.'s Suburban? Would B.B. and Burton have left anything he might use like a rope? They would have moved or hid the vehicle. If the story was traveling the highway, then it wouldn't be found out here. Probably search parties and helicopters already filled the area.

Perhaps it was more a hope than a probability. He looked up, straining to see the sky better above the dense canopy of tall trees.

E.J. felt a truth slice vertically through him. They were far off the main highway, far off the route anyone would search. Sheriff B.B. hadn't been trying to trick Burton's men. To the contrary, he had been in league with them from the start.

Why had B.B. invited him? The answer had finally revealed itself, far too late. He imagined B.B. holding a news conference, blaming E.J. and Cooper for Burton's escape. Is it possible for B.B. to escape without consequences? How was it possible for him not to?

Authorities would spend days searching a grid each side of Highway 69 before turning their attention to the vastness of the dense canopied wasteland comprising the Big Thicket National Preserve. B.B. and Burton likely concluded even if he and Cooper eluded a thorough search with hounds, Cooper would never survive so long without medical attention. Given E.J.'s reduced circumstances, no one would believe what would sound like a fanciful story compared to B.B.'s tale.

E.J. looked at his boots. Desperation rose from the burning sensation engulfing the muscles in his legs, then lifting through his body. Burton had outfoxed him at every turn. And why shouldn't he? Burton had nearly a quarter century to plot his revenge.

There had to be some strategy to settle upon. Something to give Cooper and him a chance of survival. If he found the creek they had traversed in the shootout, then it would lead him to the little blacktop road. Wouldn't the road be how Burton would return?

He should pick a direction as much to the opposite of where the county road lay as possible. Then move at the optimal pace he was able to maintain. Eventually, he would have to run across a home or road. As long as he didn't stray from the direction, then he had the ability to retrace his steps.

E.J. settled on a choice, then stepped fast. Was it possible for him to find help before Burton came back and found Cooper with dogs?

Chapter Twenty-Two

A Trick of Light?

E.J. stepped out of a forest of ancient hardwoods mixed with narrow pines. He struggled down a wide, short hill filled with bull nettles in the darkness before reaching a bottom of thick, blooming thistles standing as high as his shoulders.

His exhausted legs lifted, walking another incline, becoming tangled in thick briars. The undergrowth compelled him to spend greater energy with each step until his boot slid into a bog. A sweeping willow tree marked the edge of connecting slews laying before him.

An image of wide cottonmouthed snakes filled his mind. Fear forced him to halt for a moment in his tracks. How far had he come? The question didn't appear to be as important as the distance he needed to travel and if he could return to Cooper in the dark.

E.J. bent at the waist, resting his hands on his knees. His lungs flamed with exertion. He thought he was still following where the sun sank near the horizon, though he couldn't be sure. The lack of the sun's radiance did not provide any respite from the scorching heat. All the light evaporated. Gone were even the weak shadows which once extended from the long, sharp leaves of palmettos, looking as if they waited for the right moment to skewer a person. He forced himself to start again.

The darkness retreated in severity. E.J. found the moon rising slowly, sharing its poor luminesce like syrup flowing back into the bottle.

Dark-colored beautyberries offset the darker, veinlike structures running along their nearly florescent stalks, ascending into growths of hardwood trees crowned by rattan vines forming geometric rings and crooks extending into shadow backdropped against endless shadow.

Every part of E.J.'s body ached. His head splitting in pain drove him to his knees. The plan to make his best time dead reckoning in one direction wasn't producing results. How is it possible to walk for hours anywhere without encountering any sign of humanity in the modern world?

A rigorous discipline driving the pain from his mind had got him this far. In fact, the same self-determination had moved him to this point in life. A maddening thought enveloped his mind, evoking laughter. At what point in life was he at? One could hardly consider his endeavors as ultimately leading him anywhere positive.

E.J. tasted sour bile in the back of this throat. He failed, failed Cooper and her children, the same as he had failed Rebecca and his own children. The knowledge erupted from the pit of his gnawing intestines.

Through stinging eyes, he caught movement extending past a great quagmire of massive cypress trees. Above thick root balls arched angled trunk ridges, casting shadows under long, irregular sweeps of Spanish moss nearly shimmering. A flash of blue light radiated, casting a hue over the shallow water before disappearing into the nothingness.

Did he really see something, or might it have been a trick of light? Should he follow its path? Regardless of whether he had really seen something, there wasn't anywhere else to go.

Several hundred yards of trudging through the marsh took E.J. to the edge of a clearing of Indian grass. A shack of rusted tin and grayed batten board construction stood under a wide branched elm tree. After knocking and opening an unlocked door, E.J. discovered no one was at home. A cot, two lawn chairs, and a Coleman stove on a dirt floor evidenced someone lived there.

Necessity dictated he find a phone to get Cooper some help, still the act of searching someone's home made him uncomfortable. Probably the owner only had a cell phone on their person, because there was none in the makeshift house. A well-worn leather bag held a flashlight.

Eureka, a drum of water, lay on a makeshift stand. He soaked his thirst, laying his head under the spout.

Outside the building leaned a homemade wooden ladder. Would it make more sense to carry the ladder or tie what old clothes were in the house into a makeshift rope? Would either hold Cooper and his weight? A thick pile of clothes to carry or drag a rickety, though lightweight, ladder?

Retracing the path he took earlier in the dark, even with the flashlight, didn't prove easy. Each step landed in shallow water sloshed, a noise transmitting his location. Every rotten branch he landed upon gave way under his boot, making him fear he would step on a thick, dark-bodied cottonmouth ready to turn and drive its fangs into his leg.

The distant barks and howls of dogs reached his ears. The dogs would be on their scent. If he angled toward the sound, then wouldn't he more likely run across Cooper? E.J. must hope he might triangulate from the dogs and his guesses as to form where he might have traveled.

E.J. used the flashlight sparingly for fear the light might be seen for a considerable distance. Any moment he would walk into a machine-gun-toting death squad led by a pack of people-hunting dogs.

The lights swung through the trees. E.J. drove his knee into soft mud. He froze in place, hoping the thug wouldn't see him.

The illumination moved closer. Dogs must have moved ahead. E.J. sat for what felt like an eternity until the footfalls became audible in the thick grass. Even mud squished, receding and lifting, with boots landing.

E.J. leaped forward. His elbow slammed hard across teeth and a sharp chin. A hulking figure collapsed. The bridge of the hulk's nose caught the back of E.J.'s boot. In pursuit of the heel, E.J. swung the snip-toed Lucchese through the trachea and soft tissue of the neck. E.J.'s leg rebounded from the base of the outlaw's skull. The man fell face first into the mire.

E.J. swiftly made a move toward the person's flashlight. He felt for and recovered a semiautomatic rifle. Wouldn't he have a pistol or knife too? Time worked against him. Luck had been with E.J. that this hoodlum walked near him alone. The woods were full of Burton's soldiers. Sooner or later, the dogs would zero in on Cooper.

She had to be close. He could use the light, pretending to be one of Burton's people. They wouldn't see anything from a distance with his light indistinguishable from the other searchers.

E.J. kneeled over an opening in the earth. "Cooper?"

The light illuminated a bundle nearly submerged from seeping water. He judged the depth approximately ten to twelve feet while his wobbly ladder was eight. While descending the ladder, doubt flooded over him. Maybe he would be wrong about trapping both himself and costing Cooper her only chance. "Cooper?"

Cooper didn't move. E.J. feared she had died, then he felt her breath on his hand. With great difficulty, he successfully maneuvered her onto the bank as he climbed the ladder.

The lights were congregated in one area. E.J. turned off the flashlight.

Likely they were regrouping, going back to where the dogs last had the scent. If so, then it might be a matter of minutes. Lifting Cooper over his shoulder, he found the courage to step forward.

Several hundred feet later, E.J. heard the dogs moving in their general direction. He had to continue without relief. Surely, the animals couldn't track well through the marsh. Once he hit the shallow water bog, they had to lose the scent, right?

Thinking back to the few manhunts and exercises from the Texas prison dogs, he couldn't recall their limitations. The canines had impressed to the point they seemed impervious to any attempts to confuse them.

His heart lifted because these couldn't be the Texas Department of Corrections dogs. More likely these were some ole boy's hog hunting dogs. If so, then any number of animals might take them off the human track.

The shed's owner still hadn't returned. E.J.'s thoughts were focused on the restoration of drinkable water for most of the journey back from the sinkhole. The tourniquet had loosened, though thick mud had staunched the bleeding. He cleaned the wound to the extent possible using the owner's clothes. Would she lose her leg?

Cooper whispered as she moved in and out of consciousness. Her comments made no sense. E.J. searched the one room again. He found no food. It must be a hunting cabin.

The only solution making sense. A hunter might not leave food. Animals would tear a place apart looking for it. It was smarter to bring food each trip. Weeks would pass before opening day of deer or duck season.

He lay down on the floor, relatively certain Burton wouldn't risk anything like approaching a cabin in the woods. He couldn't know whether the structure contained a phone.

Best for both of them to rest tonight. Tomorrow, E.J. would figure out how to get Cooper help. E.J. closed his heavy eyelids, eager for a break.

How fortunate to discover their lodging? Did he really see a blue light? Light played tricks on people in the deep woods. He knew the fact from all sorts of strange calls he had worked in his past career as a deputy and highway patrol. People had claimed to have seen many unusual things lurking in the Big Thicket of Texas. There were even Bigfoot devotees. The mystique lent itself to the national wildlife preserve, attracting more visitors.

Something hard pressed against E.J.'s cheek, jostling him awake. His eyes fixed on a pair of barrels.

Chapter Twenty-Three

The Native American Who Was Not

The shotgun snapped against E.J.'s nose. A metallic flavor filled his mouth. His lip bled and his nostrils lifted against a thick musk of body odor consuming the room. E.J.'s eyes could only find the shotgun barrels distinguishable in dark shapes from the remaining darkness. "I'm sorry. I thought it was a hunting cabin and we—"

"Reaper not see you." The voice sounded as harsh as the slam of the shotgun barrels.

E.J. tried to continue. "I'm sorry. We had to—"

A growl of garlicky air encircled his face. "Reaper see future. Reaper not see you."

"My friend needed help. She is a Texas Ranger. There'll be a reward if you help her," E.J. said.

"How much?"

"How much, what?" asked E.J.

"Reward. How much reward Reaper get?" He stabbed at E.J.'s skull with the shotgun barrels. E.J. turned his head, avoiding further contact with the gun.

"Let us use your cell phone and I'm sure you'll get several thousand dollars." E.J. knew the shotgun barrels had moved from his head, though he wasn't sure how far.

"Reaper got no cell phone." The burning odor of a match igniting filled the air. A flipped over cooler made a table with a kerosene lamp casting a hazy light over the room.

"How far are we from a town?" asked E.J.

"Town?" A troll-looking figure adorned in a filthy Houston Astros tee shirt held an exceptionally long-barreled side-by-side shotgun.

Cooper raised up from her pallet of what were evidently Mr. Reaper's clothes.

"Reaper's clothes. Hey, you tore up Reaper's clothes." He pointed the barrel at Cooper, vibrating the firearm up and down. She raised her hands.

"I had no choice. She would have bled to death. We'll pay you back and more." E.J. stood, and the weapon swung back to his head.

"Who shot lone ranger?" asked Reaper.

Was he mocking them, or did he not understand? E.J. stared at Reaper's arms. They came into focus, and he peered closer. The man's dark complexion had made the dried blood on his hands and arms difficult to notice in the low light.

"Reaper shot a deer." Reaper turned his palms over as if somehow deer's blood was distinguishable to E.J.'s naked eye.

"An outlaw named Burton. He is an Aryan," E.J. said. Would this fellow understand what an Aryan was? A search of his face didn't reveal any appreciation. "White supremacist. Kills folks because God made them like you, Black, or for no reason we can figure."

Cooper said, "Mean."

"Reaper not Black. Reaper Indian. You drank Reaper's water?"

"Look, I'm sorry. Can you tell us how to get to someone with a car or a phone? Infection has to be eating her alive. Every minute matters," said E.J.

"Store on road," said Reaper.

"How far? Tell me how to get there." E.J. stepped forward, halting when he perceived from the hermit's expression he had intruded on Reaper's space.

"We finish deer and eat. Then I'll take you. Long way. Only Reaper know." Reaper stepped out the door without further explanation.

"I can walk," said Cooper.

"No. Eat a little deer and then he'll show me to civilization. I'll get a helicopter in here. FBI and DPS are probably already up there looking for us."

Cooper looked unconvinced. "We both understand that Sheriff B.B. lie about where he last saw us. Burton's people got rid of the unit B.B. drove. It will take days to get a grid expanded this far from the highway."

"Rest. Quiet. It's all alright now." E.J. wanted to help Reaper butcher the deer. Perhaps helping the man with the task, he considered essential, would endear them to the stranger.

Would his amateur skinning skills working in the darkness or whatever near light a kerosene lamp provided aggravate such a no-nonsense, self-sufficient man by trying to help?

Cooper lay back. E.J. feared she had lost too much blood. Perhaps he should compel this Reaper individual to guide him out forcefully. She had grown paler. Reaper appeared powerfully built. His neck was enormous, matching thick arms and thighs. The right bicep had what E.J. originally thought was a tattoo.

Later he had realized the arm had been branded, though E.J . couldn't make out the letters. A fight would incapacitate one or both of them. Cooper's best chance was to earn the man's confidence and cooperation.

The irregularities of board and tin walls showed the sun had risen. Reaper didn't fill E.J. with hope, despite his attempt to put Cooper at ease. Who talks about themselves in the third person? What kind of person lives like this? What kind of Indian was he or what did he mean? Didn't he realize Cooper needed help right away?

The only mystery Reaper revealed was he had killed a deer. Reaper needed little help to apply what E.J. was aware game wardens had dubbed a criminal dress on the carcass.

E.J. watched Reaper construct a fire between cinder blocks, then roast tenderloins over a makeshift grill. The aroma of meat roasting over an open fire called to E.J.'s empty stomach.

"We need to get Cooper help," said E.J.

Reaper pointed to the loin steaks.

E.J. pulled one off the expanded metal and bit the juicy, warm venison. He stopped urging and requesting long enough to finish the backstrap.

Reaper extended a cylinder-shaped beige gourd. A brown liquid sporting the aroma of diesel nearly spilled over the top. "Drink."

"Not a big drinker. Don't much care for it," said E.J.

"Drink with Reaper." Reaper downed a larger gourd. "Drink."

"Don't mean to be rude." E.J. suffered a small, burning swallow. "What Indian tribe are you?"

"Reaper a green." The big man unleashed a belly laugh.

"Is that an offshoot of Alabama-Coushatta or something else?" E.J. stepped awkwardly, reaching to hold the arm of a lawn chair so he could sit.

Reaper shook his head. "Green like the money."

In his attempt to sit, E.J. accidentally folded the chair onto himself. He rolled in mud from the deer's blood and entrails.

"Reaper tell your future. Skinhead boys camp near here. They pay reward. Cash."

"But you're Black." The light darkened around E.J.'s. vision.

"Reaper tell you. Reaper green. Reward your idea."

What would happen to Cooper? The world went dark.

Chapter Twenty-Four

Sheriff B.B. in the Cemetery

E.J. Kane's blistered foot slid across the gravestone slick with blood. A cloth bag flew off his head. Enough late afternoon light penetrated the forest canopy to cast light in grays and pinks. He peered across Sheriff B.B.'s neck even as he felt the prickly twines of the grass rope scratching his own.

E.J.'s head bobbed with a wooziness. The orb felt like a great pumpkin, far too large for his neck to support. E.J. struggled to keep his balance as confusion clouded his mind from whatever grog he had been stupid enough to imbibe. Brilliant move not insulting or fighting his host, instead he let the maniac drug him.

"All rise, Judge G.H. Burton presiding."

The musty scent of thick, dark, muddy earth lifted through a blanket of Saint Augustine grass.

Sheriff B.B. cast his face down and whispered, "I'm sorry."

E.J. battled the restraints, holding his hands behind his back. His mind tried to return to Reaper and the last moments before he blacked out. The details were hazy, yet he had an understanding that Reaper had betrayed him.

The green tribe had to predate all other human associations. Money cured all prejudices for the brief time the transaction took to complete. Where did B.B. come from? Was this real? The sticky blood clotting between his toes convinced him.

"How do you plead?" A red robe accented by a green scarf lying over the garment's collar ended on G.H. Burton's chest. Were the gray-haired man bearded, he would have resembled some culture's rendition of good old Saint Nick.

E.J.'s eyes swung toward a roof of interlacing branches from hundred-foot basket oaks whose thick leaves blotted out the sun. The cord rubbing against his neck moved his muddled mind to the recollection of a scratchy starched collar restraining him under a tortious button and tie in a similar tree canopied cemetery. Likewise, B.B. had stood across from him on the occasion of their great-grandfather's funeral. What was he doing recollecting memories with his life in peril? Whatever liquid the gourd had held must have really scattered his faculties, though he conceded they hadn't been ordered in years. Possibly, like Rebecca had preached so many times, he needed counseling.

In his memory, the younger version of B.B. glared at him. B.B.'s eyes ran over him with hatred. In contrast, B.B.'s father, E.J.'s uncle, had earlier good-naturedly teased E.J. about putting a rock on his head.

The same day, E.J. had heard a buzzing noise explode in his right ear. He reached to slap what he hoped was a dirt dauber. The sharp pinch of the stinger had snapped off in his skin. The flesh behind his ear pulsed, causing E.J. to gyrate to the right. His mother had snatched his hand, sending the message to stop fidgeting during the graveside service.

As an exasperated child, E.J. scanned up at the massive trees, aware the preacher's already lengthy prayer seemed destined to continue into infinity. "Amen" crashed through the cathedral of great oaks.

G.H. Burton's voice snapped E.J.'s fuzzy head back into the moment. "Dear friend." Burton sat on a heavy wooden office chair perched in the small cargo bed of a new Can-Am brand side-by-side.

"Got me good this time. Didn't figure you did business with Black folks," said E.J.

Burton shook a crooked finger. "Stereotypes can be misleading."

"Where's Cooper?" E.J.'s muddled faculties appreciated his words were slurred.

"My colleagues recruited Reaper out of Houston's homeless ranks. We have to keep a few to maintain the latrines. Though we can't let them pollute the camp, can we, dear friend?"

A brief survey revealed half a dozen white men carrying guns spaced among three large new-looking utility terrain vehicles. The act of getting transported to Beaumont must have been seen as a gift. Had Burton used his unwitting lawyers to suggest it or file a motion requesting such? Evidently, the Aryan Triangle had a training camp here. Burton set the ambush near their headquarters. Why didn't E.J. figure it sooner?

A stout drop struck E.J.'s nose. So long without rain back home. Only a hundred miles away, he had largely left the irregular Bahia grass pastures bordered by pine savannas and hardwood bottoms for cypress and sour gum swamps punctuated with an occasional elevated oak thicket. At some point in history, someone evidently deemed the latter worthy of a family cemetery.

Another tear of rainwater snapped on his forehead as E.J. finished scanning the graveyard. Wouldn't somebody come by? It looked fairly small, likely some private property in the preserve. "Where's Cooper?"

"We're patching her up. How do you plead?" asked Burton.

E.J. looked around, settling on B.B. What did he mean "How do you plead?"

"Don't look to the traitor. Traitors don't rate trials," said G.H. Burton.

"Not guilty," said E.J.

The closest of Burton's soldiers hissed. A tattooed skinhead swung back and forward, leading the others in a revelry of boos. Burton waved to the shirtless canvases of swastikas, numbers, and cryptic-looking hieroglyphics. The noise ended. Another cranked the four-seater side-by-side before the remaining thugs loaded into the vehicles.

E.J. watched the events, unsure in the dimming daylight and staccato rain if it were a nightmare, the effects of being drugged, or whether he had witnessed the surreal events. A squad of stormtroopers led by an escaped fugitive in shiny Canadian-made utility four-wheel drives had made him enter a plea to an unknown charge before leaving.

His mind swung to the more pressing concerns. How long could he stand on a headstone with a hanging rope wrapped over a big oak limb above? How did Sheriff B.B. get here, and how long had he been like this? Was there even the remote possibility of help?

E.J. pressed and closed his hands back and forth. Was the rope binding them a grass rope like the one around his neck? If only he could stress it until it stretched. He had to keep at it.

Sheriff B.B. spoke in a raspy voice. "More a crazy religious sacrament than a trial. They'll come back. Not over until we die."

"Why'd your friends turn on you?" asked E.J.

"Your fault, pretender," said Sheriff B.B.

"My fault?" asked E.J.

"Your wife got a search warrant for a dating site's records. In her probable cause affidavit, she mentioned she received an anonymous tip to check Burton's email. Actually, it turned out to be one of his jail flunky's emails, but perhaps the thread to unravel it all," said Sheriff B.B.

"So? Unravel what?" E.J. continued, twisting his wrist behind his back.

"Think? How did he get some unidentified killer's DNA on a knife held in evidence for decades?"

E.J.'s foot crashed into the granite headstone, reverberating up to his bad knee. He fought back the urge to move it. "You're not making any sense. Why would you help me? You hate me."

"Yep," said Sheriff B.B.

"I've done nothing to you." The statement operated as an assertion and a question. Something had to make B.B. hate him. What was it?

"You don't know why. I despised you for years before I figured it out. Cain and Abel," said Sheriff B.B.

E.J.'s legs weakened. His joint radiated pain. He needed desperately to sit for a minute, yet he caught himself in open laughter. "We're going to die with you hating me for a half century because you were jealous."

"Everybody fawned over you, firstborn of your generation. The most handsome, tallest, smartest. My mom used to tell me 'Why can't you be more like Elliott.' Burned me up. Till I realized you were a worthless pretender," said Sheriff B.B.

E.J. laughed so hard he caught himself from falling forward and hanging.

B.B. screamed full of the rasping grit in his voice, "What?"

"I've lost everything. God or fate or the universe or something crushed me. I mean Old Testament style Book of Job smiting down on me. Konner died half a world away. Wife hates me. Says I killed our son. Daughter is drug addicted and pregnant. The only thing I know about the father is nobody knows who he is, and he abused her. Probably doesn't matter because she aborted it, anyway. My incompetence got my people killed and the law calls me not credible. And you, fool, you envy me."

Sheriff B.B. shook his head. "Arrogance. So arrogant. Has to be the Almighty God Hisself out to get you. Always about you. The universe revolves around you. Father, Son, and Holy Ghost, all targeting you."

"Arrogant?" puzzled E.J.

"You're not Job. You're a stupid puppet like me and the rest of the world. I wised up. Got paid for it," said Sheriff B.B.

"When did you turn? Go dirty?" asked E.J.

Sherriff B.B. sneered over the top of the rope. "Day one, dummy. I was on the take from day one. You were like you always were, gullible and stupid."

"Look, we're going to die. Burton hates me. He'll never let me live. Come on, you can blame me. Tell me what Burton is really holding against you. I'll try to goad him into getting close enough to get one good kick on him." E.J. continued twisting one hand over the other, trying to stretch the rope behind his back.

"Oh wow. Now the great American hero saves me. Self-centered jerk to the end. All about you. You can't fix this one. I told you. I sent Rebecca a clue. It'll bust this whole charade open. I die because of it," Sheriff B.B. said.

At that moment, E.J. couldn't have articulated why, yet he knew Sheriff B.B. lied. "You didn't send her anything."

"Shut up. Burton might have someone out in the woods listening. Just more of his traps," hollered Sheriff B.B.

E.J. surveyed the wood line, satisfied the distance was too great to hear anything except when Sheriff B.B. shouted. "Son figured it out, didn't he? Only one you'd cover for. Kid made a detective."

Sheriff B.B. caught himself stifling a yell to a near whisper. "Shut up."

E.J. rubbed the soles of his feet on the rough hue of the gravestone's top.

"Boy worships you," said B.B.

"I'm right, aren't I?" asked E.J.

"Just shut up. Promise me this one thing. One thing, you arrogant wannabe. Let me die. You think good wins in the end. You never understood the way the world works. Burton ever suspects Son, then he kills him. We both know locking Burton up means nothing." Tears pooled and rolled from the corners of Sheriff B.B.'s eyes. "Let me be the man my son needs me to be, and I'll tell you the truth."

Chapter Twenty-Five

The Truth

"What truth?" asked E.J.

B.B. spit and cursed. "Unmitigated gall. Think God and the devil are fighting over your soul like some Sunday school story. Like you're Charlton Heston in *The Ten Commandments*. No, stupid. Wise up." Sheriff B.B.'s tears had stopped.

"I don't understand." E.J. came unbalanced, trying to press his hands against the bindings. The soft rain had soaked the grave marker, washing some of the blood from E.J.'s feet and the stone. Regaining his balance on the granite top, E.J. realized he had tightened the noose, making speech more difficult.

"Not God. Men," said B.B.

"What?" whispered E.J.

"You were right. All too right about that compound you hit. Meth, fentanyl, weapons, prostitutes, smuggling people. The whole place out there was a factory. They were connected, you understand, like the Zeta cartel connected."

Sheriff B.B. leaned his head back, softly chortling. "What were you thinking? One riot, one ranger."

E.J. wanted to shake his head, but instead he pressed his shoulders, trying to force the strands of his binds apart. He pushed the words out, explaining himself as he had done so many times prior. "They got tipped off before. Why we wanted a small force. No leaks. We needed surprise."

"You were never gonna surprise them. How you think the whole place got emptied before you got there the first time? How you think you got ambushed the second time? Wise up, you idiot," Sheriff B.B. snarled over his shoulder.

"My head wasn't clear. I had buried Konner not much before. The review board found I made a poor tactical plan. So bad they even referred me for prosecution. Criminally negligent homicide, remember," said E.J.

Sheriff B.B. smirked. "Cartel knew you were coming. Once alerted, an army wouldn't have been able to take that fortress."

"How? Who?"

"That would defeat the purpose. I tell you who and Son dies anyway because I told you," said B.B.

"Burton?" asked E.J.

"No, Burton is crazy. Like Messiah complex, Nazi-killer nuts. But crazy mean is not the real evil in the world. I'm talking about what makes the world turn. Real evil is big money. It's always big money, E," Sheriff B.B. stated.

B.B. hadn't called him "E" since they were in high school. "Why tell me now? Why tell me but not tell me who was behind it all? It's worse than not telling me at all." Heavier droplets fell on his face. E.J. nearly chuckled, discovering he lacked the breath for it.

"Because you're not a pretender, pretender. I'm dying. Can't be helped. But my money is on you getting out of this. You always survive." He laughed a mocking gurgle. "Maybe it really is good over evil.

I want to believe it, anyway." Sheriff B.B. looked from E.J. to the slick, wet carpet of thick-bladed grass beneath the headstones. "Watch over my son. My wife. Promise me. And if I'm wrong..."

"If you're wrong, then I die too?" E.J. felt like he had made some progress on the soaked cord, keeping his hands tied. Should he trust B.B. enough to tell him? Wouldn't our partnering together give us an edge?

"Still all good. I kind of cleanse my conscience because I was part of it. Not asking for your forgiveness. I've done you wrong like you can't imagine. Lifetime of wrong," said Sheriff B.B.

"Give me a name and I'll forgive you," said E.J.

"Either I'm going to nothingness, or I'll burn in hell. Not sure which. Don't much matter which. I'm not telling you to save my soul. If I can put you on the right path, I'll be bringing some hell from the grave to some of these devils. You'll kill 'em all, E. Always been what you do."

"But you're not telling me who. Who?" yelled E.J.

"Told you I can't tell you. They'll figure out it came from me, then Son and Candy die. Nope."

"Then why tell me?" asked E.J.

"Told you. You're no pretender, pretender. Son tells me you told him the first rule of investigations. There are no coincidences. Go back, look at everything you were working on at the time of the raid. All so much bigger than one way station of drugs and people. There was something going on. Something you blew off because you couldn't think big enough. You never think big." B.B. shook his head, looking back at E.J. as the last rays of the sun descended over the trees.

E.J. swallowed the rain driving into his face. "I don't understand any of it. Who?"

"I gave a clue, like Son gave Rebecca. A single thread unravels all of it. You don't understand evil 'cause it's not in you. You'll have to find it again. What you had stumbled onto. Only this time figure it out," said Sheriff B.B.

E.J. pressed hard with his raw wrist. "Again? What does 'again' mean? I'm working free." Previously mistrusting Sheriff B.B. had been easier before the man bared his soul in whatever odd request for forgiveness he had presented.

Somehow now, E.J. questioned his ability to cast stones. The image of the twisted grin B.B. had worn from the earliest points of E.J.'s recollection manifested in the near darkness before him. What was wrong with him? He needed to concentrate on getting free. B.B. had been wicked from day one. What if Burton had planted Sheriff B.B. here to find out what E.J. knew?

The rain lubricated his hands, giving him greater opportunity. Was it raining back home or only in the surreal jungle near the gulf and the South Louisiana swamp country?

"When Burton gets back, nod at me when you're loose. Think I'll be the great American hero this time," said Sheriff B.B.

Darkness came, bringing heavier rain soaking E.J.'s hair. There appeared to be no use trying to gain information from B.B. Whatever more B.B. knew, he wasn't sharing.

In one day, he had been drugged, abducted, made to stand in gallows for hours. Also, the truths underlying his life had been challenged. Challenged by a man he couldn't trust. B.B. had fabricated falsehoods all their lives, and yet the new piece ordered the puzzle. However, the more it came into focus, the more the whole thing presented a greater enigma than ever.

The events were too much for his mind to process. His immediate goal had to be unlashing his hands. The steady rain soaked his bloody wrist, lessening the friction.

He couldn't say how long after dark he heard the utility terrain vehicles. At first, E.J. debated whether his mind played tricks on him, then he saw Sheriff B.B. look in the same direction.

Sheriff B.B. blurted out, "I need your forgiveness."

What could it matter? Tell B.B. he was forgiven. Then it occurred to E.J. to garner something for the indulgence. "Give me a name."

"I'd be murdering my family," said Sheriff B.B.

"Honorable, giving your life for Son. How did a man capable of such honor choose to betray his badge?" asked E.J.

"Weren't no choice. The way of the world. You'll see," said B.B.

The exhaust from the trio of Can-Am Defenders grew louder, almost vibrating E.J.'s bones, wearily maintaining the scarecrow pose on the grave marker. The skinheads disembarked having covered their shirtless tattoos with rain ponchos. One of them lifted a tarp over a utility terrain vehicle bed, revealing dry firewood. Soon, the scent of burning wood filled the humid air. Between the illumination of a fire and the flashlights, E.J. saw Cooper in a passenger seat of one of the all-terrain vehicles.

Someone had placed a tailored bandage on Cooper's wound.

Burton smiled in the shadowy light casting through the night. "Told you, proper medical care."

Cooper looked drained, yet flush at the same time. "E.J.? Is it you? Gave me a shot of something. Think they got me hearing things, hallucinating?"

"She should be in a hospital," said E.J.

"Now, dear friend, you're not the boss anymore. She represents you. Lose your trial and she dies." Burton chuckled at the threat.

"What am I charged with?" asked E.J.

"Not charged with, charged for," said Burton.

"Arrgh..." Sheriff B.B. slid a foot off the headstone. E.J. recognized the maneuver. His legs cramped too. Sheriff B.B. was nearing the end of his ability to hold out.

Burton drew a polymer pistol from his waistband and faced Sheriff B.B. "I pay your price because it's your country. Right? But what do you do? How do you repay my love and respect?"

Sheriff B.B. glared at the murderer.

"You stab me in the back with four words. Four words. Four words so perfect I'm certain the clue didn't form in your moronic mind. *Check Burton's jail email*," said Burton.

Cooper's boots slid out from under her. She climbed back into the passenger seat.

"What did he say?" asked E.J. He determined it was best to act oblivious to the whole issue. He wasn't supposed to know, so it would be best if he feigned ignorance.

Burton laughed. "Actually typed. I tell you and it confirms it."

E.J. answered, "You're going to kill us anyway."

Burton said, "No need. Right now, you know only what the search warrant affidavit provides—"

"Let them go. You got me," said Sheriff B.B.

"You haven't told him?" Burton pointed the gun from one to another. "About your press conference where you told the world E.J. Kane and Texas Ranger Elizabeth Cooper attacked you and presumably killed me."

Cooper's head snapped forward. She must have been debating whether she heard right.

E.J. stared through rain and near darkness at Sheriff B.B., who looked away. It made perfect sense that Burton had told him that much of the plan. Sheriff B.B. lied about where they had been waylaid. Now he realized B.B. had told the world E.J. had ambushed him. Probably spun a story claiming E.J. was desperate to protect what was left of his reputation, sought to cover up his misdeeds.

Wouldn't the scheme serve Burton perfectly? No one would ever look for Burton because all would assume E.J. killed him. Burton must have derived the plan.

Wouldn't the world suspect E.J. had gotten rid of the bodies and the Suburban before hiding out? G.H. Burton could step into another identity. Eventually, even publicly leading the Aryan Triangle under a new name.

"An Oscar-worthy performance. Picture it, the good Sheriff B.B. was seated in a hospital, taking questions about how he got away from the rogue ranger and his flunky sidekick. Bravo." Burton clapped.

The rain had picked back up, though it didn't dissuade the thick mosquitos snapping at E.J. "Sure B.B. acted the part but your idea, wasn't it?" asked E.J. Red meat for Burton's ego would distract him while E.J. worked his shoulders pressing the bonds a little farther down his hands.

"What I can't understand is why you sold me out? We worked so well together. E.J.'s strumpet wouldn't have paid you? Were you sleeping with her? You can say in front of E.J. He doesn't care. She dumped him." Burton shined a light emanating from beneath a pistol barrel.

Sheriff B.B. spit rainwater from his mouth in G.H. Burton's direction. "Maybe I'm sick of watching you act like a villain in a third-rate James Bond movie or listening to you spew your kooky made-up religion."

A flash exploded between the two men, creasing the darkness.

Chapter Twenty-Six

Blasphemy

The flat thud wrapped across the night like a watermelon dropped from some height blowing apart. The bullet tore through B.B.'s belly. He looked down to see his shirt already soaked, leaking a viscous crimson liquid from his bowels.

E.J. tried snapping his hands apart, to no avail. He yelled out in frustration. "Ugh."

Cooper moved toward B.B. until Burton pressed the weapon into her belly. She wobbled back into the side-by-side. "He'll die," she said.

"He mocked the knowledge, the self-understanding which could have released him from the shadow god. It's blasphemy and there is only one punishment for blasphemy," said Burton.

"Stop. Stop. I'll play whatever trial you have going," said E.J.

"Stop. Stop?" Burton waved the gun, repeating E.J.'s words in a sarcastic tone.

"Get him down before he bleeds out," yelled a hoarse E.J. over the soft, dropping rain.

Burton stepped to Sheriff B.B., stabbing the wound with the pistol. Sheriff B.B. yelled an agonizing moan.

"Stop," E.J. said.

"Tell me. Why?" asked Burton, pressing the gun deeper into the seeping abdomen.

The odor of the open abdominal cavity convinced E.J. the wound was worse than he initially suspected.

Sheriff B.B. groaned. "Kill me."

Cooper yelled, swinging her hands in the utility vehicle.

E.J.'s head snapped with the boom. A contact explosion ripped near the same wound cavity. Sheriff B.B. slid backward, coming off the gravestone and rendering the noose taut. Twisting in the dark, wet night, his feet no longer stood on the headstone.

Burton nodded. Three big toughs lifted B.B. back onto the marker. One of the three eased the tension around B.B.'s neck, then brought it taut again. A dying B.B. sucked a breath from the night air.

The commotion nearly made E.J. fall. He rebalanced his trembling, wounded feet. Feeling the fluid of a busted blister, he moved one foot over the other.

"The truth. All I ask. Truth and I'll end it," said Burton.

"For God's sakes, stop," hollered E.J.

"'God sakes.'" Repeated Burton. "Do you have a soul, dear friend?"

"What?" asked E.J.

"A soul. Some splinter of immortality?" Burton asked, raising his voice and shaking his arms in a frantic motion.

"I guess," said E.J.

Burton stepped toward E.J. He aimed the pistol at E.J.'s wet torso. "How do you know?"

"How does anyone know?" asked E.J.

Burton threw his hands into the air, wildly swinging the weapon. "Precisely the issue before us. Are you a bag of sour gel like this pig or an infinitesimal splinter of the divine?" Burton had stepped to the left of E.J., pressing the warm, sticky gun barrel hard into E.J.'s waist.

E.J. concluded a bullet would soon explode through his belly like Sheriff B.B. He had to act now. Could one more pull release his wrist? His head lifted to the dark sky.

Sheriff B.B.'s voice boomed over the heavy droplets crashing to the earth. "You incest-ridden, bigoted pigs are—"

G.H. Burton fired.

Sheriff B.B. took this round higher, through his chest. The man's knees buckled, then collapsed. His neck snapped the noose tighter.

E.J.'s toe swung under Burton's chin. A bloody left hand twisted loose. His body rotated. E.J.'s right hand enveloped the smaller Burton's hand holding the pistol.

Sheriff B.B.'s bloody feet slid from the top of the headstone. His neck launched against the tether strangling him. Feet kicked and legs swung in, wildly thrashing.

E.J. punched Burton's finger against the trigger, sending a round through the chest of one of Burton's henchmen, then another. While Burton's hand slid off the trigger, E.J. stomped Burton's face into the lush grass.

A giant thug posted behind a dangling Sheriff B.B. tried to lift his rifle, only to catch a round in the forehead. His wingman got off a shot in E.J.'s general direction before collapsing. Like his partner, the skinhead slumped into the cargo bed. The man's head folded forward, revealing the large exit wound on the skull's posterior.

Cooper reached for the weapon formerly wielded by one of Burton's dead soldiers, finding something more valuable in his shirt pocket. She powered on the cell phone.

Burton's henchmen made for the vehicles, gathering their wounded and dead. E.J. lifted the pistol, setting the front post center of mass of the nearest man. He held the sight picture for a fraction of a second before firing. As he hoisted the noose over his head with his left hand,

E.J. leaped off the grave marker. Even loaded with adrenaline, his thigh bone crashed onto his leg bone, nearly rolling him at the knee.

E.J. turned the handgun to a stupefied G.H. Burton. Then he stabbed the barrel into Burton's forehead, causing the man's skull to yield backward, craning the murderer's neck.

"Murder me?" Burton's tone made the imperative a question, not a command.

A lifetime of law enforcement and marksmanship informed E.J. he held a Glock model 17. The trigger broke around seven pounds. His index finger, rendered slick by precipitation, held the tension.

Burton laughed, though heavy perspiration poured down his forehead. "Release me." He moved his head side to side around the gun.

E.J. looked to Cooper. If she were in her right mind, then she would stop him. Even if she had to fire on him, she would never stand by and witness an illegal execution.

An unarmed Burton knelt defenseless. "Release this mortal coil, dear friend."

As the UTVs roared away, Cooper cast a blank look to a wet Burton. She swung her gaze back to E.J. "I can live with it."

Burton's cackling infused the moisture-soaked air.

E.J.'s finger tightened.

Cooper showed E.J. the phone. She turned her back and stepped away.

Cooper's message telegraphed to E.J. couldn't be misinterpreted. Even the incorruptible Cooper would look the other way.

Burton pressed his head harder into the Glock. "What?"

"Not legal," said E.J.

"You're the law. You're legal. When we were in court, my people were the law. I was legal. Law is a tool for the weak-minded," said Burton.

"Tool?" asked E.J.

"Tool making wide-eyed fools dangle like marionettes. Should have seen you dance in the courtroom, dear friend." Burton projected another booming laugh through the wind and rain shower.

"You're laughing like you're the fool," said E.J.

"Paradox of a lawman. Kill me and you kill the last vestige of honor in your soul. Let me live and I'll reduce the principles you've sworn to uphold to mockery. Worse yet, watch me take your strumpet's career and reputation."

E.J. held firm against the pressure Burton's head exerted on the end of the pistol. The gun pressed like a lever, pinching into the web of E.J.'s hand. He slid the pad of his index finger farther across the trigger toward the first knuckle. Likely another half pound of exertion and the trigger would snap. One pop, one more round sent downrange and all the evil before him evaporates.

Why else would God deliver the vile, despicable killer, G.H. Burton, into his gunsight? The Almighty, or a chaotic universe, had decreed Burton needed killing.

Chapter Twenty-Seven

Justification

I mages of bold print from chapter nine of the Texas Penal Code flooded E.J.'s mind. Black-letter codes setting forth statutes and their bold-faced titles. No legal justification existed to take G.H. Burton's life. The fugitive no longer posed a threat, imminent or otherwise.

He had honed his familiarity with the law by investigating many local law enforcement officers. Rangers served as independent reviewers of officer involved shootings. Knowing the case law, specifically the applicable state and federal violations, didn't further tighten E.J.'s finger on the trigger.

G.H. Burton looked upward. His mad laughter crackled far too loud to be sincere.

E.J.'s mind continued to race. The only justification for taking Burton's life was the knowledge Burton would make a mockery of all those law codes and the people like Rebecca, who understood the reasoned application of such amounted to justice. Rebecca would have had a fancy Latin word for absurdity.

Locking eyes with Burton's vacant stare, E.J. placed more force on the trigger. Burton had stolen a young couple's future solely because the color of their skin diminished them. While the opinion represented an unfathomable ignorance, only through the application of reason could bigots create constructs capable of obscuring truth.

The man's existence made a cruel joke of everything good and right in the world. The mere act of G.H. Burton drawing air disproved any favorable view of human nature. Evil, like what consumed Burton, lived within the confines of humanity, filling their souls with a vile cruelty.

E.J.'s finger drew up more slack than he thought the Glock trigger capable. An image of Konner overwhelmed him, nearly causing him to send the round through Burton's skull. He remembered the last words he told his son. "Remember who you are?"

E.J. called out through thick raindrops. "Cooper."

Cooper walked back, holding the phone to her ear. "I got nine one one. I think I gave them a pin." She looked at the phone. "Can't be sure, because the signal is coming in and out."

"Thank you. Dear friend was murdering me," said Burton.

Cooper smiled. She looked at E.J.'s handgun, then back at his stoic face.

"Are you okay enough to tie him up? And lose that grin," barked E.J.

Cooper moved the phone back to her ear. She didn't move.

E.J. nodded to her.

"Good to have you back," said Cooper.

"We need a plan. Hopefully someone received your pin. What's the ETA on help?" asked E.J.

"Told me they'll be airborne, but I don't see how in this storm." Cooper checked Sheriff B.B. for signs of life. Finding none, she unbound his hands. She approached Burton before swaying. She handed the cord to E.J.

E.J. stepped to the side of Burton, squarely landing his boot on the miscreant's back before lashing Burton's hands with the gusto of a cowboy putting two wraps and a hooey on a flanked calf. "No way to know how far those thugs have to run to get to headquarters. Can't be far. Doubt Burton would tell us if there are a dozen or several hundred knuckle-dragging machine gunners."

"Think they'll come," said Cooper.

"Machine guns, rocket-propelled grenades. Go right through your helicopter, dear friend," said Burton.

E.J. looked at the phone, still at Cooper's ear. "Turn 'em around."

"He is bluffing, playing us," said Cooper.

E.J. crammed the gun in Burton's ear. "What direction are they coming from?"

Cooper's voice sounded hoarse. "They won't risk it."

"To have little Hitler back. He has convinced the world I killed him. They're all too close to the dream. Once the world believes he is dead, he can melt into society and turn up anywhere," yelled E.J.

"Dear friend, the dear friend understands. Five minutes through the woods and less by road on side-by-sides. We use this place to train pincer movement—"

Over the bellowing wind and water, they heard the whirl of rotors in the distance projecting from over monstrous treetops.

"No." Cooper leaned against the trailer to keep from falling. She angled the carbine at Burton.

"With your wound, you can't trust yourself. Self-defense is killing him when you know you're losing it. It's a necessity no different from shooting an armed evader intent on murder."

Cooper nodded.

"You'll hug your girls tonight. I promise," said E.J.

"Dear friend's true colors. Needs him a high-headed woman to do what he can't."

Cooper wiped the rain from her eyes. She pointed the rifle at Burton's chest.

"I'm taking the road. Most likely, where any heavy ordinance would come." E.J. grabbed a dead thug's rifle, then raced into the darkness.

The polymer handgun remained in his right hand while a fully automatic AR-style carbine was fixed to his left. Mud squashed under his boots, though it didn't sufficiently cushion his painful knee joint.

The helicopter grew louder, yet E.J. couldn't see any lights associated with the aircraft. Surely the pilot could find a section of the cemetery with few or no graves to put the bird down. Looked like someone had received the pin. Had Cooper been clear enough to drop it correctly? Did the infection and fever cause her to hallucinate visually, too, or had Burton drugged her?

Despite his concerns, the rotor noise spurred E.J. forward. The slick, uneven gravel crunched his thigh bone down through his leg, sliding nearly sideways, making him cry in agony. The rocky county road base provided no cushion. Each step cracked his bones. On some steps, he swore he heard a clacking.

E.J. swung forward, sliding on the heavy rainfall, because he couldn't stop, then he saw lights. The headlights were closing the distance, though they remained shrouded by darkness.

How many vehicles and wannabe soldiers were traveling to him? Should he hide in the ditch before opening fire as they passed? He had to assume this was only the first of many cars or utility terrain vehicles brimming with paramilitary troops. The strategy offered no assurance he could hold back Burton's army long enough to get Cooper out. He promised her she would hold her daughters again. Only one option offered a genuine opportunity to delay the inevitable.

Chapter Twenty-Eight

Road Behind You is Open

The heavy precipitation washed away the sweat pouring over E.J.'s taut, exhausted muscles. Oncoming headlights blinded him. He held the carbine in his left hand, braced against his hip. How many rounds were in the magazine? At the enormous rate of fire, wouldn't the fully automatic empty in seconds?

Maybe he shouldn't have held the handgun in his right hand. There wouldn't be time to change out weapons once he spent the rifle's magazine. Besides, since he had first held a pistol, E.J. had held every confidence in the ordinance.

E.J. stabbed his boots against pieces of broken rock paving. Shaky feet meant a shaky gun hand. When he heard the higher and higher pitched whinnying of the side-by-side's motor filling the night, he lifted his chin, steeling himself to what had to be done.

The noise reached a crescendo when the Polaris Ranger stopped feet before him in the road. Since he recalled a different, distinctive brand of vehicle in the cemetery, E.J. concluded these were fresh reinforcements. Two of Burton's skinheaded soldiers stared down the sights of fully automatic rifles at E.J.'s head. A third standing in the bed leaning over the top of the vehicle shouldered an olive drab pipe akin to a rocket-propelled grenade.

E.J. suspected a tube launched, optically tracked, wire-guided device known in military circles as a TOW. The weapons system had proven a holy grail to cartels and sovereign citizens' groups to guard compounds of all types. Such a weapon possessed the potential to accomplish the task, despite not being the best choice for shooting a helicopter.

The driver stepped out, arming himself with a M27 Infantry Automatic Rifle (IAR). His expert marksman son, Konner, had precisely referenced it each time he spoke about weapons with his father.

However, the antitank-wielding weaponeer spoke, "Who are you?"

"All you need know is the road behind you is open," said E.J.

The neo-Nazi towered from the high perch, raucously laughing. "Road's open behind you, old-timer. Can't even catch your breath. Why aren't you home, making geezer love to the little la—"

A hollow point bullet hammered the bigot's cranium, peeling the lead core like a banana delivering the most potential energy into the target. The formerly sarcastic racist tipped directly over, falling backward into the bed of the vehicle. His missile launcher landed on top of him.

E.J. lifted the rifle to match the angle of his pistol. He caught a glimpse of fireflies at the edge of the thick forest. "Fellow chose the path to hell. I'll say it again, road is open behind you, boys."

E.J. held his left index finger on the machine. One good spray would be all he could muster, yet it would be enough. They would all die.

A long, awkward moment passed as the fireflies danced in the distance. The driver looked at the other two Aryans. He stepped back into the Polaris before turning the utility terrain vehicle around and returning the way they had ridden.

E.J. doubled over, wanting to collapse from exhaustion, yet he found his breath. Air couldn't fill his lungs fast enough, nor would the awful tension leave his body. His mind raced. What if another group had traveled through the woods? At speed and at long distance, the helicopter held an advantage, yet slowing over the treetops the TOW system couldn't miss.

Wouldn't Cooper have warned them? This unit of Burton's army had dwindled to a handful of die-hard fools. Odds were no one volunteered to pass through briars, snakes, and sloughs to take the shot. He couldn't run another step, anyway. E.J. fell onto the hot, wet pebbles in standing water.

Some moments passed while he lay there, letting huge droplets land on his face. E.J. took comfort in not seeing or hearing an explosion. Guilt ate at him. He needed to get back to make sure another squad of Aryan Triangle outlaws hadn't reached the cemetery. The exhausted former lawman rose, putting one boot in front of the other, though he wobbled from side to side.

"E.J.," yelled a familiar voice behind a bobbing, small light in the pelting moisture.

"Hall?" asked E.J.

Hall's voice cracked with excitement. "Praise the Lord and God bless America. Rebecca and I kept telling them to search in the Big Thicket. Burton would take you off the beaten path."

"Rebecca?" E.J. reached Hall, nearly falling as his old friend grabbed him in a bear hug. "Rebecca is here?" asked E.J.

"She has threatened to sue everyone, including the president, to get more birds in the air, more boots on the ground. I couldn't leave her for fear she would get herself locked up by cussing directors and senators," said Hall.

E.J. stepped back, trying to draw breath from the warm wall of moisture. The full import of Rebecca on the helicopter hit him. How close he came to losing her made him light-headed. "Is she safe?"

Hall nodded in the affirmative. "We got Cooper flighted out."

"So, no RPGs? No attack? We still got Burton?" asked E.J.

Hall lifted E.J. by the shoulder and helped walk him farther toward the graveyard. The lights of the landing zone came into view as the thunder of rotors lifted another helicopter off.

E.J. let his head swing back down.

Hall steadied E.J. on his feet, then stepped away. "If you're smart, you'll always keep this lady on your side."

The strawberry fragrance of Rebecca's perfume overwhelmed him before he saw her. E.J. pressed into her embrace, finding her lips with his own.

The kiss consumed them. E.J. pulled back, gasping a breath. Through tears, Rebecca pressed her lips to E.J.'s, renewing the caress, though more gentle and less urgent this time. E.J.'s face fell away into the sweet aroma of her hair.

"Heard I need to be proud you're on my side," said E.J.

"Hall had already started this search grid when Cooper called. He would have found you," said Rebecca.

E.J. laughed. "I can't believe the FBI let you fly in here."

"How would they stop me?" asked Rebecca.

"Sharla?" asked E.J.

"Still pregnant and likely still sneaking drugs. She tested positive for methamphetamine."

"Not left the rehab, has she?" asked E.J.

Rebecca shook her head, her thick curls matting in the downpour.

"Changed her mind?" asked E.J.

Rebecca's eyes fell. "More like she never made it up to start. I don't feel like I know her anymore."

E.J. pulled her close. A lifetime of witnessing substance abusers needing their fix had convinced him addiction holds to no code of ethics. Once an individual permitted a foothold, the disease consumed whatever principles or values the person might have held.

"I feel so guilty for saying it, but it's like she is not my kid anymore. There is no Sharla left," whispered Rebecca.

E.J. wrapped his arms around her. "I understand. I see it too."

"He is right there," yelled Hall, pointing E.J. out to a young EMT in a flight suit. "I didn't see any holes, but he didn't look good."

Chapter
Twenty-Nine

The Hospital

Hospitals annoyed E.J. What was it about them? Perhaps the nature of people being housed in a place where the surroundings remained so blank, so sterile, unsettled him.

By the time he finally got checked out, Cooper's husband and daughters had arrived. Cooper's daughters ran to her with sincere affection and respect.

E.J. stood in Cooper's emergency room doorway before staring back down the hall. The high school-age girls were draped on each side of Cooper. Their father stood across the room. He mouthed the words thank you. E.J.'s presence intruded upon the love expressed by a family.

The recollection of human interaction like his daughter's hug warmed him. He had come untethered from humanity, spinning alone in space. He longed for his family. His fingers twisted the wedding ring. Could Sharla defeat addiction? Would Rebecca ever return to him? As he stared intensely down the empty hall, he came to the realization that neither possibility appeared probable.

Slipping past the door, he stumbled, still unsteady. After a turn, he lost his bearings. Each hallway appears so similar to the others in these places.

Ultimately, he found a coffeepot in a quiet corner of a waiting room. After swallowing the bitter, viscous liquid, he looked in the foam cup. Six hours, ten hours old. As a young trooper he had been an expert at aging awful coffee.

He took another gulp. What was he doing? Why did he scurry away from Cooper's husband, unable to accept the man's thanks for saving his wife? How foolish to thank him? Poor guy didn't know who nearly got Cooper killed. The person who nearly took a loving mom away from the girls at the age where they needed her most. Would they spiral down like Sharla if he robbed them of their beloved mother?

The guilt racked the pit of his belly, forcing stomach contents and raunchy coffee up his throat. What right had he to jeopardize another? Cooper's husband's words from years previous rang in his ear. She truly would follow him into hell. What right had he to such devotion from a person far better than him in every way? Cooper came so close to being the third to die under his command.

Why did he inspire strangers and fail so miserably to lead his own child? Cooper's high school-age daughters had been draped around her in a warm outpouring of genuine affection and respect. When did it really all go wrong with Sharla? His mind flooded with thoughts beyond his control.

In hindsight, Sharla might have been moving down the wrong path all the time. Perhaps Konner's death wasn't the catalyst so much as the final curtain revealing the person Sharla was now. An image of her as a child wrapping her arms around him, the way Cooper's girls draped over their mother. In his mind's eye, Sharla enveloped him like she was there.

Before realizing it, E.J. caught himself praying for Sharla. Nothing about the bright chartreuse Naugahyde chairs against the stark unadorned walls inspired reverence, and yet an awe overcame him. How close he came to losing his daughter made him emotional.

After rubbing his eyes, E.J. studied the room. There were a fair number of people broken into small groups throughout the huge waiting area. A calmness settled over his shoulders.

Possibilities flooded over him. What if Cooper had died? What if one of Burton's soldiers fired a missile into the helicopter? Hall and Rebecca would have been killed, and he didn't even know they were there. An image flashed through his mind of himself standing in front of a machine gun-wielding, antitank weapon-carrying Nazis. Appreciation for the danger heretofore before him momentarily paralyzed him. B.B. had been right. He had lived, and the thought motivated him to stand.

When he stood, the soreness brought him back to the starkness of his own mortality. A survey of the room revealed there wasn't a window to view out. What wild traffic scene would he see in downtown Houston, anyway?

Peace would mean watching over his cattle and horses or standing under the trees towering, rising from the dirt his fathers and mothers had held sacrosanct for generations. He squished down into the uncomfortable vinyl chair, recalling home.

The sun on his face and the smell of grass would be so preferable to the combination of bleach, urine, and scolded coffee in the waiting area. Why did people live on top of each other like beasts?

The black hands on a white-faced clock rhythmically pushed forward minute after minute, yet E.J. did not move. Sooner or later Hall would find him and help him get home. Hall's voice resounding in the heart of the Big Thicket had been nothing short of a gift sent from heaven. Hall and Amy had become his family.

As magnificent as it had been seeing Hall, such held nothing next to Rebecca's radiance in the dark and stormy wilderness. The memory of her kiss made him gasp to fill his lungs. Was it a fluke moment? A reminiscence never to be repeated owing to the former spouse's belief they might never see each other again.

Did he want Rebecca because he loved her, or was she a symbol of what he had lost? The delusive hope that with her in his arms, he could glue the broken pieces of the world into something recognizable. Had the stress of Sharla and the awesome consequences before their daughter, despite their many disagreements and the shared disappointment and pain, forced them to comfort each other?

In hindsight, Sharla's pattern of playing one parent against another since their divorce continued. Emotion rendered otherwise critically thinking cynical people gullible to their child's designs.

"Hey," cracked a stern voice.

E.J. jumped. In a moment, he realized the shout hailed from Rebecca's raspy yet melodic trial-lawyer voice.

"I've torn this place apart looking for you," said Rebecca.

The red in her face accented her still soaked hair. The disheveled appearance of the normally impeccably dressed Rebecca confirmed she had frantically searched the hospital.

E.J. made the only answer Rebecca's countenance would accept. "I'm sorry. I should have known you would be here."

A subtle upturn at the edge of her lips confirmed he guessed correct. "Rex has been worried sick."

"You told him?" asked E.J.

"You made national news. Constant national news. And he used a respite caregiver who didn't know you," said Rebecca.

"I can't believe he put it together. Last time I talked to Rex, he thought we were goose hunting in Canada," said E.J.

Rebecca made a downcast smirk, which E.J. took as proof she did not approve. Rex's good days and bad days, as he called them, meant he might know E.J. in the present one day and on another occasion might either not know him at all or his memory remained locked in the past. Thus, the doctor explained Alzheimer's.

However, for E.J. the description and prognosis presented such an inconsistency with the larger-than-life bulletproof man. E.J. had both marveled at the captain of industry's incredible achievements and business skill while on other occasions disapproved of Rex's lecherous and careless conduct. Yet both extremes made for a huge personality, bending the world to his will.

E.J. and Rebecca in the past attended a meeting in a medical plaza near the hospital where they currently stood. At the time, E.J. grew short of breath and stepped out of the doctor's office for fear Rebecca would witness an anxiety attack. What the doctor had described wouldn't be the Rex Ashe who had taken a zero-sum cruel world and made it an oasis for his loved ones and all the charities Rex funded.

"I'll call Rex's caregiver," said Rebecca.

"It's an enormous condo. We can stay and make the drive in the morning," she added.

E.J. rode with her in what must have been a rental. He wanted to ask a thousand questions about Sharla, why Rebecca had not pressed onward with the abortion and why the kiss, yet words failed him. Maybe he was too tired to think clearly. It was much wiser to keep his mouth shut than say something stupid, and he had already said something stupid to Rebecca too many times over the years.

Forty stories of light from expansive balconies rising near the Galleria and Williams Tower bespoke of the wealth Rex Ashe had amassed from a career building Devekon Energy into a worldwide conglomerate. E.J. recognized all the nurses Rebecca had hired to care for Rex by the sound of their voice. One remained on duty at all times except when the respite workers relieved them.

Eddie answered the door. E.J.'s poor opinion of urban living ill prepared him for the tall, vaulted ceilings, rich maple facades, and a great room boasting a huge hearth and fireplace.

In answer to Rebecca's comment about Rex, Eddie said, "He is streaming some *Yellowstone* show. Hear him yelling at the TV in the den."

"Sounds like the old Rex. Rebecca says you got an extra bedroom," said E.J.

"Extra five. More like suites than bedrooms. Ms. Johnson knows wh—"

"Call me Rebecca." She pursed her lips in an uncomfortable expression.

"Long as you paying my salary and I don't have to go back to the ER or travel nursing, you're Ms. Johnson."

An enormous leather chair held a small, gray-haired man shaking a small, shriveled digit at E.J. "Gave us all a fright, didn't you?"

E.J. nodded, shaking Rex's hand. Rebecca hugged the old man, surprising E.J. She had been little more of a hugger than E.J. He recalled all the arguments about the self-indulgent, immature millionaire she considered a bad influence on E.J. and her children.

"You're too old to chase outlaws. Look at you. Like someone beat you with an ax handle," said Rex. He snapped the remote, muting the TV and pointing to chairs.

"You look good," said Rebecca.

E.J. echoed the sentiment. Though he suspected prior to accepting his illness, Rex had been dying at least part of his hair. The prior dapper salt-and-pepper hair had succumbed to a snowcap dusting the top of the little man. He had always seemed so much bigger. "You telling me to take it easy?" asked E.J.

They all laughed except for Rex. He cursed and stared at E.J.

The demeanor and pale gray eyes reminded E.J. of his first impression of Rex Ashe all those years ago. A father and grandfather terrified he might lose his granddaughter. "I'm too mean to die. Ask anybody." E.J. looked to his right. "Rebecca knows."

"True. He'll turn off the lights after the rest of the hard men are gone," said Rebecca.

A glint appeared along Rex Ashe's eyes. Rex Ashe wept. E.J. swallowed when the realization enveloped him. Rex Ashe doesn't cry.

Rebecca rose, turning to Eddie. "Let's go get those bedrooms ready. Rex, we're just going to impose on you and invite ourselves to stay. Don't you and Elliott stay up too late talking."

E.J. tried to signal to Rebecca to stay without being obvious. He wanted to crawl under the couch. What to do? "I should go too."

Rebecca spun on her heel, casting a stern countenance to admonish E.J.

"I got a better idea. I'll visit for a while," said E.J.

E.J. motioned to the television. "Montana?"

Rex wept, placing his hands over his eyes.

"You look good. You seem really sharp," said E.J.

"So, I'm not crazy or calling in the middle of the night out of my head," said Rex.

"You remember calling?" E.J. asked.

"No. Eddie told me I did it."

"I'm glad to see you well," said E.J.

"Spit it out?" asked Rex.

"What?"

"Something bothering you. I'll never remember it tomorrow, anyway." The quip amused Rex into a belly laugh.

E.J. offered a weak chuckle out of politeness. The comment scared him. Was he afraid for himself or for Rex? The whole time in the Big Thicket and he had never let himself succumb to fear, until now. His old friend's eyes reminded E.J. of the once vibrant man. "It's Sheriff B.B., Benjamin Berryhill. He claims...I say, he claims I..." E.J. looked down. "It sounds crazy to say it out loud, but he says the raid I led on the compound where, well, where we lost, where I lost..." E.J.'s voice cracked and fell off several times.

Rex looked at the television. He laughed.

"What is it?" asked E.J.

"Benefit of being clear minded. The highest wood panel on the right opens like a cabinet. Bottle of Macallen. Get it for us," said Rex.

E.J looked around.

"Go before they get back," said Rex.

E.J. removed a crystal decanter and two double-walled glasses. "I suppose one wouldn't hurt."

"Pour us both one," said Rex.

E.J. poured a small shot into one of the tumblers.

"When will we do it again?" asked Rex.

E.J. finished the pour then handed a substantial drink to Rex holding one for himself.

The fruity aroma reminded E.J. of eating ripe, dark persimmons. He sipped the smooth, yellowish fluid.

"Ahh. Always had a weakness for good Scotch." Rex laughed. "And redheads, blondes. Brunettes."

E.J. laughed behind the warm pull of the liquor. He returned the bottle to its hiding place. "B.B. says I got set up."

"Set up?"

Chapter Thirty

Like the Old Rex

"Who would have set you up?" asked Rex.

"You don't believe it either?" asked E.J.

"Unsure. Sheriff B.B. is a liar, isn't he?" asked Rex.

"Was," said E.J. "Burton hung him. He spent his last words telling me. I can't see the angle he was working if he was playing me."

"Who? He must have known who, right?" asked Rex.

"He said it had something to do with some case I was working at the time. Something I investigated. But I don't remember focusing on anything except the cartel. We tried to raid them the year before," said E.J.

Rex shook his head like he didn't remember.

"FBI, ATF, they all sent in troops, even shipped armored cars by rail. Informants saw women, children, money, cocaine, meth, fentanyl, all of it. Well, word got out and by the time our little army hit the compound, there weren't two rocks left stacked together out there. Had to load all those tanks, drones, and a small army back on the train. Debacle. Big water haul," said E.J.

Rex laughed.

E.J. released a small chuckle. "I didn't laugh back then. I searched for the leak, but the spigot was too big to run down anyone with knowledge of the operation. Finally gave up."

"I been called all hat and no cattle many a time. How many dusters do you think I spudded in my day?" asked Rex, still chuckling. "I never understood why you were hitting a fortress with such a small team. Didn't want to ask you. Makes sense now. You were trying to limit the circle of information," said Rex.

"Because we got burned before. I wish I hadn't. Wish I had sent for those urban assault vehicles." E.J. heard a soft snore. He rose, lifting Rex's empty tumbler from his chest and placing it on an end table. After he took the blanket off Rex's legs, he then draped it over his old friend's chest.

Was Rex truly as present in the moment as he seemed? Rex, in the old days, was more gregarious and more decisive with his opinions in their older conversations. His friend had fooled him occasionally, looping back portions of the conversation as opposed to a true discussion.

E.J. learned from Rex's specialist that some experiencing Alzheimer's struggled to hide the condition, often developing coping skills rather than admitting their confusion. In retrospect, E.J. was able to recognize that Rex had been deteriorating for a while.

What a cruel disease to rob the powerful of their very awareness. Would Rex remember him when he woke? As he and Rebecca had agreed, one needed to be grateful for the brief moments of clarity with Rex. Take comfort in small victories.

E.J. walked through a condominium which encompassed most of the skyscraper's floor. It wouldn't pass for Rex's mansion, though the residence was palatial by any standard.

"Where did you leave Rex?" Rebecca asked.

She whispered the words from behind him in a doorway. The thick ether of intimacy enveloping him seemed so foreign, so dated, it nearly made him bounce out of his skin. He turned to face her, and she pulled his being into her hazel eyes. Greens, yellows, and blue made a magical palette offset by full lips and her clever mind-reading smile.

Rebecca had that look like she always knew more than him. She knew more than most anyone. A long silk robe adorned her form in a floral scene. "Why did you kiss me?" asked E.J.

Should he have asked? He wanted to kiss her again, yet instead he feared she would withdraw from him, admonishing him for trying to find the embers of a love, long cold and dead.

Why had he asked? Why not lean in for a kiss? Would John Wayne have asked why? When what he wanted stood before him, why would he question anything?

"No, no, no, mister. You kissed me. I didn't want to be rude and leave you out there." The long fingers of her right hand ran over his ear, twisting his short hair. She leaned closer, whispering in her spectacular raspy quality E.J. had always found so captivating. "Thought it would crush you to pull back. You never had much game."

E.J. placed his hands on her waist. He shook his head, entirely mesmerized by her eyes. He tried asking himself where this was going. Was it prudent? Could they glue the shattered delicate pieces of their marriage into any kind of vessel, leaky or otherwise? Why ask why?

Finally, her comment broke through his foggy mind and he responded. "No, I didn't." Her breath tasted soft, warm, and sweet. She pulled him through the door into the bedroom.

Chapter Thirty-One

Back in Time

A wisp of vapor rolled off the coffee wafting into E.J.'s nose. Sipping the rich elixir filled his head with a mental image of a gentleman in a multicolored poncho and wide-brimmed hat leading a burro based on a thousand Folgers commercials from his youth.

E.J. pushed a foot under a sheet back onto the sectional. The sheet slid away and E.J. immediately regretted the decision. Aromatic beans hailing from picturesque Columbian mountains gave way to the stark, crushing funk of teenage boy feet. Based on the Sasquatch-like size, he realized this one belonged to Konner's friend, Bradley.

A voice bellowed from another blob under a blanket at the far end of the sectional. "Dad, it's five a.m."

E.J. yelled, "Hit it. Can't be soar—"

"If you're hootin' with them owls," retorted Konner and his friends, finishing the quote in unison.

Konner sat up against the back of the oversized couch. "I love you, Dad."

E.J. nodded, looking down at the silver *cinco peso* on a heavy starched red dress shirt. "Got to run over to Tyler. Governor flying in and I got the detail. I need the hayfield laid down. Got the *H* hooked up to sickle."

"I love you, Dad," said Konner.

Bradley exhaled his gregarious laugh.

"Why do you keep saying that, son?" E.J. lifted his hat off the hook by the door.

"Because you don't say it back," Konner joined Bradley in the cackling.

E.J. swung the door open, then stopped. "I'm proud of you. I show it the way my father did by keeping you in biscuits, you little rascal. You better get the hay laid down. We don't have much window. Supposed to rain Mond—"

The pillow felt cool to the touch, though the unmistakable perfume he had chosen for Rebecca during their honeymoon lingered. Dreaming he had talked to Konner didn't surprise him. He understood that it all came from Konner's death because he had limited remembrance of dreams prior to Konner's passing. Maybe he didn't dream, didn't remember, or didn't care. A real or imagined conversation with Konner had been interspersed with nightmares about being unable to move since he lost his son.

Rebecca or her absence surprised him. She had been here. Her part hadn't been a dream, right? Could he have experienced a dream within a dream? He reached to the other side of the bed, comforting himself with the warmth from the sheets.

Still half asleep, he touched his lips. He didn't dream or imagine the kiss he had shared with Rebecca when she found him in the Big Thicket, nor did he imagine last night. She had enveloped him in the hallway like a tornado lifting a house.

Oh, wouldn't Rebecca relish mocking him if she heard his comparison, a tornado lifting a house. She would quip how only he would make the comparison of their lovemaking to a twister wreaking havoc on a trailer park. She relished mocking his lack of conventional romance, yet in his unique way, he respected the dignity of their intimacy.

He quickly replayed the night. Had she left because he said something stupid? Years of longing to get her back and he had blown it.

The tightness in his chest and nerves in his arms eased as E.J. recalled the sexual encounter. The night couldn't have been more magical. So where was she? He rolled out of bed, jumping into his boxers and blue jeans. Soreness grabbed at him, reminding him his time in the Big Thicket was all too real.

The hallway opened into the den. Rex Ashe sat motionless, watching the news. Rex didn't acknowledge E.J.

"Have you seen Rebecca?" asked E.J.

"No." Rex cut his eyes away.

"You haven't seen her?" asked E.J.

"No." Rex turned, yet still avoided E.J.

"Do you know who I'm asking about? Did you understand Rebecca was here?" asked E.J.

Rex raised his arm with an open palm. His face displayed exasperation. "You need to get out of here."

"Rex—"

"You're not supposed to be here," yelled Rex.

E.J. backed out of the room. It must be very unsettling to encounter an unfamiliar man strolling through your house without a shirt, asking about someone you are not acquainted with. Rex wasn't the only one feeling disconnected from reality. Had they had a genuine conversation last night?

A moment ago, he could have interpreted Rex's response as not knowing Rebecca's whereabouts. Further questioning revealed Rex didn't have a recollection of Rebecca, not today anyway.

Yet Rex seemed so lucid last night, or had E.J. misinterpreted Rex's comments? He had endured a harrowing ordeal, been hospitalized, and topped it off with a double Scotch. How could he be sure of anything?

"E.J.?"

He recognized another of Rex Ashe's caregivers, named Allen, carrying two cups of coffee. "Eddie go home?" asked E.J.

"A Hall Oglethorpe is on his way up."

"Yes, sir. Thank you," said E.J.

"Eddie and I trade out about five. He has got kids to run to school. I got Mr. Rex calmed down," said Allen.

E.J. finished buttoning his shirt. "Does Rex ever get normal anymore? I mean, where you can tell it is really him. All there?"

Allen looked down. "He has his good days."

"I know. I truly believed he was nearly the old Rex last night."

"You had a good visit?" asked Allen.

E.J. nodded.

"You thought he was making sense and able to follow you, so that is what's important, isn't it?" asked Allen.

"Suppose so," said E.J.

"I've been doing this kind of work a long time. Mr. Rex suffers. I don't mean he doesn't, but to me it's harder on the loved ones. You're the one constantly comparing, seeing the difference, forever grieving..."

A doorbell crashed through the air.

Rex shouted an expletive.

"I'll see to him," said Allen.

E.J. turned, then swung back. "Which way to the door?"

Allen gave him directions.

E.J. swung the entrance open. "Hall." He failed to appreciate the force of the bear hug Hall pressed upon his torso. E.J. leaned back from the pressure, unsure if he should provide a warning to his old friend that he would soon crush him.

They made their way to the kitchen, where they found a pot of coffee. After discovering mugs behind a cabinet door, they poured themselves a rich cup of piping hot black coffee, taking seats on stools in a breakfast nook.

"We tried to find you last night, but you slipped out of the hospital," said Hall.

"You saved me," said E.J.

Hall looked at him as if E.J. had landed from Mars on a spaceship.

E.J. laughed. "We're all alive. G.H. Burton is going back to the pen, plus he has to stand trial for B.B.'s murder."

Hall's dark eyes sank to his boots. "You're wanted for questioning."

Chapter Thirty-Two

I Wanted to Be You

"Wanted for questioning. Wanted for questioning. Who wants me?" asked E.J. Pale sunlight slipped around the edges of the opaque curtain into the sterile white kitchen of the high-rise condominium.

"Who doesn't? FBI, rangers," said Hall.

"I don't understand. You saw it. G.H. Burton hung B.B. He had an entire compound of killers going after us," said E.J.

Hall sipped the coffee. "They'll be here soon. Rex's place is the obvious choice for you in Houston."

"Because I'm not hiding. I expected to give a statement. But questioning me makes it sound like I'm suspected of something." The coffee's aroma rose from the heavy cup in E.J.'s hand.

"You left the hospital without checking out. I tried to find you last night. Finally occurred to me to call Rebecca," said Hall.

E.J.'s head nodded upward. Despite the confusing nature of the events Hall was describing, E.J. could only think of Rebecca. "Where is she?"

"Concentrate on being interviewed. You need to understand how this shakes out before they talk to you," said Hall.

"Where is Rebecca?" asked E.J.

Hall exhaled. "I trust everything you told me during the flight out of the thicket. But my superiors—"

"Rebecca?" insisted E.J.

"Crime lab in Tyler. Between what she had and the pieces you told us last night, she thinks she figured out a sizable chunk of the puzzle on Burton's writ. Okay?" asked Hall.

"Okay, what?" asked E.J.

"Okay, concentrate on what I'm telling you. I'm trying to explain your story doesn't pan out," said Hall.

"Truth—"

"I have no doubt it's the truth. But it doesn't add up with the scene, and it's a little wild," said Hall.

"Wild?" asked E.J.

"You got attacked by Burton's skinhead army, met a homeless man pretending to be an Indian, and then, conveniently, the innocent guy you falsely convicted murders your mortal enemy. Have I hit the highlights?" Hall's tone had turned snarky.

E.J. wanted to know why Rebecca had left him without a goodbye, but to ask would be to reveal they were together. Together seemed far too much. The word struck him as small, yet it denoted more intimacy than he could fathom. Did sleeping together one night mean anything? He couldn't talk to Hall about what really mattered.

"Sheriff B.B. gave a big press conference before Burton abducted him. Of course, no one except you and Cooper knew Burton had abducted him. At the press conference B.B. says you went rogue. Says you led your old pupil Cooper down a dark path to take vengeance on Burton and cover up your evidence-planting sins," said Hall.

"All crazy. Nobody will believe it. Didn't his wife or Son report him gone?" said E.J.

"Either he wasn't gone long enough, or they don't keep up with him," said Hall.

"Maybe about me, but no one would buy it about Cooper," said E.J.

"Of course, they will. It makes a great story, much more plausible than Big Thicket Nazi troopers. Actual innocence. Innocent man condemned by rogue cop. Even a love interest if we read between the lines, right? Only reason an attractive idealistic ranger would fall under your spell." Hall raised his arm in a theatrical gesture.

"Bull," said E.J.

"Burton, the media darling in all his backwoods broken English pretending intellectual disability tells his story last night to the FBI. His story matches up with Sheriff B.B.'s press conference to a tee. And of course, they couldn't match up unless it was true because Burton didn't see the press conference because you had him prisoner—"

"They match up because Burton wrote the script for B.B.," yelled E.J.

"Your story is all bad. It's politically incorrect to claim an ID person isn't really ID, much less a master criminal heading up a white supremacist gang. I believe it, but it is a wild story."

"But the training ground, the dead gang members. You saw it. Looked like a war zone," said E.J.

"There were no bodies other than Sheriff B.B. I'm guessing they drove them away with the wounded and dead in the off-road vehicles you told me about."

"Nothing?" E.J. raised his voice and twisted his shoulders.

Hall matched the tone. "Tropical storm near a hurricane out there last night. Whatever blood or DNA was washed away in the deluge."

"Tracks?" asked E.J.

"You got to be kidding," said Hall.

"My name is mud and has been for years, but Cooper is a Texas Ranger in good standing. When she makes her report, all will be set right," said E.J.

Hall threw back a generous gulp of coffee, then looked away, grinning.

"She never lies," pleaded E.J.

"She has already admitted to seeing and hearing things. Besides, it has nothing to do with her being a ranger. She couldn't lie to save her life or to save your life. Not who she is." Hall turned back, staring into E.J.'s eyes. "But it won't matter. They will lean on her, anyway. I tried to get you to understand, to see years ago. You remember what you said the major told you."

"I understood. He told me he had to look to the ranger service. He told me I had to protect the good of the ranger tradition. It's why I resigned," said E.J.

"I watched you die a little more every time I saw you. I'd come home and tell Amy. It crushed both of us watching you lose what you were, who you were. They put you on trial. Blind loyalty to people who stopped being worthy a long time ago," said Hall.

"I don't understand. What are you saying?" asked E.J.

"I'm saying, neither of you went rogue like B.B. said in the press conference. But he also said Cooper pushed him to take you and her on the Burton detail to Beaumont—"

E.J. blurted, "He's lying."

Hall said, "Of course, he lied. Probably spent forever memorizing what Burton told him."

"Then Cooper tells the truth—" said E.J.

"About how you got her to do you a favor because you needed backup. Right? She made a statement already. Admits she didn't tell her superior," said Hall.

"She doesn't need to tell her lieutenant every time she assists law enforcement," said E.J.

"You're not law enforcement and Sheriff B.B. says she invited herself. Violation of policy, isn't it? What does the ranger service do when you violate policy? They're like any other political bureaucracy. The image, budget, fundraising, and you move up by keeping your head down and never volunteering."

Undigested coffee backed up in E.J.'s stomach and throat. He had led Cooper where she had no business going. His throat constricted, and he swallowed, nearly choking.

"One riot, one ranger gets you a lawsuit or worse these days. You know, like when you decided the only way to raid a huge drug and human trafficking outfit was by keeping it close to the vest instead of clearing the raid through channels and waiting on backup," said Hall.

E.J. dropped his head, trying to add up what he had done to the protégé he would have died to protect. He wouldn't wish what he had endured over the last several years on anyone, yet he had inflicted it on the person he loved like a daughter.

"It's a modern world. Crimes are cries for mental health services and the last thing we should ever do is punish supposed wrongdoers. Law enforcement, at every level, is adapting. The ranger service has told you repeatedly who they are. You don't listen. It's no different from Cooper is who she is, and you?" asked Hall.

The tone made it sound like a question, though the look in Hall's eyes told E.J. he meant the statement as a challenge. When it came to a choice, E.J. would stand with Cooper, though Cooper would never buck the Texas Ranger service, the sacred Department of Public Safety she had served her entire career. "So, they're not getting a warrant for B.B.'s murder."

"Not for Burton," said Hall.

"For me?" asked E.J.

"No, but view it from the outside. You and Sheriff B.B. hated each other. Nobody knows why, but we all know it goes back forever. Burton accused you of planting evidence and falsifying a confession. What my boss calls a twofer. You got even with Burton and Sheriff B.B."

E.J. threw his head back, trying to draw a deep breath, taking in the artificial lavender scent from air fresheners plugged into the electric outlets. "I can't believe this is happening." A mild chuckle came to him, still unable to fathom a world gone mad. "'Your boss.' They sent my oldest friend to bring me in."

Hall shifted back in his chair. "I volunteered after I shared my opinion of him, the bureau, and his lineage in explicit terms. Probably my last assignment."

E.J. recalled the old days when Hall's cursing could make sailors blush and Rebecca stepped aside in sheer admiration. "What about your retirement? You and Amy have all these travel plans. And your big conversion. You gave up sinning."

"Nobody gives up sinning. I'm ashamed to tell you I thought about my retirement. Then it hit me. I was no better than your old major. If I were under fire or even a stranger, you'd run to the sound of gunfire. It's who you are. I decided I didn't want to be me. I wanted to be you."

"Do I have time to get cleaned up a little?" E.J. asked.

"Sure. No one knows I'm here. Came to see you get a fair shake. To be certain, no scared, wannabe kid playing G-man draws down on you. We ride to the office. You give a statement. I will drive you home. You have my word."

Chapter
Thirty-Three

The Eulogy

On the drive out of Houston, Hall said few words. E.J. welcomed the quiet after the lengthy interrogations.

Most special agents like Hall were attorneys. They didn't try cases, though they perfected interview techniques.

The route took them west of the swamps comprising the Big Thicket National Preserve. Like so many times prior, they rose onto the East Texas Freeway from the Gulf Coast Plain into the pine curtain. Even the spindly evergreens morphing into great pine plantations occasionally alternated into brown needles, evidencing a long-term drought.

"I have to bring something up," said Hall.

E.J. turned to face him. Could he take anything more? Hall literally set his world upside down earlier in the day. Cooper was disgraced and sold out. Federal authorities thinking he might have killed a sheriff. G .H. Burton still playing his actual innocence and intellectual disability card. He fought back the urge to ask, how can you make things worse?

Hall's Lexus sped through Lufkin as the sun fell away into darkness. "While they interviewed you, Rebecca called."

For a moment E.J. considered, what if Rebecca would have Hall tell him their night together had been a mistake? He moved the vent to turn more cool air in his direction. Of course not, she would tell him directly. Did she want him to call her?

"Candy called her looking for you," said Hall.

He caught himself before asking what Candy. The only one he knew and had known all his life was Sheriff B.B.'s wife.

"Why is she looking for me?" asked E.J.

Hall drew in a deep breath. "She wants you to deliver her husband's eulogy."

E.J. snorted, "Me?"

"What I thought," said Hall.

"He never missed an opportunity to berate me. Guy nearly beat me to death. Sheriff Benjamin Berryhill stood for everything I despise. One of the lowest, crookedest individuals I've ever known."

"Probably wouldn't lead with that line," said Hall.

"I'm not doing it," said E.J.

"Rebecca says you should. For the same reason, Candy wants you," said Hall.

"I mean, Son surely can say some great stuff about his dad. I can't," said E.J.

"Rebecca expects Candy can't imagine you ever would have killed Sheriff B.B. She says with the entire world thinking you're a murderer, it would be wise to show Candy is right." He pressed a presetting on his satellite radio. The smooth voice of Jimmy Ruffin asked "What Becomes of the Brokenhearted."

E.J. stared out the window. "So, I lie about a man I hated because it makes me look like I didn't kill him. I would have seen such a ruse as a sure sign of guilt if I were investigating. Especially if I'm watching an old boy struggle to say something nice."

"Not the reason to do it anyway," said Hall.

E.J. looked at Hall, trying to surmise if his old friend had lost his mind while the Motown hit continued the catchy melody.

"Because it is the Christian thing to do," said Hall.

"After six decades of heathenism, you're now the authority for the 'Christian thing to do' because you halfway gave up cussing," said E.J.

Hall's upper lip raised, opening his mouth. E.J realized he had gone too far. He felt guilty insulting his old friend. Who was he to question the sincerity of a conversion? Though E.J. must have harbored questions about whether the whole newfound faith had been to appease Amy more than a heartfelt conversion.

"I mean, it's not about you. The widow asks you to do something, then you do it. Yes, the Christian thing to do." Hall's tone shortened.

"I appreciate you driving me home." E.J. let the words linger, though they seemed small compared to Hall's frequent support. He suspected Hall likely fought the entire FBI to get the search grid expanded, then picking him up so he didn't get hauled into headquarters in cuffs. He owed Hall and not only for this time. "I'm sorry. I know you're risking your career."

Hall's countenance lit up, signaling to E.J. that he accepted the apology. "Not sure I still have an FBI career. Besides, I'm near mandatory retirement and I'm ready to take on something new. You hungry?" asked Hall.

"No, I might take a glass of tea." E.J.'s mind grappled the rest of the way home and afterward trying to add up the strange turn of events. How was it possible for Candy to ask?

He recalled as a kid growing aware Candy at the time held a romantic interest in him. Why she had fallen for B.B. escaped him. Though time had proven, E.J. presented no prize.

While B.B. had spent his adult life carrying out assorted crimes and scams to turn a dollar from public office, Candy had been a pillar of the community. She raised Son and an older daughter, Christy. Christy followed in her mother's footsteps in cheerleading, teaching school, and coaching cheer.

E.J. watched Hall swing the Lexus back onto the highway. Facing an empty travel trailer prompted him to check on Sunshine. After some initial trepidation, E.J. had passed many conversations with Sharla's horse.

He should call Sharla, but what to say? Admit he liked the fact she didn't abort the baby, yet what possible chance did a drug addicted baby have? She wasn't even able to quit long enough to give an innocent kid a fighting chance.

He hated her. The thought slapped his forehead like a two-by-four before he had the ability to prevent it. It wasn't true. Wasn't the real problem he loved her too much? He didn't walk away even when she repeatedly chose her addiction over him.

No, he would fight for her. Were the evil consuming Sharla tangible, he would shoot it. She had to win this battle. There was nothing he was able to do to safeguard her from herself. E.J. remembered begging Dr. Meecum to pray for Sharla as he pressed her name on his phone screen.

"Sharla?"

"The news had me so worried. Mom said you were okay, but I'm so glad you called."

"Your mom tells me you've had a setback," said E.J.

"I don't want to talk about it. Talk about anything else," said Sharla.

Of course, she wouldn't want to talk about it. She didn't want to face the truth. Should he risk alienating her? Perhaps she wasn't responsible for some of the consequences confronting her, yet here now she made fateful decisions about another life. He had to try. "I love you, but I need you to listen to me. Let me say one thing and we can talk about anything else. Okay?"

"One," she said.

"Once you commit to bring a child into this world, life stops being about you. Do you understand?" asked E.J.

"I do," said Sharla.

E.J. noticed Sharla let out a breath like she had avoided a real lecture. How could he ever reach her? "Sunshine misses you. I'll put you on speakerphone." E.J. caught himself motioning to the phone for the horse as Sharla spoke. A whiff of the hay reminded him of better days and wet saddle blankets with Sunshine. Both he and Sharla owed the old gelding more attention.

The skewbald horse swung its head at the voice emanating from the cell phone sitting on top of a post. "Do you have a treat for him?"

E.J. worked a brush untangling the horse's mane. "You know I don't believe in treats. People shouldn't spoil horses like..."

"Like children." The words amplified in the stall then died on thick, dry air. "I'm really better."

E.J. asked, "Trying to talk me into coming to get you?"

"No. I know I'm not ready," said Sharla.

"Soon as things settle down a little. I'll try to get down there and see you," said E.J.

"Bye, Dad."

E.J. found it impossible to restrain the elation growing in his heart. True enough, everything remained problematic. Sharla came across as genuine. The sincerity of her childhood had been almost totally replaced by a mixture of fraud and sarcasm. What were the odds they have turned a corner and finally gotten through to her?

E.J. chided himself for letting hope expand to the size of a hot-air balloon. Still, the parent of a child battling addiction didn't have many victories, real or perceived. E.J. stepped lighter, moving toward the trailer.

He stopped. Someone had parked a beige Land Rover about ten yards into his yard. Couldn't the idiot see the pavement had ended? E.J. stepped quicker over the uneven ground, nearing his camper.

Though not seeing anyone in the vehicle, E.J. continued making direct for the big sport-utility vehicle. He walked around the end of the travel trailer past his favorite old lawn chair. A hammering blow whomped his skull forward. E.J. toppled, trying to regain balance. Nearly crashing face first into dead grass, he caught himself.

His mind spun, crashed, and reilluminated like a computer rebooting. Instinct demanded he reach for the pocket pistol. Fear gripped the hollow of his belly when he realized he didn't have it. His captors had taken it in the Big Thicket. Dizziness led to a curdling nausea, forcing his mouth open. E.J.'s weak knee collapsed under him.

Chapter Thirty-Four

Attacked

E.J. slammed his hand on the sugary sand, halting his forward momentum. The back of his throat filled with regurgitated coffee, making him gag and spit.

From his peripheral vision, he saw gray untied moccasin-style shoes. Above the casual footwear appeared bare ankles rising into a sea of beige-and-white seersucker material. Rage swarmed E.J., driving his body around. He rose into a crouch for the first time, facing his attacker.

The shovel hammered toward E.J.'s head. Successfully deflecting the pummeling handle bouncing off his forearm bone, E.J. surged forward on his injured knee. He propelled himself into the iron part of the shovel, forcing it up and backward over his attacker's head.

The assailant's arms were pinned above him. E.J. tackled the pin-striped bushwhacker. The man's feet lifted off the ground. His shoulders smacked the earth. E.J.'s torso rotated, bludgeoning a right fist into the attacker's snapping cheekbone.

"Stuart?" E.J. yelled the name as a question, yet all doubt had been eliminated. It wasn't enough the sockless fop had carried on with his wife.

"Have you gone crazy?"

Stuart exhaled guttural yelps, tears, and slobber in a seemingly endless series of nonsense. As E.J. rose, he saw a dark, wet stain on the sheer white pajama-like pants. Immediate recognition of urine confirmed the vulgar whiff E.J. hadn't placed until now.

"Ugh, Stuart," grunted E.J.

Stuart rolled on the dead vegetation. His body writhed with agony.

E.J. found the cell phone Hall had loaned him and called 911. He reported the emergency and his address. No doubt the operator heard the wailing in the background. She asked E.J. to remain on the line. He ignored the request, ending the call.

Stuart had contorted onto all fours. Tears poured past his cheeks. Blood fell from Stuart's open mouth into the sandy loam.

"What is wrong with you?" asked E.J.

"Me?" Stuart slurred and stuttered, spitting blood.

"You gone crazy," said E.J.

Stuart turned his head toward E.J., still not rising. "I love her." He repeated the phrase, louder at each pass.

E.J. dropped into his favorite web-backed lawn chair. His sweat-soaked arms rested on the cool aluminum frame. He had put little thought into Stuart. To the contrary, E.J. had tried to forget the interloper.

Stuart's mere pathetic presence demanded E.J.'s attention. The metallic odor of blood coated the fool. How was it possible for him to fight back pity for this lovestruck dunce now?

Stuart rolled onto his butt. The man's fingers coated in a chalky mix of gore and powdered dirt struggled for a hold to raise himself. Slumping back, Stuart exhaled a deep moan.

"You don't understand. I love her so much," said Stuart.

E.J. stepped inside the trailer and threw Stuart a dish towel to hold against his bleeding cheek. "You don't know her."

"She's not your wife anymore." Stuart stabbed at the words in a starting, stopping staccato cadence through wild crying.

"Why now? Why attack me now?" asked E.J.

"She dropped me. So, I had an investigator follow her. I can tell the two of you've been together."

For a split second, E.J. wanted to deny it. He was uncertain of the reasons, whether it was to safeguard his privacy, uphold Rebecca's dignity, or shield Stuart's sensitive emotions. True, an investigator might have discovered they had both spent the night at Rex's condo but to conclude they had sex took some conjecture or an obsessively jealous mind. Though if the conclusion had been conjecture, E.J. suspected his face confirmed it.

Maybe he should lie. Perhaps this buffoon made Rebecca happy. Obviously, E.J. couldn't do it anymore or she wouldn't have left so early and refused his calls. If they couldn't work it out, then shouldn't Rebecca have the opportunity at love? "Take some advice." E.J. motioned his hand in an arc at the tear-soaked, bleeding Stuart.

E.J. added, "Rebecca is a trial lawyer. She lives to fight injustice, and she hates weakness. You giving into rage, attacking me, blithering and bawling won't work. She won't have it."

"I love her so much," pleaded Stuart.

A siren filled the dry air, trumpeting the arrival of the orange-and-white ambulance. Two paramedics briefly elicited what happened, then went to work on Stuart. They took vitals and strapped him onto a gurney.

E.J. remained motionless in the old yard chair, suffering from a head still throbbing. The flashing lights didn't help. Shouldn't he get checked out? Who needed an ambulance bill or worse, to get taken to a hospital for observation?

Lost in contemplation, he was oblivious to Son's presence until the sturdy young man materialized above, enveloping E.J. in shadow. "You're settling scores with everyone, aren't you?"

"He blindsided me with a shovel," said E.J.

"Stuart?" Son pointed at the shriveling blob of bleeding and bawling humanity, packaged in what amounted to pajamas passing for a business suit in the Deep South. "Stuart took you out?"

"I said he hit me with a shovel," said E.J.

Son turned, walking to where the paramedics were loading the patient. "You really catch him unawares with a shovel?" The tone showed a new respect for the gentle lawyer.

"I love her," said Stuart.

"I'm taking that as a yes." Son leaned his head around the ambulance door to face E.J. "Pressing charges?"

"No." E.J. projected the answer for Stuart's benefit.

"He's not pressing charges?" asked a groggy Stuart.

"Guess he don't want everybody to know his wife's glam boy toy whopped him. Old man has pride." Son stepped aside, and the ambulances backed out of the drive.

On other occasions, a smile would have followed the quip, yet here Son's flat countenance concerned E.J. The ambulance motor rumbled into the distance.

"Ought to arrest you anyway," said Son. The younger man's hand fell toward an ornately tooled leather gun belt.

There were rare times when Son reminded E.J. of the elder Berryhill, though as a general rule, they were surprisingly different for father and son. "Way you see it?" asked E.J.

The ambulance noise trailed off. E.J. rose in near darkness, heralded by the sound of cicadas. The insects' soft chirping noise constantly increased and subsided, reminiscent of a snake moving to strike. Wouldn't Son assume E.J. had a pocket pistol? Both were known as gunmen. Each had witnessed the other's prowess.

"Then what?" E.J. asked.

Son put his hand on the hilt of the semiauto pistol rig. "You kill him?"

Chapter Thirty-Five

You Kill Him?

S on wouldn't draw on an unarmed man. Though wouldn't Son assume he secreted a pocket pistol? The notion made E.J. feel uneasy. How could Son ask if he killed Sheriff B.B.?

True, E.J. hated the man, yet the miscreant was Son's father, Candy's husband, and a distant relative E.J. had known all his life.

Daylight's absence didn't cool the air. E.J. felt a drop of sweat rolling across his face. He dared not make a sudden movement of any kind. Son wouldn't kill him, would he?

The awkward cicada song played in the background like a well-executed symphony supporting a theatrical production. The Son he knew, the one who backed him in Shreveport against the outlaws who held Sharla, would never harm him. It wasn't in the man's makeup, his character.

In the dark, he couldn't see that Son in the young man's eyes. If Son thought E.J. killed Sheriff B.B., would he retaliate with E.J.'s life? No doubt grief and some misplaced guilt for not saving his father must be consuming Son. E.J. had witnessed grief crush many a good heart, many an otherwise strong character, and make one capable of all manner of wickedness in the name of revenge masquerading as love.

The thought of one movement ending everything danced through E.J.'s mind. He witnessed Son shoot in competition. In a heartbeat, he was able to draw and fire accurately. So odd he didn't feel fear. In fact, a strange relief gripped him.

The bead of sweat fell from E.J.'s cheek. "I didn't kill your father. Did you need to hear it from me?"

"Got to admit there's plenty of reasonable suspicion on you. And I understand you had a good reason," said Son.

Was he baiting him? Possibly employing an interview technique to obtain a confession. The plan to make an admission more palatable and then draw on him? "G.H. Burton hung your father. He became convinced B.B. double-crossed him."

Son yelled, "You're lying—"

"I'm no liar." E.J. snapped the words, trying to calm his tensing body and unballing his fist.

"Then there's more to it. My father may have been a lot of things, but he played outlaws, not the other way around. No way Burton got to him. So why? What happened out there? You're not telling something?"

Son presented the total package for a great lawman. Despite his big lug appearance, he possessed a keen, questioning mind. The young detective ascended through the possibilities in his mind. E.J. couldn't reveal the truth.

In point of fact, E.J. didn't know the whole truth. B.B. had been hamstrung, refusing to escape his fate because he needed to protect Son from Burton. Yet Sheriff B.B. confirmed a far more insidious and cunning killer than G.H. Burton had robbed E.J. of his career and his good name.

The immediate cause of Burton's ire against Sheriff B.B. had been Son leaking information to Rebecca. He wouldn't saddle Son with the guilt. Better to remain a mystery. "Burton hung him. You've been around some. Murder rarely makes sense except in the twisted mind of a murderer."

Son raised his hand above his beltline. "I'm not drawing on you. You've outlived the wild West, old man. Take your secrets to your grave. When we bury my father tomorrow, we bury any respect I ever held for you." Son spat the words, turning on his heel toward the patrol car.

E.J. fell back into the yard chair. The cicadas' song mellowed in intensity. Dry night air carried a musty smell like it had been locked up too long. Son was certain that E.J. had been the one to kill Sheriff B.B. Such an impression disturbed E.J., because it carried truth imbedded in it.

Did he not have any other options to try to save Sheriff B.B.? Taken back further in time, shouldn't E.J. have foreseen whatever forces must have robbed him of his standing, his dignity? Wasn't there some Bible verse about binding a strong man before someone robbed him? The tangent temporarily derailed his thoughts.

The struggle to remember consumed him. Was Son right? A lawman who outlived his era. A trick of time had suspended him in darkness, out of place, out of connection to everyone. He didn't understand anyone or anything anymore. Worse, he couldn't even fully appreciate what was gone. How much of what made him a talented investigator and a good person was gone? The sinking sorrow of not even knowing who or what cost him all he had lost washed over him, casting a sourness in his mouth.

E.J. pressed the button, calling Rebecca.

"Hello."

"I tried calling you. You left kind of unexpected," said E.J.

"I'm busy," said Rebecca.

"We have to talk sometime," said E.J.

Rebecca made a mock laugh. "Well, look who wants to talk."

"Your boyfriend tried to kill me," said E.J.

"Stuart? Stuart couldn't hurt anything. He is a pacifist."

"Your pacifist, commie, swung a shovel into my skull," said E.J.

"You didn't hurt him, did you?" asked Rebecca.

"Appreciate your concern, I'm fine," said E.J.

Rebecca said, "We broke up and he hasn't taken it well. Is he alright?"

"Stuart is still Stuart. He'll be okay. Why would I do B.B.'s funeral," said E.J.

"You should," said Rebecca.

"Why?" A long silence filled the night. No cicadas, nothing but stars in the sky and silence from Rebecca. "I'm not going to do it," said E.J.

"I left because I expected you'd think we were back together. One night and all is forgiven," said Rebecca.

What did he need to be forgiven for? The question would set a fight off, and he didn't want to fight. He had mostly called to hear her voice. She had been right about him concluding one night and everything would be better. A start to salvaging his marriage, and a step toward taking old life back.

Only now he would appreciate how he continued chasing an untethered hope. The way forward would be the way backward into whatever he had been investigating near the time of the raid on the cartel compound. The path wouldn't put his life back together.

However, it might reorder the pieces of himself, fashioning himself into something right, something he could respect.

"I'm sorry I called. You were right to leave," said E.J.

"First time we've spoken and not argued over Sharla in years." Rebecca exhaled before continuing. "You should do the funeral."

"Son accused me of killing B.B. and half the world is convinced I did," said E.J.

"The leads are panning out. I'm knocking down Burton's writ. Soon I'll have the complete farce uncovered. Of course, you didn't kill B.B., and once you speak, everyone will know," said Rebecca.

"And us?" asked E.J.

"I'll always love you, but there is no us. Get it through your head, E.J. There can't ever be an us again."

Chapter Thirty-Six

Stay Away from My Wife

"I did not conduct Sheriff B.B.'s autopsy. Easier to take the body to Beaumont." Dr. Meecum voiced the answer in his unique accent.

The bleach smell from the autopsy room down the hall stung E.J.'s nostrils. "Figured so, but you read the notes, right?"

"Nothing inconsistent with what you've described—asphyxia, by closure of passages in the neck from compression because of the body's weight," said Dr. Meecum.

E.J. studied the photos adorning the walls in Dr. Meecum's office. The pictures of family sharing special events at church comforted him. He turned to face the doctor. "You have a beautiful family."

"How is your daughter?" asked Dr. Meecum.

"Facing a lot of challenges," answered E.J.

"My family and I have been praying for her like you asked," said Dr. Meecum.

E.J. looked back at the wall. "I didn't mean for you to take us on as a project. I figured you might, kind of the onetime..."

"You honored me by asking. Have you thought about why you asked," said Dr. Meecum.

A silence settled over the office. Like the autopsy room, the bare cement floor stretched from one end to the other. It appeared Dr. Meecum didn't stand on pretense or carpet.

Dr. Meecum raised and opened his hands. "Thought, thought it might be the real reason you came."

E.J. looked down at the desk. "I got asked to do the eulogy for Benjamin Berryhill."

A grin jumped across Dr. Meecum's face. "You will bring comfort to so many."

"There's the problem." E.J. looked into Meecum's ebony eyes. "I grew up with him, worked with him all his life. He would have sold his momma's dentures for a nickel."

Dr. Meecum shrugged. "I don't understand."

"He took payoffs, from anybody and everybody. Like a crime boss, if you wanted to do business in his county, he took a piece. Drugs, prostitution, gambling, whatever turned a buck. Killed untold numbers the same as if he put a needle in their arm or a bullet in their head. Even when I doubt God exists, I believe lawmen like him earn a special place in hell's fire."

Dr. Meecum pushed himself away from the desk, leaning farther back in his chair. "I wasn't very familiar with the sheriff. Though I appreciate the dilemma, most certainly."

"Dilemma, huh? What would Walker do?" Conscience pangs erupted in the pit of E.J.'s stomach. Dr. Meecum idolized the iconic television character originally portrayed by Chuck Norris. Meecum had done him no harm, and he insulted the man. Why was he mocking something good, like the Walker character? Shouldn't people at least try to believe in nobility? Before E.J. could apologize, the doctor's response took him aback.

"Walker would," said Dr. Meecum.

"Walker would what?" asked E.J.

"Give the eulogy. Because it is not about you," said Dr. Meecum.

"What?" asked E.J.

"Who asked you?" inquired Dr. Meecum.

"Candy, his widow. We grew up together. I'm being told she wants people to know I didn't kill him," said E.J.

"And you didn't kill him?" asked Dr. Meecum.

E.J. shouted, "No."

"Then she needs to hear the truth. Even the most wicked soul has value. If God in his righteous glory can see the value in the one and leave the ninety, then why can't you find some quality Sheriff B.B. possessed? God will judge. Whether the man was a saint is not for you to determine," said Dr. Meecum.

The bleach odor had dissipated. E.J. stood to leave. "Must be something finding all the answers in one place?"

"The greater understanding comes from discovering the questions," said Dr. Meecum.

"I knew to come here, though for the life of me sometimes I don't understand what you say," said E.J. rising to leave.

Dr. Meecum looked up at E.J. "The older I grow, the more I think life is about the questions."

E.J. normally liked the drive through the Attoyac Bayou as it meandered into the Angelina River bottom, though the vibrant green bloom had given way to dulling beiges. The drive provided an opportunity to order his thoughts and try to organize a speech.

How do you say something nice about Sheriff B.B.? A real writer and speaker couldn't pull off such an impossible task, much less a fellow who conceded he lacked oratory skills. Rebecca would have equaled the task.

Above the road a massive peppermint looked as if untethered it would fly across Highway 59 at any moment. E.J. parked behind the plastic confection. On the front of the dark glass door, letters stated "Sweets for Sweet." The candy cane had originally begun as a joke until the owner took a shine to it.

Two old-timers E.J. recognized as retired Louisiana State troopers and the operator, Mr. Sweet, looked up from a counter of pistols. Behind them stood a wall of long guns.

"'Tis the man hisself. You know these webfooted beanie weenies are not gonna buy anything, anyway." Sweet placed a lever action pistol on the counter. "Mare's leg." He turned and dribbled a syrupy dark liquid mostly in a wastebasket.

E.J. briefly studied the curious firearm before nodding in acknowledgment to the Pelican State officers. "Need another P938. Fellow stole mine."

"We heard," said one of the former officers.

"Travels fast, don't it?" said E.J.

"Bad news do," said the grayer haired of the two men.

Sweet's cheeks moved back and forth, crushing tobacco prior to spiting again. "Feared you were bringing in your old compadre's ranger rig," said Sweet.

"What?" asked E.J.

"They didn't even let her get home. They sent a lieutenant colonel to the hospital to drum Cooper out," Sweet said.

"Not old DPS. All new DPS. Y'all act like a bunch of church ladies or something," said one of the Louisianians.

E.J. stiffened. What kind of insult was he making? "You are aware that Cooper is a woman—"

"He means what I tell you 'bout old DPS versus new DPS. Rangers done become more about looks than business. If still old times, man or woman, either, the service would close behind 'em not over 'em." Sweet worked the rest of the wad out of his mouth, then frowned.

E.J. had spent enough time with Sweet to know the frown denoted the former Dallas Police Department officer and current gun shop owner's opinion of the Texas Department of Public of Safety, as well as having to waste good chewing tobacco talking. "Cooper did nothing wrong."

"Yeah." Sweet smirked, reminding E.J. the old SWAT commander had been shuffled out of his department into early retirement, though E.J. had never inquired into the backstory. He felt a kick in the pit of his stomach.

In his mind's ear, E.J. listened as Major Fenton emphasized the importance of prioritizing the well-being of the ranger service. The grimace on Sweet's face evidenced he felt a similar betrayal by his old department.

At the time, E.J. couldn't fathom not falling on his sword. Like a corollary to his oath, if the good of the organization demanded his career, then he surrendered it. Duty demanded those actions necessary to fulfill one's obligation.

Likely Sweet and these gun store flies spent too much time gossiping. The story always exponentially improved with each telling until the truth had been wrung from it like liquid from a washcloth. Cooper would have had a little heat to fade, but nothing serious. No more honorable lawman or woman ever pinned a badge. E.J. surmised silence would send the message he would take no more frivolity at the expense of the department, Cooper, or the ranger service.

Sweet broke the awkward silence. "Sure, I can order you a little Sig, but let me show you what I got. Aluminum frame, fifteen-round mag, G10 grips, three-pound trigger pull..."

The superb balance of a well-machined pistol never ceased to please his hand. The cocking seriations made charging the slide a joy, revealing a fluted barrel. He lifted the weapon into easy alignment on the red TruGlo post.

Sweet nodded. He replaced his standard smirk with a smile of jubilation at E.J.'s delight. "Feel the trigger pull."

"Can't afford a Wilson," said E.J. staring at the four digits written on a white tag tied with cotton string around the trigger guard.

"Never stopped me," said one of the Louisianians.

"Thousand down and you pay rest out monthly as you can," said Sweet.

"Done." It didn't take long to complete the transaction and put E.J. back on the highway.

Back on the road, the task of Sheriff B.B.'s eulogy weighed E.J. down again. The euphoria of the weapon purchased had been erased by the task of writing a speech praising Sheriff B.B. Likewise, the events of Big Thicket replayed in his mind, bringing to the fore his concerns about Cooper. Sweet's gun shop talk hadn't helped. It had to be gossip, right? Was she still in the hospital? He should check on her.

"Call Cooper."

A gruff voice peppered curse words through the stereo system. After the tirade subsided, Cooper's husband yelled, "Stay away from my wife."

Chapter Thirty-Seven

Draw a Hard Line

E.J. slid his heels back in the stirrups and Sunshine took off. Concern filled him as the old horse sped up, kicking out as it did so. Sooner or later Sharla would ride him. Maybe it would be better if he worked the animal in the round pen. He wouldn't slow the mount.

The speed with which the gelding gobbled up the shriveled vegetation of the pasture caused a breeze in an atmosphere where nothing stirred. Welcoming the relief from a shirt soaking with sweat, E.J. pressed his knees and the geriatric critter turned loose in a rare gallop.

After giving the animal its head for a suitable distance, E.J. slowed the beast. He hopped off, folding onto his bad knee.

E.J. secured Sharla's pet to a tall pin oak along the edge of a dry branch with a lead rope. He flipped his hat using the brick crease as a makeshift water trough filled from his canteen. By walking over a rise, he gained a good view of an old slough which snaked back and forth before absorbing the dry branch he previously left.

Upon discovering the desired topography, E.J. positioned himself before higher ground ascending from the low country. E.J. unrolled a feed sack he had tied behind the cantle of his saddle.

The reeds of the slough made a crunching sound as his boots stepped. He tried cross drawing the weapon from inside his waistband, finding it clumsy the first dozen times. Settling on a pattern, E.J. raised the semiauto and launched the contents of a magazine into the letter *O* of the printed feed company's name.

Shooting always freed his mind. A way to unplug, gain perspective, and view issues from new angles. He didn't have a speech written, and the funeral was at eight tomorrow evening in the football stadium. A current sheriff murdered in the line of duty would garner honor guards, mounted patrols, even Canadian Mounties, literally officers from the entire continent.

Only a high school football stadium could seat the size crowd the sendoff for a peace officer killed in the line of duty would draw. The Texas heat wouldn't pass until evening, so a late start made sense. What would he say about a man who needed killing twenty years prior?

Wrestling with the dilemma didn't present him an entrée to approach the problem. His thoughts turned to Cooper. If only he could speak to her.

Cooper's husband was clear. Jefferey, or Jeffie as Cooper called him, hadn't ever come to terms with the career his high school sweetheart chose. Cooper was sensitive to his overprotection because of all the challenges she faced in a male-dominated profession, though E.J. defended Jefferey. He explained the man hadn't been any more protective than any colleague, supervisor, or friend and her career choice would take a toll on any marriage.

E.J. had been racking his brain to answer so many old riddles he couldn't have foreseen a couple of days ago. Despite the stillness of the secluded bottomland, his mind filled with conversation. Repeated lines from old friends pleading with him those years ago to wake up, to see he was being made a scapegoat. Devotion caused blindness.

Families of murdered officers and civilians, incapable of extracting justice from an amorphous, invisible, and all-powerful cartel, needed to hold someone accountable. Agencies desperate to preserve their legitimacy and political standing scrambled to put the deaths at the doorstep of another. Phrases like the good of the department, necessary to preserve the service, and an organizational duty confused the simplicity of right and wrong.

Though E.J. never conceded his actions were criminal. Thanks to Rebecca's skill in the courtroom, a jury later agreed. She had been adept at strategies to deal with his admissions his guilty conscience made him make on the witness stand.

E.J. took responsibility for what he believed hindsight proved were errors in judgment. After all, he had captained the ship. The one entrusted by the great state of Texas with the lives of other junior officers.

The revelation from Sheriff B.B. changed his life, expanded his worldview, compelling him to reexamine everything. *Cartel knew you were coming. Once alerted, an army couldn't have taken that fortress.*

In Sheriff B.B.'s words, didn't E.J. have a gift? In fifty years of ill treatment, had B.B. in death done him a good turn?

The consequence of the words trembled his legs, forcing him into the tall, dry weeds. E.J. went down from the weight of the guilt pushing over him. Tears both surprised him and soaked his cheeks as he clamored for breath. It wasn't his fault.

For the first time, the realization falling on his sword hadn't been noble. The act only served to further blind him to the real evildoers. Worse, the people and institutions he needed to rely upon instead threw him under the bus for their own expediency. A sense of betrayal twisted, then knotted in his gut.

Graying, dried mud filled both his hands. Cooper faced a similar fate to what E.J. had suffered, though on a smaller scale. When would she wake from the web of guilt and false obligation spun around her? Somehow Cooper must appreciate she had done right, not wrong.

Seeing the world in absolutes and unwavering loyalty to ideals blinded Cooper to the insidious truth? She would be unwittingly condemned to a path of injustice, and she would pay the price for accepting such a path.

Orange rays from a setting sun struggled through distant pine and hardwoods, casting a surreal hue over the winding sloughs stretching in the distance. The legacy of the real property lay before him. A heritage he always hoped to pass to Konner and Sharla. Did his ancestors include this parcel in their original grant because the great bowl held moisture in times of drought?

As he rode back on Sunshine, E.J.'s mind constructed the beginning of tomorrow's speech. A sleepless night fueled by percolating coffee brought trepidation and later some relief.

The necktie constricted his airway. E.J. hadn't donned the suit since his trial. He pulled at the button while watching Cooper's husband and his daughter load their Bronco for the drive to school.

Rex Ashe never skimped, even on the company truck, so the cowboy Cadillac appeared far too showy. Besides, Jefferey had seen the vehicle on other occasions. Instead, E.J. therefore opted for his old 1964 Ford pickup.

The old truck stood out to a lesser extent among automobiles of suburbia. Cooper's house stood nestled in a long line of similar houses along streets named for types of flowers in a bedroom community outside Tyler. Ducking down below sight, E.J. caught a glimpse of Cooper's husband's sport-utility vehicle.

The big V-8 Y-block sparked to life and E.J. drove down the street. After parking he called Cooper on his cell phone, though showing up on her door still surprised her. A big, ornate front door opened. Cooper's color and forceful presence had returned to normal from her poor condition the last time he saw her.

"You're looking well," said E.J.

She laughed. E.J. assumed because she wore no makeup and wore a terry cloth bathrobe over her nightgown. "Come in. Want some coffee?"

There wasn't much point in answering the question. He hadn't turned down the elixir even when it had been heated for hours in nooks of courthouses or the break rooms of many a law enforcement agency. The Cooper family kept their living room neat and modestly furnished. Photos of the daughters' volleyball, basketball, and softball teams' victories adorned the walls.

E.J. followed her into a kitchen painted pastel blue. Cooper pulled two coffee cups hanging from a decorative ceramic tree, obviously made by one of the kids as a project. E.J. had feared Cooper would throw him out like Jeffie. Her kind smile showed she appreciated the visit.

A comforting aroma wafted from the silky, black nectar. The taste revealed a rich, dark blend warming his throat.

"Jefferey seems a little upset." E.J. understated the drama normally so far outside of Jefferey's character.

"Think so?" Cooper chuckled.

"Can't fault a person for protecting his family," said E.J.

"Sometimes I worry he needs to be the big man protecting his little lady," said Cooper.

"Probably not a man thing. You know nothing phases Rebecca but when I stayed out all night without a phone call, she always waited so she could read me the riot act about the dangers of police work," said E.J.

Cooper stared down at the cup. E.J. drew a deep pull on the coffee. The hot, rich flavor likewise satisfied the second time.

"Lt. Colonel Fenton came by yesterday," said Cooper.

E.J. grimaced. He suspected what might have transpired based on Sweet's gun shop talk. Likely Cooper didn't tell anyone. A number two in the Department of Public Safety coming to Tyler from Austin could cause reverberation and rumor as far as the Louisiana line. "What did my old friend Craig have to say?"

Cooper looked away, her expression of disapproval at the sarcasm. "The lieutenant colonel wanted me to understand the last thing the rangers need is bad press. We're coming off the bicentennial. District attorneys and mayors in urban areas are trying to paint us as white-washing officer involved shootings. Puppets of the governor and the party dominating state politics. Plus, the bad press we got on that other matter."

E.J. didn't have to ask. He was the other matter. Yet wasn't there always another matter? Like there were always allegations. Ranger whitewashed political corruption and uses of deadly force by officers. Fenton needed more to convince Cooper to sacrifice her career. "What sin did you commit?"

"You know I shouldn't have gone with you and Sheriff B.B. without having discussed it with my lieutenant—"

"Bull. The sheriff of one of your counties decides he wants to carry a capital murderer back to prison and does so with a reckless disregard for proper security. You were exactly where you should have been. Otherwise, a capital murderer would be in the wind," said E.J.

"Where you wanted me to be," said Cooper.

Tilting backward, he attempted to evade the sharp jab. "Fair enough. I put you there. Doesn't change the fact it was where you should have been."

"The lieutenant colonel explained the perception to me."

The blood pulsed quicker in E.J.'s veins. He was aware that rumors of him and Cooper being more than colleagues had circulated among certain individuals for years. "Perception?"

"I didn't know you personally called the governor to get me my ranger appointment—"

"Common knowledge, we all know the governor from doing security when he is in our area. The rangers have always received far too many qualified candidates. There is necessarily a political element, you symbolize Texas. I explained to him how the department had the opportunity to promote a brilliant officer of absolute integrity who would serve as a role model for a generation." Suddenly cognizant, his voice must have risen far too loud, E.J. quieted. "I did it more for the future of the rangers than I did for you."

"Yes, but from Burton and B.B.'s press conference, it looks like I was a love-sick schoolgirl. I have to think of the good of the service. When one of us stands in the way of the mission, then we have to step aside," said Cooper.

"He asked you to quit?" asked E.J.

"You resigned," said Cooper.

"You're not me. Your feet aren't made of clay and you're in the right." E.J. balled a fist. This conversation wasn't going the way he had played it out in his head.

Cooper shook her head. "You had the courage to step aside. I'm finally seeing what you have tried to explain since I've known you. Right and wrong isn't always black and white."

E.J. leaned farther back in his chair and swallowed hard. Even in a gray world, occasionally we have to draw a hard line.

Chapter Thirty-Eight

Trade the Devil Offered

E.J. parked on the street over two hundred yards from the football stadium lot. He walked past crowded rows of cars, including many police units. A pair of fire ladder trucks hung enormous Texas flags from their extended ladders.

Golf carts scurried back and forth, carrying dignitaries. The walk wasn't the problem—rather, sweating like a pig in a dark suit posed a concern. Heat persisted, despite the sun descending in the distance. Once an extended gas-powered rig slowed for E.J. until the driver could get a closer look. E.J. surmised without a badge, no one considered him important.

He entered the field house. Glass comprised nearly the entire interior wall, providing a splendid view of the field and stands. People filled all the home-side stands under a massive press box. On the field, the funeral home employees had arranged a couple hundred chairs by rows three quarters of the field length. A large, raised flatbed trailer normally reserved for transporting heavy equipment made a dais on the fifty-yard line.

Though full, the field house wasn't crowded. E.J. recognized the official blue blazers and matching pink pastel ties of the Gibson-Margrave Funeral Home. E.J. called one of the directors by name and the man greeted him with a powerful handshake and a bear hug. "I'm so proud you're doing this for Ms. Candy."

"Couldn't really say no, could I?" asked E.J.

"You'd be surprised. Water?" asked the funeral director.

"Got any tea?" asked E.J.

"I'll find you a glass." The dapper dressed man took off down a hallway.

From his periphery, E.J. saw a smallish middle-aged man wearing a heavy, starched dress shirt making a beeline for him.

Lt. Colonel Fenton sneered at E.J. causing instant recognition. "You're a walking, talking cluster, Kane. The word former never sounded so beautiful as in former ranger when associated with you."

"You're out of line leaning on Cooper. She's good police. It's a handful of hard chargers like her who you cowardly bureaucrats should thank for being able to stay on the public dole. Why don't you go shiver back under the rock you slid out from?"

Fenton grimaced, then a broad smile expanded over his face. "Make sure you say hello to Jenkins and Aldner. Brought them up from Company F on temporary assignment to enhance the case against you."

E.J. recalled the same snarky glow on Major Craig Fenton's face when taking the witness stand during the criminally negligent homicide trial.

"You remember how close they got to convicting you last time? Hope you sparkin' a new alley cat lawyer. I caught wind that your old lady is getting disbarred," said Fenton.

E.J.'s chin raised, and his blood pressure hummed so loud he heard the throb in his ears. Fenton provoked him into a fight, and it would only validate all the lies, making Cooper's predicament even worse.

His mind raced back to when Fenton asked him to call him Craig, then sold him on resigning for the good of the service. E.J. clenched his fist, recalling the entire routine and the tears he had fought back while contemplating one solid punch at the pompous fop. E.J. closed the distance to an uncomfortable point with Fenton. "Back Cooper or I'll come after you. No Jenkins and Aldner, no ranger service, no army can protect you from me, you understand?"

Fenton stepped back. He chuckled, mocking the statement. "You'll come after me. I'm supposed to take it you're threatening a peace officer, Mr. Private Citizen Kane."

"You're a bureaucrat putting himself and his station in life before his duty." E.J. smelled the familiar scent of Fenton soaked in Aqua Velva.

"Gentlemen," the recognizable voice poured like silk as a hand touched E.J.'s back. "Your voices are too loud. Much too loud for this discussion."

"Not the time, cluster." Fenton turned to face Larence Kutnick. "Mr. Speaker, I speak for all law enforcement when I tell you it is an honor to have you here."

"Do you feel the same way, Ranger Kane?" Larence Kutnick stared at Fenton like he dared him to correct the reference.

Fenton turned on his heel, walking away without comment.

E.J. couldn't restrain himself from breaking into a small grin. "Laying it on a little thick, isn't he?"

"We'll need a new colonel for DPS soon. What do you think about your old major?" asked Larence Kutnick.

E.J. had spent a fair amount of time with Kutnick years ago, yet he had never been able to read the man. Was this an attempt at a joke? Kutnick's demeanor did not indicate sarcasm. E.J. chose not to respond.

Larence Kutnick said, "Possibly someone outside of the department. New blood, new perspective. They've done it before, like a career FBI agent."

Could he be suggesting Hall? What a perfect choice. Should he lobby for Hall? Would it do any good?

Kutnick changed the subject as quickly as he had made what E.J. took correctly or otherwise as an implied reference to Hall. "Besides starting the family construction business, my grandfather organized the first fire department in this part of the world. I watched a lot of houses burn. See, I thought you tried to save every home. Suppose it might be what they do now, but then there was no way."

E.J. wanted to walk, find a place to review his notes one more time for the speech. Even for a man who no longer stood on the conventions governing state employees, when the speaker of the Texas House of Representatives spoke, one didn't walk away.

"Had a bad one over in Stien's Quarters. I probably wasn't twelve yet. Ash fell like snow. A dark gray paste covered all our faces." Larence Kutnick's eyes searched E.J.'s blue orbs.

E.J. knew what he meant, though he recalled no fire. Kutnick had some years on him, likely the events transpired before E.J.'s time. The poor inhabited Stien's Quarters and no doubt they always had. Poorly constructed wood-frame homes made potent fuel for a conflagration.

"My grandfather picked a street, Murchison. I'll never forget it. They bulldozed a firebreak. Meanwhile, the fire engulfed more and more homes. People screaming, begging, and running in and out of collapsing homes. I didn't understand. Why Murchison? 'Cause it had to be some street? Saved the quarters."

The intensity of his gaze seared E.J. "Cooper is an acceptable loss, like I was? Way I'm supposed to look at it? Just shut up and take it for the greater good."

"I'm trying to explain the way Fenton sees it. You know, in Stien's Quarters, the big field where the older-timers play dominos. Hear they going to make it a soccer field."

"Murchison Street?" asked E.J.

"I learned. I looked at my grandfather differently. Not an old man who life had worn down. In those wrinkles, I saw a soul burdened by a lifetime of acceptable losses. God wasn't helping, so he took the trade the devil offered because it saved lives." Larence Kutnick's eyes plead for understanding while unwavering in their lock on E.J.

E.J. stepped aside for the funeral attendants. Flowers, from sprays to ferns, were transported past them, perfuming the air. "Your point is he had to draw a hard line, and it made him who he was?"

"Stien's Quarters stands today because my grandfather didn't battle the fire at every house in flames. He saved a community because he took property loss, even causalities for the greater good. Destroyed some homes to save others," said Kutnick.

Even, if necessary, who chooses which street, how, and why? E.J.'s memory conjured an image of the quarters with new images, painting the carnage on one side of the neighborhood. Charred ruins and blackened grass in contrast to white frame homes in neat rows with green yards of thick grass-blades. Did those folks on the wrong side of the old firefighter's line agree?

"'Drawing a hard line,' I like the way you put it. It's important to me, you understand," said Kutnick.

E.J. stared at a row of funeral sprays. "Defines us, doesn't it? Where we draw those lines and when? I mean, one side of the line is life, the other death."

Kutnick's face turned, revealing a partial grin. "Aren't you overlooking the most crucial aspect?"

Chapter Thirty-Nine

Whom Shall I Send

E.J. looked out an enormous window. Assorted honor guards displayed their splendid uniforms, garnering attention.

A soft voice lifted behind him. "Thank you for doing this."

He turned to find a recognizable girlish face disguised by blonde hair, age, and makeup. "Candy?"

E.J. took her hand in both of his. "I'm sorry for your loss." His initial awkwardness faded when the corners of Candy's lips turned up, because it reminded him of her youthful smile. The smile hadn't changed since elementary school.

"How is Sharla?" Candy followed the question before E.J. answered. "My Sunday school class is praying for her."

"Thank you. She improves a little, every so often." E.J. looked away. Answering the question forced him to bite back emotion and push it away.

"Rebecca and I play mah-jongg on Tuesdays," said Candy.

E.J. nodded, appreciating Candy likely had a wealth of information about Sharla.

"Can I ask you something?" asked E.J.

"Why?" said Candy.

E.J. nodded, grateful he need not say more.

"I watched you perform the greatest act of Christian faith I've ever witnessed. Preaching Konner's service. Why I chose you."

"B.B. and I weren't close—"

Candy erupted in laughter. She caught her mouth with one hand, then surveyed the room. Certain she hadn't caused a scene, Candy leaned closer. "He hated you."

"Why? I never figured out the why," said E.J.

"I expect it went back to his father. Benjamin never felt good enough. His father didn't help. Remember Leonard, 'Roly Poly' daddy's little fatty. He sang it all the time."

In his mind, E.J. registered a correct portion in Tommy Duncan's immortalized voice. *Bet he's gonna be a man someday.* The old Fred Rose and Bob Wills tune played in his head thanks to the silky voice of Tommy Duncan.

"Leonard sang *Don't you want to be a man someday.* Then he held you up as the example. Benjamin never compared in his dad's eyes. Even as kids, I felt sorry for Benjamin," said Candy.

"Why you married him because you felt sorry for him?" asked E.J.

"No, he had his moments, though it's no secret we grew apart. Son joins the best of both of us. Why I wanted you to speak today? Boys revere their fathers. They have to. He needs to salvage something decent from his father. He needs someone he respects, you to tell him his father was an honorable man."

"I can't—"

She stepped closer. Her perfume captured the fauna of a spring garden after a heavy rain. Candy placed her tiny hand on E.J.'s enormous paw. "Son's all I have in this world. I knew you would understand."

E.J. nodded. He wanted to tell her what she must have known no matter how much she deluded herself. B.B. possessed no honorable trait. On the contrary, every time B.B. had an opportunity for good, he searched out an opportunity to profit from wickedness.

A woman wearing a funeral service uniform pantsuit appeared and escorted Candy from E.J.'s side. The service would start soon. E.J. crumbled the speech notes in his hand. After throwing them into a wastebasket, he walked to the door slammed by the hot, thick air.

E.J. looked past the throng of funeral goers to the setting sun. In theory, a good idea trying to catch the point when the heat of the day dissipated. However, the balminess failed to subside. The act of walking the field in the dark suit caused him to remove a straw hat heavy around the band with soaking sweat. Once he reached the dais, E.J. took his seat next to Lt. Colonel Fenton. Who came up with this arrangement?

On his far right, a preacher started the service with an invocation. Then Fenton rose, placing his white Stetson on his head only to remove it within steps. Observing the entire stadium, his focus centered on the group of television cameras.

The program indicated Fenton introduces Speaker of the House Larence Kutnick. E.J. knew the stage would prove irresistible to Fenton. In addition to the over-the-top praise for the speaker, Fenton shared his recollections of Sheriff B.B. None of the remembrances hinted at the truth.

Kutnick rose, reaching the podium in a quick series of steps. Unfolding his reading glasses, he turned to face Candy and Son. A crowd of somber people punctuated by uniforms filled the bleachers. He preached a short sermon on Isaiah chapter six, verses eight through thirteen.

The traditional calling for law enforcement—*Whom shall I send* followed by *Send me Lord*. E.J. sat recalling Kutnick's oratory. Before taking the bench, the man had been the kind of lawyer folks walked past the movie theater to see argue a case. E.J. wished Kutnick would continue. The speaker had regularly conducted eulogies from the time he served as judge.

Were there a desperate battle calling for the faithful to march into a steely curtain of gunfire then Kutnick would inspire the troops. E.J. would have preferred taking B.B.'s hat and gun out of the coffin and running into the night, shooting bad guys to facing the stained oak of a lectern podium. Why would he face an army, yet a speech made his fingers tremble?

"I have the great privilege of introducing someone who embodies the highest measure of this awesome calling. To commemorate our glorious hero, Sheriff Benjamin Berryhill, I give you legendary lawman, Ranger E.J. Kane."

E.J. nearly stumbled rising from the carpet-covered folding chair on the platform. One boot stubbed the back of the other. Kutnick's flattery had caught him off guard. A deep breath inflated his lungs with the oven-dry summer air.

Standing before the microphone made the sea of people appear even more vast. They all waited for some words of wisdom to explain why a convicted murderer had been provided an opportunity to reassemble his racist army and take the life of their hometown hero. There is no question that many were familiar with Sheriff B.B. as a disgrace to the badge, yet they would never acknowledge it today.

Probably most of them thought E.J. had killed Sheriff B.B. There had to be some who came secretly hoping to hear him admit it or make an implied admission. The others expected lightning to strike E.J. when he delivered the obligatory praise of the deceased.

E.J. avoided surveying the crowd because it made him dizzy. Seated in the first row beneath the flatbed trailer serving as a stage, he spotted Candy. Son had his big arm around his mother's shoulder, ready to pull her closer if necessary.

Candy's eyes, red from crying, held back more tears. He remembered the kindnesses she extended to him in grade school. Never remembering his pencil or tablet, she extended him her extras. The sainted Candy probably garnered more votes for Sheriff B.B. than the corrupt favors he extended to those he called friend. If E.J. had the ability to alleviate her suffering, then it was his responsibility to do so.

E.J. forced himself to speak the words. "Benjamin Butler Berryhill was a hard man..."

Chapter Forty

Know I'm Coming for You

"Benjamin Butler Berryhill was a hard man. He kept the peace with an iron fist. Old-time knocking heads because it was the way he learned to keep order. More than once, I ended up on the wrong side of what B.B. considered right. For a long time, I thought he was a cruel man. I realize now I was wrong."

E.J. swallowed hard and turned his gaze back to Candy. "He wasn't a cruel man at all. B.B. taught me the difference between a hard man and a cruel man. A cruel man knows no love in his heart, his family, his friends. Inability to accept and return love keeps a cruel man from appreciating it in anyone, or even witnessing it. Cruelty motivates and begets cruelty, consuming everything within and outside of the person. A pathetic and harsh existence is the inevitable result."

The weight of the crowd's eyes nearly forced him back. Several thousand people watched him. All waiting for him to say something.

E.J. looked back to Candy. Her lowered eyes red from crying. She peered up and met his gaze. Women crying pulled at E.J. like nothing

else. Struggling against the overwhelming sense of hopelessness engulfing him, E.J. raised his head in a feeble attempt to pray for words. He
needed something to ease her pain.

While swinging back and digging the heels of his boots into the
carpeted floor of the big trailer, he looked again at the early night sky
above the stadium lighting. E.J. fought to avoid the pull of his own
mother's memory. He recalled her cool hand turning back a child's
warm tears. The edges of his eyes burned with water because she
poured tears instilling within him the helpless, hopeless feeling of a
child incapable of protecting those he loved. Son must be suffering a
like pain.

"Can be difficult to determine the difference between a hard man
and a cruel man. Battling desperately against perceived enemies, they
both strike powerful blows, destroying everything in their wake. Except, except...

"The hard people are forged solid in the crucible of life, making
them capable of all the world requires of them to protect those they
love. It was solely through death that I was able to genuinely comprehend the connection B.B. and I shared. His death provided the opportunity to witness the humanity within Benjamin Butler Berryhill.

"I lost what seemed like the world, my son. Lost him because he
chose a path honoring his father, honoring his mother, and his country. It was not fair. It wasn't right. I couldn't fix it. I couldn't mitigate
the consequence for the people I loved, the people God entrusted me
to protect. Made me hard, cold, capable of things I never saw within
myself.

"When my remaining child suffered, then I discovered I could justify anything in the name of protecting what I loved. I lashed out in
ways inconsistent with the values of my youth, my people, my home,
and the faith in which I was raised. It's like an abyss. Once crossed,

the way back disappears into the ether. To view your own image so far from who you were that you can't appreciate the difference is indescribable."

Strawberry hair drew him to Rebecca on the last row of folding chairs behind B.B. and Candy's family. "Capable of justifying killing, killing them all without thought to the morality of it."

Rebecca, teary faced, looked down.

E.J. drew a breath in another long pause. "You see, B.B. brought me back. B.B. didn't kill them all. I wish he had. Maybe I could have brought him home to Candy and Son."

E.J. waited until Candy's gaze met his before continuing. "B.B. had to draw a hard line. On one side, life, on the other, death, his own death. He died far more noble than simply fighting the evil surrounding us every day in this world. No, B.B. backed down the devil, consuming all of us from within. A wickedness so dark and constantly closing on us all. We can't help but take it in until we find it has blighted our soul.

"B.B. feared for the safety of others, though I didn't understand why. B.B. had no more weapons left to finish the fight. I can't identify the threat because he told me nothing of it. All I know is he had convinced himself he had to protect another. I faced loss when my son..."

Stopping to end the cracking he heard in his voice, E.J. drew a long breath broadcast by the sound system. "At Konner's service, I quoted John fifteen thirteen about the power of sacrificial love. B.B. wasn't cruel. Wickedness didn't motivate B.B. The hardness B.B. showed the world. A hardness he deemed necessary to protect what he loved—his child, his wife, the community he swore to protect.

"We didn't always see eye to eye on how to protect those we served, we loved. I didn't understand why he had to sacrifice himself. Evil knows no limits, forcing hard men, lawmen and women to hold fast. Not knowing if the threat is behind or in front of us, nor all the sources and extent of inequity and depravity in the world, we have to draw a hard line, prepared to fight ahead or behind us. My grandmother called it covering the ground we stand on.

"I can't say he lived his life like a saint, though I can attest in those ultimate moments B.B. sacrificed his life for another. Greatest death a man can meet. He battled back the lesser nature within him. Takes far more courage than fighting back an army we can see."

He tried envisioning the discarded notes in his mind's eye. None of the scribbles on E.J.'s note pages made much sense to him. He had left any prepared remarks long ago and his eyes stung, fighting the overwhelming memory of Konner.

Then he envisioned B.B. sliding from the grave marker and the rope catching taut. "I can see B.B. standing strong, turning back evil. An evil, battling to consume the heart I never realized B.B. had. A heart for his wife and child." For the first time, Son's eyes locked with E.J.'s. Son must never find out his father died to protect his identity from Burton and his minions. More than Burton in that moment, B.B. had feared a far more powerful monster possibly hiding in plain view.

E.J. stared into the crowd. Was the person B.B. had been afraid of now looking back at him? He should apply pressure to force the adversary into the open, yet not enough to endanger anyone except himself. Understanding that it was possible for anyone to be involved caused frustration to consume him.

"You can't hide any longer. Mark my words. Hear my promise to a dying man. I'm a hard man, too, and I'm coming for you."

Chapter Forty-One

Objection

"Why not call me?" E.J. meant to whisper. Glares from the opposing counsel's table and the first row of the gallery proved he failed.

Rebecca's stony stare proved E.J.'s position was untenable. Not only did the world consider him crooked, but he had unwittingly decimated Cooper's reputation.

E.J. studied the room full of people, including reporters. News camera operators filled the jury box. He lowered his head and slinked back into the gallery.

There was no chance to really probe Rebecca on why she had hurriedly left after their night together. Her earlier answer had been too short a quip falling back on circular reasoning. You don't want me to think we're together doesn't explain why we're not together.

Continuously replaying the night repeatedly provided no clues as to what drove her away. In reality, the night turned out perfectly. Could their night together have been too perfect? Did renewing their intimacy scare her somehow? Is that what she meant?

Turning to stare at her now, another question arose. How close they had seemed and now how could they be more distant? E.J. would have preferred her cursing to the silence. Her eyes had appeared so cold, holding neither love nor hate. Now from behind he saw them only in his memory and they clashed with her fiery reddish-blonde hair.

E.J. tried to blend into the gallery, stepping behind a reporter. Positioned on the edge in the rear, he became conscious of a presence fixedly gazing at him, as certain as if he had heard the words "dear friend."

Despite his best efforts, E.J. couldn't tear himself away from the poisonous path. He couldn't concentrate on any other subject. As if his mind were tied to a railcar and the steel wheels forced him down the track.

Why had Rebecca left after their night presented only the most recent installment in a never-ending torment? How did they end up so far apart from each other? He remembered so many couples like the Blakes. So many parents seemed to have tried to find what comfort possible in each other, though some had separated. Did cracks exist in the foundation of their marriage before Konner's death?

Once the funeral was over, Rebecca completely dedicated herself to her work. For reasons E.J. never understood, she mounted a freedom of information campaign telling anyone who would listen the full truth about Konner's death had been kept from her. No matter how many documents were provided, she complained to everyone. She demanded more, insisting something must be hidden. As if there must be some grand conspiracy to merit her son's life. Whereas E.J. had withdrawn from everything and everyone.

Rebecca's voice rose in argument, startling E.J. back into the moment. "I get no discovery, so how can I foresee every rebuttal witness? They are the ones proving up the purported actual innocence," yelled Rebecca.

"Your Honor, the prosecutor's theatrics hide the worst form of trial by ambush. The great and majestic, all-powerful state of Texas can't provide a witness list?" objected three-piece blue suit.

"At least let me present a bill for the appellate record and then you can make a ruling with all the evidence. The witness must testify either way," said Rebecca.

The judge raised an open hand in an exasperated fashion to Rebecca. "Call him then."

"State calls Conrad Beams."

The crowd grew quiet, looking at the door. Even the air conditioning kicked off for the first time of the day. Into the open door walked a young, overweight man donning a maroon sports coat over a white shirt, black slacks, and tie. Rebecca's longtime investigator, Jacobs, stepped behind him and continued to the gallery while Beams took the oath.

"Please state your name," said Rebecca.

"Objection, Your Honor."

"She has a right to make a bill for what the testimony would be, if admitted," said the judge.

"Simply asking to take the witness on *voir dire*, Your Honor," said three-piece blue suit.

"Alright," said the judge.

"Why?" asked Rebecca.

"Because you called him, and no one knows why?" said the judge.

"Mr. Beams, how are you connected to this case?" asked three-piece blue suit.

The witness smirked and struck out in a loud voice. "I'm not."

"I renew my objection."

"Permit me a question." Rebecca's terse words were more admonition than inquiry, and she didn't wait for an acknowledgment. "Where do you work?"

"Garland Lab."

"Garland DPS Lab. The lab where the DNA testing in this case was performed." His smug demeanor collapsed. Conrad wiped his pudgy face with the sleeve of his suit coat.

"I didn't work on this case," said Conrad.

"Not the question I asked, Mr. Beams. I asked you whether it was the same lab and the answer is yes, isn't it?" said Rebecca.

"Yes," admitted Conrad Beams.

"And you had access to the evidence in this case, didn't you?" asked Rebecca.

Three-piece blue suit and his entire gaggle of lawyers erupted onto their feet like a choir singing the same word. "Objection!"

Chapter Forty-Two

She Died

"**Y**our Honor, can't you see what she is doing? They have found some putz willing to take the fall and say he contaminated or transferred or something," yelled three-piece blue suit.

Conrad Beams stared stone-faced, looking ahead.

"Judge, two minutes ago it was the worst 'trial by ambush' yet now counsel knows exactly what I'm offering. Please admonish counsel to stop with these spurious objections," said Rebecca. E.J. drew strength from the tone of her voice. She relished the moment.

"Perhaps she makes her bill, so we can move forward, Mr. Weatherstine," said the judge.

"Mr. Beams, do you have any other names you use?"

Conrad Beam's expression looked as if he suffered from nausea.

"Let me help you, Mr. Beams. You go by 'Dudlydogood' on an adult dating site, don't you?"

"What?" asked Conrad Beams.

Rebecca raised her voice, taking any levity out of it. "It's more for hookups than dating and you had fifteen supposedly female profiles with whom you regularly chatted, correct?"

"*Supposedly*?" Conrad Beams swung his head back, displaying the same unpleasant countenance.

"One of the two took a particular interest in you. Recall someone using the tag line, 'Bored living in the middle of nowhere.' She told you she was a schoolteacher, right?" asked Rebecca.

A red-faced Conrad Beams looked away.

"Do you recall Melinda?" asked Rebecca.

Conrad Beams turned back, casting a stare of absolute hatred at Rebecca. He rubbed his reddening eyes.

"You even went on a real date with Melinda. She couldn't teach high school because she attended high school, correct?"

The witness closed his arms over his chest, ignoring the question.

"She wasn't as attractive or as old as SexKitty01, was she?"

Conrad continued to look away. The judge leaned forward.

"Do you not remember SexKitty01? Perhaps a photo will help your memory. May I approach the witness, Your Honor?"

The judge motioned.

Rebecca stepped forward, holding a glossy sheet of paper she held where only the witness could view it. Holding the photo before a trembling Conrad Beams, he reached for it then pulled back vibrating fingers.

"You know her as SexKitty01. She told you her name was Kitty Karlson. And sometimes, it was, wasn't it?" asked Rebecca.

"What do you mean, 'sometimes'?" asked Conrad.

Conrad Beams looked from the light glinting off the vulgar picture to his shoes. He sank lower in the chair, nearly sliding into a crouch.

"Sometimes the IP address matches a Kitty Karlson living at a residence in Huntington, sometimes a cellular number which couldn't be fixed to a permanent location?" asked Rebecca.

"I don't understand?" said Conrad Beams.

"Stationary, fixed, permanent as opposed to something like a mobile hot spot linking back to Houston, but with no concrete positioning of its whereabouts. No way for anyone to trace it down to a certain place?"

"You're trying to trick me. She used the app on her phone?" For a moment, Conrad Beams leaned up in his chair before adjusting to continue his slide.

"Not many people live in Huntington and work in Houston, do they? Possible yet not likely, right?" Rebecca shrugged her shoulders, walking back to the prosecution table.

"No," said Conrad.

Rebecca paused, letting every eye fall on her. "Here is what is interesting. In Ms. Karlson's phone records, there are a huge number of calls from her cellular number to a number billed to the Huntington address owned by Kitty's husband, a high-ranking officer in an Aryan gang. Do you know where that phone number leads?"

"Question calls for speculation and it's irrelevant. How would he have knowledge of who might reach out to whom?" said three-piece blue suit.

"I mean, what numbers other than your own had been called and texted from this phone associated with the high-ranking lieutenant, though likely used by someone else?" Rebecca stared at Burton.

Conrad Beams nodded in agreement that he was unaware.

"Judge, bill or not, you have to stop this absurd departure from jurisprudence," said three-piece blue suit.

Rebecca lifted a document as if she were reading from it. "One such number is the personal cell phone number of an accomplished Houston trial lawyer, one Ray Weatherstine—"

"Objection, this is an impermissible interference with the attorney-client relationship, a violation of the fifth and sixth amendments and more Constitutional provisions than I can articulate without review." Three-piece blue suit slammed his fist into the counsel table. Law volumes and laptops bounced in response.

"I have reviewed no content, counselor. I'm using the register of the numbers only to identify your client, G.H. Burton, masquerading both online and by phone as Kitty Karlson." She made a production of straining to lift a banker's box from under the desk to on top of it. "Numbers tying to numbers. We tracked his use of phones, including cell tower triangulation, even approved Internet usage, though not all approved." She stared at three-piece blue suit to show she had anticipated his objection. "It leads to the cellular phone and hot spot establishing G.H. Burton as SexKitty01."

"Am I witnessing supposed evidence before a tribunal reduced to the equivalent of clickbait? This ignorance amounts to checkout line tabloid headlines." Three-piece blue suit stepped into the well of the courtroom as he yelled at the bench.

"I object to counsel's presenting a purported objection of low-rent hyperbole masquerading as an objection," said Rebecca.

The judge opened her mouth until three-piece blue suit raised an open hand. "Please, Your Honor, not only is a prison inmate gaining unfettered access to cell phones and adult Internet sites, but he is cat-fishing Mr. Conrad Beams all the while he is scoring in the intellectual disabled range on the IQ test given by professional psychologists." He swung his arms high, then turned to the gallery. "I mean really?"

The crowd launched into chants of "liar" and "free Burton," cascading in loud sound waves, banging the walls.

The judge's gavel slammed, flipping the pedestal. She hammered onto the bench until the noise subsided. Raising her hands and turning to three-piece blue suit, she stopped then paused for a long moment. "Overruled, you may have a running objection on the issue."

"Not satisfactory, Your Honor," said three-piece blue suit.

"Not satisfactory. I'm certain all those bank boxes stacked under the prosecution table are cell phone records showing numbers calling and texting other numbers. Probably raw data for maps of towers triangulating phone signals showing us the location of each phone when the calls were made. I expect she has two weeks of investigators and communications company records custodians and the DPS experts who make triangulation maps. Do you really want to sit through all of it or let her ask this witness her questions?"

"You're assuming this sea of paper is genuine? We've proven E.J. Kane creates false evidence out of whole cloth," said three-piece blue suit.

"E.J. Kane did not know why the investigation developed this way, nor did he ever work on any part of the case leading to the discovery of Conrad Beams." Rebecca stared into the gallery finding E.J.

E.J. met her gaze. A clever strategy to keep him in the dark. His heart lifted. Had she avoided him for strategic reasons? Did she regret isolating him or were the courtroom theatrics timed with the cold shoulder all a coincidence?

Wasn't he overlooking the more important fact? Rebecca's theory shredded the whole writ. Further, she had proven the truth by substantiating the accounts he and Cooper had related from the Big Thicket.

"You appear not surprised, Mr. Beams, because you aren't surprised, though I suspect it astounded you when you first discovered SexKitty01 was more than one person, right?" asked Rebecca.

Conrad Beams's sad expression transformed into a stronger demeanor than his prior teary countenance. "I don't understand."

"The female sex kitten you lusted after turned out to be a white supremacist gang leading capital murderer, at least some of the time, correct?" asked Rebecca.

Conrad Beams tilted his head to the wall. "I didn't know."

"Didn't know what?" asked Rebecca.

"I didn't know any of it. All stupid, complicated, ignorant, stupid, and crazy. All of it." Tears poured down Conrad Beams's cheeks. He yelled, "I didn't kill anybody."

"What happened to sweet little schoolgirl, Melinda?" asked Rebecca.

Conrad Beams whispered, "She died."

Rebecca leaped toward the witness stand. "She didn't die. She got murdered, right?"

"I didn't do it," cried Conrad Beams.

"No, but you're responsible, correct?"

Chapter Forty-Three

Gone

"Yes. Yes," screamed Conrad Beams.

Three-piece blue suit jumped to his feet. "Your Honor, Mr. Beams should have counsel. She has him admitting to felonious conduct."

"Do you have an attorney, Mr. Beams?" asked the judge.

"I talked to one, but I didn't have enough money for the retainer," said Beams.

"You need one now. I will appoint you an attorney." She turned to the bailiff. "Let him wait in the law library."

The judge called a recess. E.J. pressed his way to Rebecca. After forging a path through the throng of excited trial goers, he found her in the hallway. He yelled above the crowd, "Why didn't you trust me to tell me any of this? So this kid monkeyed with the results—"

Rebecca ignored him, taking a double step into the district clerk's office. She nodded to the clerks. E.J. followed her into a small conference room, where she shut the door. "I didn't tell you because I still wasn't certain, plus you see how much more effective to keep you out of the loop."

"Okay, you just sneak out in the night because you don't think I can keep a secret and it looks better." E.J. had rehearsed how to raise the subject. He wanted to sound cool and aloof, so she wouldn't be aware he put too much hope into the meaning of one night. Wouldn't it be better to appear perturbed over the insult to his professionalism than the stabbing wound to his heart?

"No, I departed because I understood that you lacked the capacity to comprehend that sex has no meaning. We're not together. I'm not your wife. You can't understand. We're divorced."

"I know but...We could work. I mean, I'm willing to go see any counselor you want to see. I'll do anything." Nothing sounded like he wanted it. E.J. suspected he looked crestfallen. He had called down this thunder, yet it didn't make it any easier to accept.

"This is what I mean. One night and you assume we'll live happily ever after," Rebecca remarked.

E.J. looked up toward her bright eyes and flaming hair. Her demeanor conveyed a finality he found disturbing. She stood so close, yet the distance between them extended farther than ever. How was it possible for them to be together just a few nights ago? It might as well have been a million years in the past.

"If you want to ask me about the case, I'll answer, otherwise let me go back over my notes before we start again," said Rebecca.

E.J. spilled his questions in quick succession. "I don't understand any of it. Did Burton pay the kid off? Is this the same Melinda as the unsolved Son worked on? How does it tie in? For the moment, you're killing them, but have you really proven anything?" He literally stood on his feet a little straighter. Hurling questions like a detective had regained his footing.

"Like you and I discussed, DNA tells us nothing except there is a chain where one item came into contact with the skin cells from a person or one object came into contact with another object which in turn came into contact with the skin cells of a person or we could have an even more attenuated chain."

"Right," said E.J.

"An attenuated chain where only the swabs taken from the object come into contact with another object or even a swab taken from the other object. I had an expert hypothesize the only way to be certain of the result was to contaminate the swabs after the technician created them. See, I'm figuring if we retested the knife, we wouldn't get the same result. One of many questions I still have." Rebecca leaned against a wall of files. "How does DPS afford so many scientists? I mean, math and sciences are the degrees that pay."

"They hire young people like Conrad Beams," said E.J.

"Young people leaving their little sheltered lives for new communities, few with spouses or kids. For the first time in their life, they are on their own with no one watching them. A real chance to howl," said Rebecca.

Did she have it figured out or was this all some elaborate hunch? It wasn't like Rebecca to display such scattered reasoning. "What do you know?" E.J. asked.

"I'm certain G.H. Burton pretended to be SexKitty01 part of the time. Likewise, Kitty Karlson also SexKitty01 used the name to meet and plan liaisons with Conrad Beams at hotels where he used his credit card to pay for the rooms. Woman is a porn star and biker model. Way out of Beam's league. Her husband, Lewis Karlson, aka Timber Wolf, served as Burton's chief lieutenant. We suspect you probably killed him in the Big Thicket."

"But they never found any bodies out there?" asked E.J.

"No, but all of the sudden he fell off the grid," said Rebecca.

"So, this Wolf leaned on Beams for courting his wife?" asked E.J.

"Not courting," Rebecca exuded a small grin. "Low-end hookups courtesy of a website for people who share the same sexual interest and fetishes. I know Conrad Beams found Kitty Karlson and our high school student turned pretend teacher, Melinda Blake. Of course, under the law, it doesn't matter if Melinda chased him. Anyone having sex with an under seventeen-year-old commits sexual assault by Texas law. I'm also certain someone murdered Melinda Blake."

"So, you think Burton pulled Beams into the deep end? Murdered Melinda Blake using the Karlsons?" asked E.J.

Rebecca leaned her head back and rolled her eyes. "No. I'm questioning what drives a man who successfully clears a polygraph-enforced background check to put everything at stake to aid an unknown murderer? Underage girl is good. Law doesn't care if she told him she was twenty-five. Spends the rest of his life as a registered sex offender even if he doesn't go to the pen. Pretty good, right?" asked Rebecca.

"You're thinking it was enough, but not for an ask this big. Sexual assault wasn't enough. Murder on top of it, right? Then a last step to pull out all the stops," said E.J.

"Right, why frame Beams for murder when you can frame him for capital murder?" asked Rebecca.

"Stakes can't get higher than murder in the commission of the sexual assault of a child. Burton unlocks the lab door with Beams as the key," said E.J.

"In hindsight, we can see it all hatched. DNA testing and actual innocence claims have exploded since Burton's trial ended. He hires Weatherstine who inadvertently runs his mouth, explaining to a guy he believes is unable to grasp his reasoning on how to overturn an old conviction. Burton formulates a plan. His top thug, and the thug's wife troll for and find a pigeon, our Mr. Beams. Easy enough to see online where Beams has found a girlfriend, Melinda—"

"Though he keeps playing around, enter SexKitty01," said E.J.

"Then, when the girlfriend gets killed, she has the oddest DNA result from the rape kit. It puzzled Son and I'm not sure you see it," said Rebecca.

"The mixture? Three contributors?" asked E.J.

"My investigator got Beams's trash. Private lab—"

"Conrad Beams is the male contributor?" said E.J.

'Rebecca nodded. "Bingo. Left only one unknown until we figured out the many locations of SexKitty01."

"This Kitty Karlson, the wife of Burton's number one henchman?" asked E.J.

"The female DNA traces to Kitty Karlson. You remember my investigator, Jacobs? He dubbed her Ms. Kitty like in *Gunsmoke*. He followed her round a fitness center until she used a towel," said Rebecca.

"What do you and Jacobs think? I'm still not understanding how the lab found her skin cells in the rape kit," said E.J.

"You remember our surprise when we discovered the jurors who hung up our first child sexual assault case were women because they were certain a hymen couldn't be intact? Grown women with odd notions about female anatomy aren't uncommon," said Rebecca.

E.J.'s mind flashed to the time of the trial she referenced and the heartbreak of watching the little girl sent home with her rapist.

"The goal was framing Beams. She likely followed Beams and killed Melinda after he left, yet how could she be certain they had sex, or a condom hadn't been used? Kitty Karlson made certain there would be trauma she would assume was evidence of rape," said Rebecca.

"Why fentanyl?" asked E.J.

"Remember, the legislature made an additional definition of murder, providing the drug to an overdose victim. Think about it. The ambiguity of a possible suicide or accidental overdose would keep anyone from digging too deep—"

"Until and unless Burton wanted them to dig," said E.J.

"She murders the girl right after Beams and Melinda had a liaison. Whether at that point or later, Kitty spells it out for Beams and gives him his marching orders. They had to have Beams's role planned out beforehand," said Rebecca.

"It would be too messy to contaminate the knife with anything but unknown DNA," said E.J.

"Right, because they needed a profile, but nothing we can ever disprove like an unforeseen alibi from a known individual. Which is prone to occur when framing someone. No, unknown DNA is best and what works better than sub-Saharan African. Stands the entire theory of the motive on its head and precludes Burton being connected as an accomplice. Racist don't conspire with minorities," said Rebecca.

Reaper came to E.J.'s mind, though he decided it was too strange to explain. "Most important is with unknown DNA from an unknown suspect. There is no way to disprove the alternate perpetrator hypothesis, thereby Burton is always absolved," said E.J.

Warm bile regurgitated in the back of his throat. In thirty years, there had been a lot of kicks in the teeth. The callous indifference to life sometimes still took him down like a kidney punch. "It's too perfect. Every angle covered," said E.J.

"Exactly how you would describe Burton. We know the man runs a racist crime syndicate from the penitentiary," said Rebecca.

Ellie Ruth and Steven Blake conceived a baby, nurtured the child for sixteen years only to have her reduced to a slab of meat. Would the mire of humanity's wickedness have overcome E.J. physically prior to Konner's death?

He and Rebecca had shared Konner from conception to death. How could parents sharing so much over the years grow so distant?

E.J. watched Rebecca peruse her notes. It made no sense how she could turn her passions on and off? At Rex's Ashe's condo, her fire had enveloped E.J. with warmth, yet now all had turned to the coldest lake of ice.

"He's gone." The voice yelled from the hallway. E.J. couldn't be sure he heard the words. He stepped from the room while the speaker repeated himself.

"He's gone," yelled Son.

E.J. asked, "What are you saying?"

"Conrad Beams. He jumped from the law library window." Son shook his head in astonishment. "I didn't even think those windows opened."

Chapter Forty-Four

Ya Basta

E.J. followed Son into the law library. The musty smell of leather volumes further weighed down the humid air, lethargically moving from the open window. His peripheral vision caught one of the dozen or so grand chimneys transforming the Romanesque brick into a castle of justice facing the main street. "Would have been easy for Beams to shimmy down the side of the chimney even if he jumped. It's probably not fifteen feet."

"You expect he was stupid enough to go to home?" asked Son.

"Lives off Grande in Tyler," said Rebecca.

"Got to figure he wouldn't have come here today if he had a plan to run," said E.J.

"No. Likely curious, then discovered enough to surmise we were on to him. Panicked, don't you figure?" said Rebecca.

"You ruined his whole day," said Son.

"I worry he is suicidal. I wouldn't want Tyler PD to turn out a SWAT team or half a dozen patrol cars on his house. Might push him right over the edge," said E.J.

"If we run code, then we won't be far behind. Ms. Rebecca, if you could stall reporting it to the judge. We might can get over there before it blows up," said Son.

"Stall?" Puzzlement turned to fire in Rebecca's eyes.

"We'll get him back." E.J. turned to Son. "Get a unit. I'll meet you out back," said E.J.

About a block from the courthouse, Son's lights and siren erupted on the Tahoe. He had already laid the accelerator to the floor.

Despite being no stranger to high speed, E.J. fought the urge to tell Son to slow. He vastly preferred driving at high speed to riding in the passenger seat. Although Son drove with the same proficiency that he fired a weapon. E.J. hated to see the world flash by at speed without his hands on the wheel.

Wouldn't they catch Conrad Beams at this rate? The sudden halt propelled E.J. forward, causing the seat belt to tighten across him. Son slowed in an intersection, then took off. They repeated the process at all traffic control devices and the road was wide open on the highway.

E.J. knew they were somewhere south of the loop in Tyler when Son turned off the lights and siren.

Son yanked the wheel hard, pulling into the parking lot of a series of white steel-roofed apartments accented by green balconies. They both studied the numbers on buildings, looking the same from one large complex to the next before parking in the adjacent lot to one designated number five.

"You take the door. I'll jump onto the patio," said Son.

E.J. frowned, then smirked. "Yeah, you do that." Pride made him take the stairs two at a time, crunching onto his bad knee. He had no idea what vehicle Conrad Beams drove, so no way to know if he was there. Why didn't they run a twenty-eight on the way and find out? It occurred to him doing so would have resulted in discovery of Beams's disappearance.

Should he slam his shoulder on the door or crush his leg bone into the thigh bone? E.J. raised his boot high, stepping into the knob and shattering the jamb. The door swung free. Sharp, shooting pain crushed him, making him buckle at the waist, yet he froze. "Son, don't come in here."

Seated in his recliner, Conrad Beams's head sat perched on the chrome barrel of a revolver. E.J. recognized the stainless Smith & Wesson as a K-frame, likely 357. His vision lowered to the cylinder and the cocked hammer.

Through tears and slobber, Conrad Beams announced his opinion of Rebecca in rank terms. Surely the kid had no idea he was maligning E.J.'s former bride, and E.J. decided telling him made no sense. "Lawyers trying to win cases don't always consider the lives they damage."

"Enough is enough. I couldn't do anything. They told me it was capital murder with my DNA in the rape kit." Conrad Beams's index finger slid inside the trigger guard.

E.J. saw a picture of Conrad Beams with what must have been his parents and brother on the wall. He swung his gaze back to a sniveling, crying young man.

The kid didn't want to die, right? E.J. recalled the last suicide he had seen. Like most hanging victims, the young woman had clawed at her neck, trying to release the ligature. He was certain that they always regretted the decision.

Besides, if Beams really wanted to die, wouldn't he have shot himself already? "Least you got enough sense to blow your head off."

Beams's eyebrows raised, and he turned his head toward E.J.

"Seen a few hang themselves. Pitiful critters. Always scratch marks round the neck." E.J. used his hand to point at his own. "Figure they get regrets, start trying to get whatever they used for a noose open enough for one more breath. Torment their momma. Same with the jumpers. Can hear 'em begging before they splat."

Beams stopped crying and nodded.

"Put the gun under your chin, not on the side of your head. Seen too many from the side live. Not pretty. Folks like vegetables lying around with open shunts draining their brain juice."

"You thought about it yourself." Beams raised his trembling free hand.

E.J.'s throat passed a little macabre chuckle. "I ought to have. My son is dead. Wife and daughter blame me. Oh, my daughter is committing suicide the long way. She pumps poison through her veins. And now she's torturing the baby in her womb with the same smack killing her."

"Sounds like I should shoot you," said Beams.

"'Preciate it if you didn't. I'm not better than you. Some would say worse. I just never thought about suicide. Might be I seen way too much death. Life is a precarious thing. Consider it all so delicate. Whether you believe in God or some cosmic accident slamming microscopic particles together in absolute harmony, the whole thing is crazy. Tomorrow amounts to some kind of gift. We got no right to claim."

"Tomorrow my family will know I'm a pervert. A coward. They killed a girl to get me to doctor the swabs. Everybody knows. I can't live with the guilt. Can't do it. Enough is enough," said Beams.

"*Ya basta.* What my Mexican friends say. Always seemed to me they didn't mean enough is enough. What they meant was any was too much. Been chewing on it for a long time. I don't have the answers, Mr. Beams." E.J. took a deep breath.

Beams did likewise. E.J. took it as a good sign. Perhaps he reached the young man.

"All I can tell you is people got to turn from misery and wickedness or it'll swallow 'em whole." E.J. extended his hand. "People got to step toward tomorrow."

E.J.'s open hand mesmerized Beams. Beams's whole body shuddered. E.J. leaped forward, snapping his right hand into the back of the revolver. The webbing between his thumb and finger caught the hammer, pulling the barrel off the target.

His left hand hit the pistol's handle and Beams's wrist. The gun exploded, sending bullet, gas, and soot upward. E.J.'s ears popped, no longer processing the deafening noise.

Son kicked through the patio sliding glass door, sending shards of glass bounding into the room. In the wake of the pieces, he moved closer to the chair where E.J. stood intertwined with Beams.

E.J. had the weapon. Conrad Beams slumped onto the carpet. All three inhaled the firearm's soot deep into their lungs, shocked by the event.

Beams rolled on the floor, relinquishing any semblance of composure. "I made it worse."

"No." E.J. shook his hand in the air, dulling the pain the hammer inflicted. "Son, tell the neighbors it was a mistake. The gun never should have gone off." E.J. looked back to Beams. "You'll go back and tell what you did with the DNA and why. Son will keep you in protective custody in the jail tonight. In the morning, we will all drive to your family. Which is where?"

"McKinney."

"We will be there with you when you see your family. I can't brush over what you did like this accidental discharge today, but I can sure tell your folks it took courage to come forward," said E.J.

Son's face resembled that of someone who had experienced an offensive scent. E.J. realized Beams had soiled himself. "We got time for you to get a shower and get cleaned up," said Son.

Beams leaned against the arm of the recliner to stand up. He made a wobbly production of walking to the front door.

Son stepped toward the door. They could hear the neighbors making a commotion outside. Son turned back to E.J. "Can we trust him not to ice himself?"

"Probably," said E.J.

"Think Burton's people will try to kill him."

"Definitely," said E.J.

Chapter Forty-Five

The World According to Sharla

The golden circles opened against the blue background. Sharla's heart pounded, broadcasting through her skull. She redoubled her efforts to ignore the spheres. They weren't real. Nothing was real.

The air had a hot flavor. It took maximum effort to breathe. Repeatedly pushing the rings off of her, Sharla's heart pounded like a drummer playing without rhythm. What if she turned her back to the circles? It was possible she might ignore them. They weren't real.

She sensed their tiny mouths on the back of her neck, opening to bite shards out of her. Their jagged teeth dug and stabbed into her skin before sawing away at her flesh. Her entire back cringed at the first of many continual painful spasms. Nearly leaping out of the bed, Sharla kicked the comforter farther away. If she possessed a knife, she would be able to stab at the tiny, animated objects. What if they were attached to the people waiting for her in the mattress? There must be people inside. It only made sense. Their mouths were chomping at her.

Sharla shivered from a piercing, high-pitched scream. Were the people in the mattress yelling at her? Someone would hear them and come. Even so, she couldn't tell anyone what really happened. No one would ever believe her. They would think she was high, but being high had nothing to do with it.

The scent coming from her takeout container of kung pao chicken on the nightstand made her stomach convulse. How long ago had she eaten it? She had to act before the people in the mattress read her thoughts again. The more she hesitated, the more likely her body would be chewed or worse. Sharla flung her hand at the plastic dish, taking the plastic fork like a weapon.

While plunging the plastic utensil into the mattress, she stabbed with all her strength. The malleable object contorted before snapping into pieces, sliding the wielder of the weapon off balance.

The hard floor came up to slap Sharla in the face. She reached to her nose, touching the sticky, warm blood.

Unibrow stepped into the room. "I could hear you on the other end of the hall, shrieking and yelling. What's wrong with you, fool?"

"Go away." Sharla's voice turned shriller and higher pitched. Her throat scratched and burned.

Unibrow battled to make eye contact with Sharla. "Look at me. Look at me. You're high."

Sharla kicked, trying to break free of the vastly bigger woman's hold. The woman pushed all her weight down on top of Sharla. Awareness came to Sharla that she couldn't breathe because Unibrow had her ribs pinned against the floor.

Unibrow's thick hand fumbled with the phone. The device dialed the number, and a voice answered. "Help. Room number eleven."

Sharla positioned her leg beneath her, using the support to exert force on the weight above her. She filled her lungs and broke free, running into the door. The flimsy wooden door bent before cracking to reveal a hollow core.

The shell of the door flung open, laying over Sharla's nose. Her senses were overwhelmed by the metallic scent and flavor of an abundance of blood, followed by a sudden onset of darkness.

"You need to remain calm. We're on the way to the hospital."

It dawned on Sharla she had asked "what" repeatedly. The world blurred in busy movements around her, and she swung her head back down. The car door opened, and the odor of garlic and fish assaulted her nose. Unibrow came into focus.

"Can you walk?" Unibrow's head moved closer then farther back and swung to the side.

"You stink," said Sharla.

Unibrow jerked her head back and stared at Sharla before pulling and pushing the girl out of the car. Sharla slid onto the asphalt. After lifting herself onto her skinned knees, she struggled to stand. The formerly white, oversized tee shirt displayed the dirt and grime of a brutal night.

Bright lights blinded Sharla, though averting her eyes led to spots appearing and floating in her peripheral vision, causing her heart to beat rapidly. She stepped over the threshold of the wide, automated metal and glass sliding doors.

People massed everywhere. She looked down at a floor filthy with muck, grime, and hundreds of steps by people from all sorts of locations and stations of life. Movement cascaded and blurred the world around her.

She tried to anchor herself by turning past two partial walls staring at the black-and-white linoleum squares. A dark plastic in faux woodgrain connected to an orange Naugahyde cushioned chair in line with many others against a glass wall. Unibrow must be trying to find the nursing station.

Sharla splayed into the chair. The vinyl against her skin and the thin nightshirt clung to the sweat soaking her. She wiped her forehead with the shoulder of her shirtsleeve, causing grit to prickle her skin. Thirst cramped her throat, drying her tongue to the point. Only the air outside her mouth in some small way satiated it. Did they even have water fountains anymore? She might have the chance to find a water cooler with a cup somewhere.

After forcing herself upward, she walked to the edge of a hall. Everything compressed into lights and sound blinking then snapping at her. Her head twisted on a swivel, trying to take in the surroundings. The world swirled in circles around her like she centered a whirlpool.

Halfway down a glass wall, she saw a huge drinking cup. The woman holding the beverage looked small and old, perhaps forty. Sharla swung sideways, losing her balance. Did anyone see her? What did it matter? Her dry tongue raked across sandpaper lips.

The red, thick plastic cup moved until the red resembled an eye staring back at Sharla. She tore the straw aside, slinging the container over her mouth.

"What's wrong with you, you freak?" The old woman yelled as she stood.

Sharla's knee turned against the ungiving arm of the chair, taking her legs away from her control. Her butt slammed into the smooth cushion, pressing it flat.

"Can somebody help this crazy girl? We need a nurse here."

Chapter Forty-Six

Tweaking Like No Tomorrow

The mass of humanity around them looked and then went back to their miseries. The low, dull hum of disparate conversations slowly bubbled throughout the room again. Sharla saw no hospital attendants in the area.

The older woman had a hand on her hip, then drew in a monstrous breath. She spoke in a softer tone. "Are you here with someone?"

Sharla studied the old lady's round face, realizing she really wasn't all that old. The woman might not be in her forties. The lady's dark eyes were pools of chocolate pudding moving clockwise in a mesmerizing fashion.

"Where is the person who brought y-o-u? You came here with someone, didn't you?" asked the woman.

As if in slow motion, the woman's mouth opened in an ever-increasing circle. The act of slowing her speech increased the hypnotic effect. Her massive lips snapped shut in front of Sharla like the jaws of a bear trap.

A brutal splash of profanity spewed like vomit from Sharla's mouth.

"Uggggh..." The woman grabbed Sharla by the arm. "Let's get you cleaned up, and then we'll try to find where you're supposed to be."

A short distance later, the door to the women's restroom swung open. Sharla leaned onto a counter of double sinks under a mirror. The room ended at an inner door past the vanity.

She forced water from the faucet to her lips, taking as much as possible. Her image stared back above the sink. "I'm hideous."

As she grabbed towels from the dispenser, the lady made an effort to remove regurgitated stomach matter from Sharla's hair. Sharla turned her head to draw fresh air, slowing the process.

Sharla cupped her hand back in the cool running water, trying to eliminate the foul taste and odor from her mouth. "I'm sorry." The face in the mirror looked sallow, like death. She had dilated pupils. How long before she didn't look high anymore? Why did she ever think she had fooled anybody?

"Are you going out for the evening or you starting to come down a little?" asked the lady.

"What?" asked Sharla.

She pulled Sharla against a small sofa on the opposite wall. "You don't fool me. From the looks of you, probably only fooling yourself anyway."

Sharla told herself the woman's earrings weren't snapping at her. "What do you mean?"

"What do I mean? You're wearing a nasty nightshirt, wondering around a hospital, tweaking like no tomorrow."

Sharla drew her hand back from behind her head. A bloody goo coated her fingernails. She reached to her neck, touching the open sore. As her gaze met the woman's eyes, she observed a piercing and knowledgeable stare. The woman's inky eyes held some knowing quality. She didn't appear like she was in the life, though. "You a user?"

"My little sister. Why I'm here," said the older woman.

This time, Sharla dug at a bloody spot on the side of her thigh. "She overdosed?"

"I wish," said the older woman.

Sharla snarled, assuming she hadn't heard right. "Huh?"

The older woman stared into Sharla's green eyes. "You know your baby will have color eyes. Always wanted a kid with colored eyes."

"What is wrong with you?" Water on the counter crawling toward the sink drew Sharla's attention.

"What kid is this?" The woman pointed at Sharla's pregnant belly.

"Huh?" said Sharla.

"What number? What number, kid?" asked the woman.

"Nothing you say makes sense." What number, kid, color eyes, and she wants to kill her little sister? All made Sharla think this was one crazy woman. The unblinking stare of her eyes reminded Sharla of the women in the documentaries who murdered their whole families. She had been nice, though, but they all started nice.

The annoyed older woman raised her tone. "Must be number one. Surprised you haven't already had it. First one comes early, real early on meth."

"I don't do drugs," snapped Sharla.

The woman cackled with laughter at the point of tears. "Baby comes before it's ready. My sister's first one didn't have his insides finished, couldn't pee like regular people. Kid has had four surgeries since then and we're back for another one."

"I'm sorry," Sharla looked at the door, hoping someone would come in and save her from the crazy woman.

"No, you're not. You can't imagine the tiny little hand of something you love suffering treatments and surgery. A little person wrapping its little fingers around yours. All the while begging you with its eyes to make the pain stop. All the while, you want to knock the nurse and doctor down so you can hold your baby."

"I'm sorry." Sharla stammered, looking for words and a way out. The room appeared dimmer now.

The woman yelled through tears, "Stop. Because if you cared, you wouldn't be wasted and pregnant. You don't know. You stupid, selfish pig."

Sharla jumped from the seat. She yanked the stainless-steel handle on the wooden door, swinging it wide. The hallway looked empty both ways.

Her hand bounced around the stainless frames of posters lining the hallways. To the right, a pair of large doors automatically opened. Momentarily confused, Sharla looked to see if she had pushed a button or stepped on some sort of mat. She became aware of the orderly's gaze on her shoulders and cringed.

"Can I help you?" asked a young man dressed in scrubs.

Sharla rubbed her running nose. She must appear dreadful. "Which way back to the ER?"

His eyes widened and hands raised. "Like five floors below us."

Chapter Forty-Seven

My Body, My Choice

"Rebecca, this is different." Sharla hadn't called her mother, mom, since Konner's death. Whereas E.J. wouldn't tolerate it whether the reference was to mother or father, the comment drew a lecture about being disrespectful.

Sharla awaited the lecture, though E.J. only stared. The small bouquet her father had brought stood on the food tray, brightening the barren white hospital room. He wasn't bad, just dumb.

"It's always different. When are you going to learn it's not," said Rebecca.

Sharla felt E.J. touch her hand. Guilt washed over her. He must have thought she had really overdosed and was going to die. Telling him she had suffered worse wouldn't help. "It is different." She looked to E.J. for validation.

Rebecca stared at E.J. "We've talked about it. It's different now. Your father agrees with me. He has stopped fighting the inevitable."

Sharla dropped E.J.'s hand.

E.J. said, "I don't want you to die. We've crossed a line."

"Crossed a line," repeated Sharla, exhaling a huff. He looked weaker, lesser than the great, powerful man he had always projected.

"You nearly died. I'm choosing you..."

All Sharla's attention focused on her father. Tears welling in his eyes. She had never seen his tears. He didn't even cry for Konner, and he loved Konner. Konner was his favorite. What was wrong with him? Her shoulders shivered.

Sharla insisted, "I told you about meeting the woman. Then my doctor walked me through the NICU. I'll never watch my baby suffer. I'm serious this time."

Rebecca stepped toward the inclined bed. "It's not a doll, baby. You can't set it aside when things get tough—"

"I wouldn't—"

"You've done it all your life. Stop this mess. We're scheduling the procedure," insisted Rebecca.

"My body, my choice," Sharla screamed several times at the top of her lungs, salting the chant with expletives.

A nurse opened the door and Rebecca yelled, "Get out!"

The caregiver looked to E.J. "I have to be certain everyone is alright."

E.J. gave Sharla an intense gaze, and she came to a halt. "We are—"

"Out," demanded Rebecca.

The nurse ducked behind the closing door.

"I'll take out a guardianship and force you." Rebecca spoke through gritted teeth in a much softer, though more deliberate, tone.

Sharla drew in a gasp. She stumbled in her mind, trying to think of a response. Her mother had proven herself a formidable trial lawyer. She knew the words rang false as she said them, but she had to respond. "I'll get a lawyer."

"You'll get a lawyer. With what? My money?" Rebecca laughed. "No one will cross me. You'll find no one to take your case. I'll crush—"

"Stop," E.J. snapped the word and both mother and daughter peered at him. "We're gonna crush our baby girl? You've made your name fighting fair, seeing everyone got a fair shake. This isn't you."

Rebecca stepped toward him. The look Sharla knew well. Her mother vibrated with rage. "You know what I see when I look at you?"

E.J. looked away.

"I see Konner's eyes, his nose. Desperate to prove he is a man to his father. I see Konner. The son who was part of me but always idolized you. Then I see the man who took my son's life, just as if he had pulled the trigger himself," said Rebecca.

"War killed our son. Terrorists shooting at him killed him. You think I don't stare in the mirror every day and ask myself why?"

"Then why? Why does the great E.J. Kane walk through bullets, stare down cartel bosses, and defuse bombs, but his boy dies? Dies alone in a hellhole half a world away for nothing," screamed Rebecca.

"Konner didn't die for nothing. He died drawing sniper fire, trying to draw out a killer to protect his brothers and the decent people in that village. Our son gave his life for others protecting our nation," said E.J.

Rebecca's hand jammed into his chin, forcing him backward. "There are no decent people in that village. Our beautiful Konner wasn't 'protecting our nation.' He was cannon fodder for a war machine. You're too dense to comprehend it."

Sharla wanted to crawl under the covers. She had no ability to hide, and this battle had been a long time coming.

E.J. raised his voice, matching Rebecca's tone. "Why? Why do I walk through bullets, but my son dies? I don't know. For the longest time I couldn't figure out why when I got in a tough spot, I would lose myself thinking inane things, but what I'm really doing is trying to die. I'm trying to end it. So, I won't miss him anymore."

Rebecca leaped farther toward E.J. "Then do us all a favor and have the courage to die."

Sharla witnessed her mother swing a hard fist, though E.J. avoided most of the strike by raising his hand and closing his grasp around Rebecca's forearm.

E.J. motioned toward the hospital bed. "Sharla. She matters. She is real. And you can't treat her this way."

"Thank you, Daddy," said Sharla.

His eyes pierced her. "No. No 'thank you, Daddy.' Don't divide us—"

"I'm not," said Sharla.

"This incident proves you can't handle it. You'll kill the baby and yourself. When it is you or the baby, I choose you." His breath was strong with coffee, heat, and life washing over Sharla.

He wasn't on her side. For the first time, she couldn't manipulate him. Maybe there had been other times, though she had never felt so weak. "You're both wrong. I swear."

Rebecca exhaled, locking her gaze with E.J. "You're witnessing it, she is incapable of rational thought."

"She is our daughter," said E.J.

"My body. My choice," yelled Sharla.

Rebecca retorted, "You're a junkie. A danger to yourself and others—"

Sharla screamed over and over, "I hate you."

Rebecca lifted her phone, pushing the device to record Sharla thrashing across the bed. Then the force of E.J.'s arms pressed Sharla down.

"Stop. You're giving her what she needs for court. Stop," said E.J.

Chapter Forty-Eight

A Poem

"**M**om."

Rebecca held her hand on the stainless-steel door handle. Her back remained to Sharla.

"Mom, please." The tension in her father's tone eased. Sharla turned in the hospital bed to better face her mother, though she only saw the back of the woman's expensive suit.

"'Mom, please' what?" asked Rebecca.

"I'm sorry. I'm really sorry. Please don't do this to me."

Rebecca nodded her head, then peered over her shoulder. "You don't understand. And you don't want to have an actual conversation. Because so far, you've been trying to play your dad off against me." Rebecca pointed to E.J.

Reaching as far as she thought possible, Sharla lost her balance. Her father's big hand caught her at the shoulder. Sharla's other arm reached the cool of the drawer knob. She lifted a yellow spiral notebook.

Rebecca took it. "More of your poetry about your mean, hateful mother. You had no life because your mom was living your life. She couldn't have her own, so she had to control your life." Nearly tearing at the pages, Rebecca lifted to read from the spiral.

Hot tears trailed down Sharla's checks. She mouthed the words from memory, as her mother must have read them to herself.

Too late, I find purpose.

The goal my mother, the lawyer, so prayed I would discover

Too far gone she wins my writ of habeas corpus

Buying my maturity with the flesh of my fetus

Too certain my baggage is surplus.

A life so fragile, entrusted to a vessel too frail

Soon, my tiny one, I commit you to the stardust

The fruit of the womb: a loving God's reward or

Too much the fulfillment of wicked man's lust.

Rebecca's stern countenance drooped. The spiral fell to the white linoleum. E.J. looked at her, his face evidencing a puzzle.

Sharla didn't know for sure which one Rebecca had read. The act of composing poetry had been her passion before methamphetamine. At first, the meth made it seem like her life was a poem. Beautiful, free verse where everything fell in place. She tried to write, only to read illegible gibberish after she crashed.

The door closed behind Rebecca. Sharla fell back against her pillow, pouring tears. Her father's rough hands held her, though they weren't strong. This time, his hands trembled. Maybe he couldn't see it. She felt the noticeable shake consuming E.J.'s entire body, evidently beyond his control.

After a long silence, he rose and stepped toward the door. E.J. lifted the book off the floor, though he didn't read it. He handed it to Sharla. "What was your poem about?"

"Not sure which one she read," said Sharla.

"Probably the most upsetting one. Did you write anything mean about your mother?" asked E.J.

"No, one of them is about how I want to be a mother like my mother. There are a lot where I'm trying to apologize to my baby. I couldn't finish those." Her father's shoulders rolled forward. He turned a dirty granite-colored hat in his hands.

She recalled the man of her youth wearing starched shirts and big badges on a puffed-out chest under an enormous white hat. This man slid and shuddered like rocks crushed him as each one fell over him.

E.J. handed Sharla a box of tissues. "I want to believe. What makes this time different? I don't know the person you have become."

"I understand." Sharla's tart tears wet her upper lip as she tried to clean her face up. While shouting a series of continuous apologies, she made an effort to cease her tears, but it was unsuccessful. "Is she really going to start a guardianship?"

"No," said E.J.

"Then where is she going?" asked Sharla.

"You and your brother had a way of making the most rational person I know depart from reason. She used to tell me all about whatever had occurred as a way to compose herself."

Sharla watched her father open the curtains. "Aren't you going to get her?"

"I only aggravate her suffering. She should have peace," said E.J.

"What do I do?" asked Sharla.

"Take your notebook and start writing a plan. Who will be your doctor? Stay at the center until released. You can stay with me. What kind of job will you find and how will you get it? What are your long-term plans to improve your employability?"

Sharla turned the page and started at it. She filled her lungs with the hospital air.

"Doesn't mean you can't write poems. Means you show your mother you have priorities based on a life more important than your own. You understand your mother is the kind of mother who put you first every time. I didn't always. I regret it," said E.J.

Anxiety gripped Sharla. Her father didn't reflect on his conduct. He didn't admit mistakes. The man didn't question or doubt. Her father stood like a giant, grabbing the world and bending it to what his sense of honor demanded.

For the first time in years, she looked at her father. He was like a grand jigsaw puzzle, yet instead of coming together, more and more pieces fell away. Like snips of cardboard disappearing off a coffee table until no one could decipher the picture anymore.

Chapter Forty-Nine

What Winning Looks Like

"He can do that," said E.J.

"He did it. We're done," said Rebecca.

"That's crazy," said E.J.

"No, it is the law. His writ. Burton is the applicant. He can withdraw it any time he chooses," said Rebecca.

"What about his lawyers, the whole legal team?" asked E.J.

"I believe Weatherstine has reached his limit. He is a true believer, but not an idiot. The writing is on the wall and this case hurts his cause. This is called winning, Elliott." Rebecca looked out the conference room window. In the few minutes since she departed the judge's chambers, the courtroom cleared out.

E.J. hadn't been able to place what was different until now. It was an absence. Rebecca didn't wear her normal perfume. If it was indeed a signal, then it was not required. "What about B.B.'s murder? They aren't going to charge Burton."

"They will not charge you either. A special prosecutor will investigate and prosecute," said Rebecca.

"You?" asked E.J.

"Attorney general," said Rebecca.

"He's a political hack. Probably hold an opinion poll on who to charge," said E.J.

Rebecca shook her head. "I'm telling you how it is."

"What about Cooper?" asked E.J.

"Uncertain. I expect Fenton doesn't want any bad press behind him. She lies low. He will probably let her finish out her career," said Rebecca.

"She did nothing wrong. She was the pride of the service before all of this," said E.J.

"Yes, she was..."

They stared at each other in silence. No doubt, Rebecca meant the comment as harsh as it reverberated in his mind, not stemming from an intentional insult but rather a matter-of-fact assertion. He had crushed a promising career and cost the world a skilled investigator.

E.J. thought of Fenton. A cautious man by nature, he would conclude it was best to sell Cooper short. The stigma of the Big Thicket and her association with E.J. would cast a dark shadow over her forever.

Rebecca slipped out. She slinked away without saying goodbye or telling him off.

E.J. stepped into the empty courtroom. The air conditioning gave the room an artificial flavor. He gazed downward at the stately carpet. The red-and-gray loops made an unusual pile, forming an erratic pattern.

All anticlimactic, wasn't it? Burton went back to the penitentiary waiting to see if he would face murder charges for Sheriff B.B. Yet what was the point? He served a life sentence and the odds of anyone really facing the death penalty these days were slim.

What if Burton faced capital murder? The man already demonstrated how easily the system could be stood on its head. More travel and attention for the prima donna. What else did he have to do?

The back bench caught his eye. He had sat there when Burton made his "dear friend" remark. The entire courtroom had turned and stared at E.J. Might he have been the only one who believed in Burton's guilt?

Rebecca was right. He was ungrateful and stupid. This is what winning looked like. The empty courtroom at this moment was dazzling as if in oil captured on canvas by a brilliant painter. He stood in a portrait of justice.

Outside the back window, an oak tree had largely given up its leaves to the drought. The thought of how he would get Sunshine and those worthless longhorn cattle through the winter crossed his mind.

He should sell the cattle before they fell out and died on him. Rex wouldn't understand, anyway. E.J. felt convicted by the unkind remark. Rex couldn't be blamed for his mind failing him.

There was another bright spot to withdrawing the writ. Likely Conrad Beams would have a shorter press cycle, though he would certainly face prosecution for tampering with evidence. Surely, he could get himself a lighter deal by rolling over on Kitty Karlson and her husband. It's possible that Burton's lieutenants would turn against him for commanding the killing of Melinda Blake.

All assuming Conrad Beams didn't kill himself. What had he told the boy? Something about tomorrow was a gift we got no right to claim. At the moment, it had seemed like something to say to stop a suicide.

He gazed up at the impressive seal of Texas, which consists of symbols representing strength and peace encircling a solitary star. The realization struck him tomorrow amounted to a promise. Tomorrow we will have justice.

A tomorrow when people like the Blakes won't bury their baby because human beings are capable of such gross callousness. In a world rebelling against all the values of our forefathers instead of only rejecting those time has proven false, there were still people who carried right and wrong written on their hearts.

Men and women like Son and Cooper, who battled to hold evil in check until the end of time. Was he ever such a lawman? Really worthy of their respect and capable of leading officers like them.

Since B.B. had first told him someone had sold out him and those under his command, in his heart, E.J. had entertained the prospect of justice. It started as a whisper he dared not repeat and now the blood cry deafened him.

E.J.'s head tilted above the olive and live oak branches. *Whom shall I send?* The scripture came to him as if the heavens had opened.

"Send me, Lord. Send me."

Chapter Fifty

A Personal Favor

"I need a date." E.J. held the phone with his neck, trying to throw the scoop of feed into Sunshine's bin. The feeder dominated the corner of the stall, though the barn appeared too dark for the middle of the day.

"This how you woo your prospective partners in redneckland?" asked the movie star.

He dropped the scoop in the bin. The horse shook his head upward, irritated by the distraction from his feed. "I was in San Antonio this week and saw you on one of those morning shows—"

"*Good Morning San Antonio.*"

"Said you had been in Austin shooting a new film. Well, my event is in Austin. So..." said E.J.

"What event?" asked the actor.

"The event I need the date for. And I remembered you gave me your cell number." E.J. studied the clouds in the distance then caught himself trying to twist the wedding ring no longer on his finger.

"I remember telling you to call if ever your lawyer wasn't your lawyer anymore," said the actor.

"She is not. She is not my lawyer anymore." E.J. looked down at the stall. He turned to the wall, reaching for the manure rake.

"Well, I promised. Am I the first woman to express an interest since your wife?" asked the movie star.

"No, but the other one really didn't end well," said E.J.

"Where do you need this date?" asked the movie star.

"Barbecue at a big hunting ranch in the Hill Country. Close to Austin," said E.J.

"You need a date to a barbecue at a hunting camp? I can't understand how my publicist missed the event of the season," quipped the movie star.

"Not, not a...not a barbecue or anything like you think. Fundraiser a big banker throws every year at his ranch for Speaker of the House Larence Kutnick. Very formal. Black tie kind of deal. I need a date because people will know I wouldn't go on my own. They will accept it if I'm with you," said E.J.

"Did you forget I'm a naturalist? I don't get invited to the speaker's fundraisers. And I believe your speaker and his friends are destroying humanity and all life on this planet for greed and power. They are disgusting."

"From what I've seen, people of all political persuasions have to kiss the speaker's ring if they want something done for their cause or a little less done to hurt it. More Republicans, but there will be all kinds," said E.J.

"Absolutely, I'm going. Don't worry, I don't always resort to drastic means. I can charm people into seeing the movie because the message wins hearts and minds. You should watch the movie," said the actor.

"Thank you," said E.J.

"Why is a fundraiser so important? You don't strike me as hardcore either way," said the actor.

"The speaker and I go way back. I need to look at some old files from my days in law enforcement, and I've burned most of my bridges." E.J. wouldn't risk asking anyone in the rangers. Burning more old friends like Cooper was too much. Kutnick could order anything he wanted brought to his office and no one would even know E.J. had requested it. Not knowing who or for what he searched, it made sense to keep it under wraps.

"You think you will be incognito with Vanessa Wooten on your arm?"

"No, I won't. Can't say I've been thinking everything out as clearly as I should for a long time." E.J. heard silence over the connection.

She spilled into her natural accent and cadence. "Call me Millie. It's my real name. And yours."

"Everybody calls me E.J."

"Elliott Jacob Kane. I have a publicist. She can find out anything about anyone. When do I need to tell her to clear my calendar?" asked Millie.

"Saturday afternoon," said E.J.

"Cowboy up, right?"

The expression took him back to a moment after the bomb scare when she had collapsed on top of him. He was glad she couldn't see him, in case he was blushing. "Not sure it's the right expression."

"Cowboy up." Millie ended the call.

He had better work on his poker face. Millie must be having fun, making him uncomfortable. E.J. was the rube she enjoyed teasing, yet he sensed no meanness in her quips.

A little breeze hit his face from the north. Rex Ashe's longhorns in all their white and red or white and dark variations grazed the short vegetation.

"Ever going to build your house back?"

E.J.'s head snapped high and back. "Hall."

Hall snapped E.J.'s hand into his own. E.J. pulled his palm back, then closed it around something solid and round.

When he unclenched his fingers, E.J. caught the dull shine of a cattle ranger's badge. "What is this?"

"You know what it is," said Hall.

E.J. set it on top of the fence post, ignoring the dark clouds in the distance. "Not mine."

"Yours if you'll take it," said Hall.

Had Hall lost his mind? Maybe he had never been familiar with the Texas and Southwestern Cattle Raisers Association? "They're private rangers but under DPS. The governor appoints special rangers with the approval of the cattle raisers and the DPS colonel."

Hall stepped back, pointing to a circular badge on a holder clipped to his belt. "Proper title is director of the Texas Department of Public Safety."

"Governor passed over Fenton?" asked E.J.

"Technically, the governor appoints the commissioners, and they appointed me, but yes. Governor wants a change. I want a change too. I'm bringing back what works," said Hall.

"No. I'm thrilled for you and you're the right choice, but I'll never wear another badge. Besides, I have so many enemies, like Fenton. They would undercut you before you ever started. You're going to need all your credibility to return Cooper to duty." E.J. held his gaze in Hall's eyes, trying to convey his earnestness.

"My first order overturned Cooper's suspension. Remember the story I told you about Timpson, Bobo, and Blair," said Hall.

"You were a young FBI agent, and I earned your respect by not treating that section of U.S. fifty-nine like a toll bridge to line my pockets." E.J. felt a wet drop strike his hand.

"You didn't need a law school course in due process because it was innate, intuitive to you." Hall made a fist and shook it in front of him. "It's part of what we must be if we are going to win the future. You'll chase stolen livestock and equipment, but you'll also be able to help me. In time, I can move you on to my staff." Hall's shirt evidenced sprinkles.

E.J. pointed at a spindly legged red-faced longhorn calf standing in the pasture. "First time he has ever seen water fall from heaven. Curious about what he'll do." He exhaled, then drew a deep breath. "If I could..."

"Here's the holder. I'm leaving the badge with you. I would consider it a personal favor if you pick it up." Hall's dark eyes stared at E.J.

Hall's coal-black eyes bored through him, reminding E.J. of all the markers he owed his closest friend. "I owe you a lot. I know I do but..."

Chapter Fifty-One

Seems Perfect

"You were right." Millie nodded toward a woman wearing a string of huge pearls. "Very formal. Glad I brought a little black dress. There was nothing in Austin."

"You look great. And you fit right in." E.J. moved forward in the receiving line.

"I'll take the insult as a failed compliment. No one here is environmentally conscious," whispered Millie.

"Some folks here might be kind of woke," said E.J.

Millie giggled. "What did you do? Look slang up on the Internet so you could use it in conversation?"

"Worked, didn't it?" said E.J.

Her blue eyes peered through him, sensing his mockery. "Might—"

Millie picked up on the photographer assistant's motions while the young woman had to physically move E.J. to the side of Larence Kutnick.

"Ranger, an unexpected pleasure and the talented Vanessa Wooten. You two make an impressive couple," said Kutnick.

"I really need to talk to you about a personal matter." E.J. saw Kutnick already motioning to the next couple.

Kutnick put his hand on E.J.'s shoulder, moving him forward. "I need to keep this line moving. Give me till right after they start serving dinner and we'll talk."

They ended up in another line, though E.J. wasn't sure what kind of line.

"What do you think when in Texas, margarita?" asked Millie.

E.J. grinned, adding up he was in the drink line. "Not a big drinker."

After picking up the curvy glass, Millie and E.J. stepped to a tall table. They stood in a great room decorated with incredible examples of taxidermy. A bobcat snapped at a pheasant as a centerpiece.

"Fill me in on all the details about the legendary E.J. Kane?" asked Millie.

"Legendary?" E.J. cackled.

"You should tell me about the great movie star, Vanessa Wooten," said E.J.

"The first rule of being Vanessa Wooten is you absolutely must check Vanessa Wooten's makeup and hair, darling. In my element, there is a team. Here I'm on my own. Excuse me." She raised her handbag and stepped away.

Hot, foul breath stung the back of E.J.'s neck. "Out of your league aren't you, mall cop?"

E.J. turned carefully to step back, distancing himself. He pronounced the person's identity before he completed the maneuver. "Fenton. Is Hall letting you ride out the year, or did you have to clean your desk out?"

Fenton stepped closer. "Lt. Colonel Fenton to you."

"You must have me confused with one of your feebleminded lackeys," said E.J.

"No, you're not under my authority. Not anyone's authority. Nothing to keep you from hauling off and hitting me." Fenton stepped closer, pressing his chest into E.J.'s.

"Sir, is Mr. Kane creating a disturbance?" Cooper cut an impressive vision in her starched white shirt, ribbon tie, and white cowboy hat.

"No." Fenton snarled.

"Your mic is open," said Cooper.

"Nearly got your butt whipped over an open channel," said E.J.

"Another time." Fenton backed away.

E.J. faced Cooper. "Looking good. You know, as good as an ugly woman can fix herself up."

"I missed you too, Kane," said Cooper.

"What brought you down here?" asked E.J.

"I've been assigned to provide security for Kutnick. He was at home in the district. We drove here this morning. I'll take him back tomorrow. Hall is looking for you," said Cooper.

"How did he know I was here?" asked E.J.

Cooper shook her head, smiling. "We get a list. He and Amy bought a house in Georgetown already."

"Did he tell you what he wants to rope me into?" asked E.J.

"Seems perfect to me," said Cooper.

"Suppose I should speak to him," said E.J.

"I got him moving this way. We got word when you posed with Kutnick. How do you think Fenton snuck up on you? Better give Hall the right answer. So far, no one has told the new director no." Cooper started stepping away.

E.J. held his cell phone, reluctant to strike the screen, denoting Rex Ashe's phone number.

"Who is this?" demanded Rex Ashe.

"It's me, E.J." He cupped his other ear to reduce the noise of nearby conversations.

"Who? Who?" asked Rex.

"I want you to know anything you ever need I'll be there for you, even—"

"We don't want any here." Rex Ashe ended the call.

E.J. placed the device in his suit pocket, then turned his head, searching for Hall.

Chapter Fifty-Two

Biggest Cowboy Hat Wins

H all Oglethorpe had donned a tall, crowned white hat reminiscent of John Wayne in *The Man Who Shot Liberty Valance*.

"That's a stout hat. I figured you would start out with one of those short-brimmed LBJ jobs," said E.J.

"Realized people direct their attention to the man with the biggest cowboy hat. Amy says I'm foolish," said Hall.

"Suppose we all are. She'll get used to it. What is your daughter's opinion?" said E.J.

Hall jostled the glass of tea in his hand. "Loves it. Aren't you avoiding something?"

"Grant me one request?" asked E.J.

"If it's within my power," said Hall.

"Give me a free hand to review my case, access to all old records and reports, and a free hand to investigate what happened," said E.J.

Hall extended his hand. "Why didn't you name your terms when I first asked?"

"Thought it was selfish to put you at risk fighting my battle, then I realized it's what you've always done. Put yourself at risk fighting other people's battles. It's what you do. How you lead," said E.J.

"Done," said Hall.

E.J. gripped Hall's hand. "Can't believe you let old Fenton stay on?"

"Oh, I figured you would pick up the badge just to aggravate Fenton." Hall released his grip. "God bless you, Special Ranger Kane."

E.J. nodded. "Thank you."

"Better check on Kutnick. Got to protect my budget, right? What brought you to a political event?" said Hall.

"Doesn't matter now. I won't let you down," said E.J.

Hall nodded and stepped away.

As they moved toward a vast, open sliding door, E.J. became aware of a familiar face coming closer to him.

"I'm seeing everybody here," said E.J.

"My wife, Kerry," said Dr. Meecum.

"The advisor to Chuck Norris?" asked Kerry.

E.J. wanted to change the subject instead of rehashing the inside joke Cooper had perpetrated on Dr. Meecum and E.J. "I understand *Walker, Texas Ranger* is big in Ghana."

"We met in Knoxville during undergrad." Her head twisted, following a passerby. "Excuse me." She stepped away quickly.

"Out of your stomping grounds aren't you, Doc?" asked E.J.

Dr. Meecum motioned toward his wife. "Kerry wants to be included in high society and since we live in the speaker's district, he put me on his reelection committee."

E.J. spied past the doctor to the landscaped grounds and covered arena flanked by a horse barn. "Society, Texas-style anyway. Big hair and barbecue guns." E.J. led them toward the stables.

"You don't approve?" asked Dr. Meecum.

"Not my business. I envy people who are comfortable at these hootenannies. I had to provide security at a bunch of them. Never cared for it."

"Then why are you here?" asked Dr. Meecum.

"I need access to my old notes and reports. Reason to think I didn't have a breakdown like I assumed. Someone took me out," said E.J.

"And what will you do if you find the person?" asked Dr. Meecum.

"Let's say they won't be filing any jailhouse writs," said E.J.

Dr. Meecum turned his attention to a board fence bordering the stables enclosing a pair of sorrel horses. "And you'll trade your life to kill this man or men or women?"

The odor of the horses reminded E.J. of home. "Didn't ask your approval," said E.J.

Dr. Meecum exhaled. "What about the Blakes?"

"Who?" asked E.J.

"Ellie Ruth and Steven Blake," said Dr. Meecum.

"I didn't realize you had met with them," said E.J.

"Son called me several times trying theories and other detectives' advice before he went to you. All their efforts yielded nothing. Nothing until you started working on the case," said Dr. Meecum.

"Rebecca solved their case, and it didn't bring—"

Dr. Meecum raised his voice. "You put the pieces in motion. You provided the opportunity for the resolution of knowing and gave them what measure of justice we can do for each other as humanity. Because of you." He pointed his long, narrow finger at E.J.

"Resolution? There is no resolution, no peace when a parent buries a child," said E.J.

Dr. Meecum scanned the area, likely making sure his tone didn't draw stares. "The Blakes found it in their faith, but only after you gave them enough certainty to look for it. God has delivered you. Granted, your victory over your enemies to put you in the exact moment with the unique set of skills necessary to bring justice to those suffering."

"Maybe I'll find my certainty," said E.J.

Dr. Meecum's head fell. "I fear you'll only find strife and bring about more death. Death brings death."

"I've made it this far down the road. You excuse me, I should find my date," said E.J.

Did Dr. Meecum know something or was the warning based on some biblical admonishment? Calling or curse, E.J. would carry forward and find the truth.

THE END

Epilogue

E pilogue

"Please, please hush." E.J. already kneeling, turned his head sideways in front of the car seat.

"The worm ate." Sharla stopped reading the book. "Nothing works. Did you call mom?"

E.J.'s tone turned sharper. "Keep trying." Marveling at the perfect tiny fingers before him, E.J. added, "Josey is getting out of this place."

A nurse making notes on a chart looked at a monitor above them. "She is okay." The nurse pressed a button on the machine, then stepped away.

He shook the brightly colored toy in front of the blaring baby. E.J. whispered, "Come on, please stop already."

The familiar factory tone of a cell phone rang out among the shrill crying. Millie struggled to make her voice audible over the constant shrieks. "E.J., are you still in the NICU?"

"We haven't been able to leave," said E.J. "They won't let us."

"Why?" asked Millie.

Struggling to hear Millie's soft tone over the deafening noise exasperated E.J. "I can't hear you."

"What are you doing?" yelled Millie.

"We're trying to keep the baby quiet so we can pass the car seat test," said E.J.

"The baby doesn't need to be calm. They are trying to make sure she doesn't stop breathing in different positions in the car seat," said Millie.

"Are you sure?" asked E.J.

"Yes, I have one more day in Toronto and then I'll fly in. But I'm not staying in your trailer—"

"Of course not. I got a new fifth wheel and a builder putting up a metal building. Probably already dried in. Barndominium, latest style, will open up into a little arena and overlook the stables."

"A barndominium? You want it overlooking animal stalls?" asked Millie.

"Yes." E.J. smiled, seeing the plans in his mind.

"I just wanted to make sure I said the word right so I can tell my girlfriends. They will be so jealous, first a fifth wheel and now a barndominium with livestock," said Millie.

"Hashtag jelly movie stars," said Sharla.

E.J. placed the phone on speaker.

"Is Josephine a family name?" asked Millie.

"No, I named her after a lady I met here at the hospital," said Sharla.

"They're motioning for me. E.J., call me when you get home and let her cry," said Millie.

E.J.'s knee buckled under his weight. He slid to the side, though eventually rising. "I'm going to get some coffee. Millie has two daughters. She knows these things."

"Mom does too," said Sharla.

"Your mom will come around, you watch." E.J. walked back through the neonatal intensive care. Once he had poured a cup of coffee, he enjoyed the relative peace of the nurse's station. A lounger in the waiting room called to him. He woke to a nudge from Sharla and a cold cup of coffee.

"Dad, get the truck. I want to get out of here before they change their mind," whispered Sharla.

The walk carrying the seat to the parking garage gave him lots of time to consider all the reasons this wouldn't work. But so far, he knew this was Sharla's longest streak without using. Wasn't that a win in and of itself? None of us knew what tomorrow held.

The big Ford pickup took up two spaces at the hospital entrance. As soon as he opened the door, a blast of chilly air engulfed him. Walking past the tailgate, he saw Rebecca stepping toward Sharla. Josey's bundled face was barely exposed, her closed eyes squinting hard, evidencing her displeasure at the cold. No matter how dark, how ugly the world turned, creation kept pushing through proclaiming every moment of every life an unearned gift from the Almighty.

E.J. stepped back around and into the cab. He pulled the truck out of line, then watched them in the passenger mirror. He would circle the parking lot, then return after Rebecca, Sharla, and Josey finished their embrace.

E.J. spoke a silent prayer that Sharla always appreciates what it means to have another life depending on her.

Also By

Micheal E. Jimerson https://michealjimerson.com/
https://www.goodreads.com/author/show/15248216.Micheal_E_Ji
merson

WHITE GOLD
A hard-boiled cowboy detective thriller about choosing the lesser of
evils in an imperfect world. E.J. Kane Mystery Number One.

WHERE NO MAN PURSUETH
An award-winning inspirational fiction murder mystery set amongst
the backdrop of the Great East Texas Oilfield.

About the Author

Micheal E. Jimerson is the sixth generation to live on his family farm in the Oakland Community of Rusk County, Texas. Micheal and his wife Mona raise their son, David, on the same property. Micheal graduated from the Baylor University School of Law in 1993. *Pro Bono* work for the Kilgore Crisis Center and other victim advocacy groups lead him to be elected office as the County and District Attorney of Rusk County, Texas. He has appeared in documentaries such as *Cold Case*, *On Death Row*, *Snapped*, *On the Case*, and an article in the *Texas Lawyer*.

9 798218 377724